Beware My Lovely

With the letter and diary in hand I closed
the trunk. Then I let myself back down through
the trapdoor, lowered it into place, and hurried
along through the tunnel. But when I mounted
the steps and the flight going up loomed, I
stopped dead. Were there secret openings into
the rooms on the other floors? A hidden door
to my quarters?

It took several minutes to gain a semblance of control over my emotions, then I sat
down on the chaise and opened the diary. Heart
in my throat, I turned to the final entry, penned
on the night before Charlotte's death . . .

THE CURSE OF BELLE HAVEN

IRENE M. PASCOE

JOVE BOOKS, NEW YORK

THE CURSE OF BELLE HAVEN

A Jove Book / published by arrangement with
the author

PRINTING HISTORY
Jove edition / September 1991

ISBN: 0-515-10667-4

Jove Books are published by The Berkley Publishing Group,
200 Madison Avenue, New York, New York 10016.
The name "JOVE" and the "J" logo
are trademarks belonging to Jove Publications, Inc.

PRINTED IN THE UNITED STATES OF AMERICA

10 9 8 7 6 5 4 3 2 1

For my friends in Seannache Writers' Workshop,
with love and appreciation

1

Charleston, South Carolina, 1850

FOR nearly two months now I had lived with the cold, heart-shattering fact that the stepsister who had been so dear to me was dead.

Repeatedly throughout the long voyage home to America from France, I had told myself that it just couldn't be true, until the words of denial ringed my head with tight bands of pain. Charlotte was gone! I had to accept what her husband, Matthew Steele, had made so clear in his letter.

In the open carriage I had hired to drive me out to Belle Haven, the Steele plantation, the grizzle-haired driver flicked the reins at the chestnut mare. I was nearly pitched off the seat when the animal lurched forward and one wheel plunged in and out of a deep rut. "Slow down, sir," I entreated, grabbing my slipping bonnet with one hand, while the other hand flashed out to clutch the side of the rattling conveyance.

"It's gettin' late," he threw gruffly over his shoulder in a thick Southern accent. "I aim to be back in the city before dark." He glanced up at the gathering dusk in the slate-gray sky. It was barely visible through the overspreading branches of moss-draped oaks and pungent pines that lined the lonely country road. "It ain't much farther now."

If he'd meant that last remark as a measure of reassurance, the attempt fell flat. I could hardly be anything but apprehensive when we were moving at a dangerous speed that turned the damp spring air from cool to cold and the trees and dense, subtropical undergrowth into a blur. "You're going to land us upside down in a ditch!" I shouted over the sound of pounding hooves. "Slow this carriage at once!"

The driver muttered an expletive, and after several more hair-raising seconds he reluctantly obeyed.

By then my gloved fingers were gripping the lacquered buggy so tightly that I practically had to pry them free. How foolish I'd been to hire this slovenly man who smelled of spirits. Not that I'd had much of a choice. Only he and one other driver, of the handful I'd approached at the Charleston harbor, had been willing to journey the short distance out of the city in the approaching dark. And the other man had looked me over with a lascivious gleam that left no doubt he'd been mentally divesting me of my cloak and matching burgundy traveling dress.

Suppressing a shiver that had nothing to do with the dampness, I settled back on the leather seat and returned my attention to the lush panorama. The city, with its teeming port, elegant homes, quaint shops, and cobbled streets was a good fifteen minutes behind us. And the smell of bracing salt air had given way to the sweet fragrance of jasmine and honeysuckle that intermingled with the scent of pines. So far the only other person we'd seen since leaving the city was a robust Negro man driving a heavily laden cart toward Charleston. As we'd come upon him, he had slowed his vehicle as if he had expected to be stopped. Slaves, I'd heard, were not allowed in public without a pass, which they were obliged to show any white man upon demand. I was more than a little relieved when my driver did not stop and issue the unjust order.

From time to time we passed long drives that led to magnificent clapboard and brick homes, with handsome columned verandas. Spacious lawns, stretching in every direction, edged striking flower gardens, magnolias, and weeping willows. Beyond the lawns were outbuildings, slave quarters, and endless acreage planted with rice or cotton.

To me, the picturesque countryside was a wilderness compared to congested Boston, where my stepsister and I were born and reared. Through business acquaintances Charlotte had met Matthew and married him after a whirlwind courtship in that city. Mere weeks before their initial meeting I had sailed for Paris to study under Madame Fontaine, the renowned *couturiére*. Now three years had come and gone, and Charlotte, just twenty-two, a scant ten months older than myself, was also gone.

My throat tightened on a surge of overwhelming emptiness. The only immediate family I had left was my stepsister's six-month-old son, Rory. Now he would be partly in my care. While

I yearned to see the little boy and hold him near, just the thought of the tremendous responsibility I had inherited made my stomach flutter with unease. I knew nothing about caring for a child. On top of that I couldn't even imagine that Matthew Steele would want me, Alexandra Chandler, under his roof any more than he'd come to want his wife there.

A painful jolt snapped me back to the present, and my lips compressed when I saw that the driver had cunningly inched up the speed again. I was sympathetic to his wish to start back to the city before nightfall, but I wasn't willing to risk life and limb for him to achieve that end. I leaned forward and was about to tap him sharply on the shoulder when a brawny dark-dressed rider whizzed by. Hot on his heels was another male rider, also darkly attired and with his hat pulled low.

From the way the men sped past, without so much as a sideways glance, I got the impression they were either engaged in a race or being pursued by someone. To my horror, the driver must have assumed the former, for he laughed with the glee of challenge and slapped the reins forcibly against the horse's flanks.

We shot forward, and I was flung violently back against the seat, knocking the wind from my lungs. Before I could catch my breath and order this madman to an immediate halt, one of the front wheels dropped into a cavernous pothole, and I heard a snap.

The carriage teetered wildly. I gasped and hung on, my eyes wide with fright. In front of me the driver jumped clear as the creaking vehicle tipped, then crashed onto its side with a thunderous racket that echoed with the sharp scream of the horse. In the terrifying tumble I was flung out and hurled into the thick growth of ferns and tuberous vines that blanketed the ground beneath the roadside trees. On impact every bone in my body was jarred and my head reeled as my temple struck a moss-covered rock. Bright colors swam before my eyes, disappeared in a moment of blackness, then reappeared. I lay sprawled face-down, one arm pinned awkwardly beneath me and tendrils of ebony hair spilling across my cheek. My cloak was a twisted, constricting vise about my body, and my lungs strained for air.

Above my labored breathing I heard a man with a slight Southern accent shout, "Keep going! You know where the entrance is!"

I tried to lift my head and call for help, but excruciating pain, and the blackness that faded in and out, rendered me immobile and mute. Scalding tears surfaced.

Strong masculine hands came down on my shoulders, then moved beneath my ribs, slowly over my torso, and onto my limbs, fingers probing for what I dazedly prayed was nothing more than possible broken bones.

"Where do you hurt, miss?" a man asked with concern. Gently he turned me onto my back. Just as gently he brushed away my tears, and I looked up at the wavering, hat-shaded face just inches above my own. Involuntarily my eyes closed against the unrelenting pain. I tried to speak, but the words refused to come. I blinked and looked up again, right into the inky eyes dominating a strong face. Then the world spun, and I slipped into the black hole of unconsciousness and disjointed dreams. In some of the visions I was in Paris, at work alongside Madame Fontaine and then laughing with friends in that fabled city. But the most pleasant scenes were of childhood days in the big house in Boston. I was born in the stately home, and my stepsister had come there in her third year after the marriage of our widowed parents. I saw beautiful, blond-haired Charlotte with her former fiancé, the only man she had ever loved. In an instant he vanished. A moment later she, too, was gone, and I once again felt the utter emptiness.

The hollow sensation startled me awake. My eyes opened for a second, then shut against the savage drumming in my head. I ached all over, as if I'd been trampled. What had happened to me? That question had scarcely penetrated the fog in my brain when a picture of the carriage accident loomed and my lips parted in renewed horror.

My eyes flew open. Through a blur I saw that I was in a canopied bed, in a dimly lit room. Blinking, I cleared my vision. The mahogany bed was large and draped in a rich apricot color. From what little I could see of the room, it was immense and lavishly appointed. I tried to lift my head to survey the unfamiliar surroundings, but shooting pain compelled me to lie still. The moan that escaped my parched lips must have signaled someone, because I glimpsed movement from beyond the foot of the bed.

Squinting, I brought into focus a tall, broad-shouldered man in dark clothes. He was turned partially away from me, his profile hidden in shadows, so I couldn't see his features clearly. He put something down on the chest of drawers beside him, then came toward me. "It's good to see you awake," he said and added in a soft, reassuring tone, "You're safe and being well cared for."

Across the room the door opened. A round, middle-aged Negro maid entered. She went to the man's side, the starched white trim of her black skirt whispering over the muted carpet. When she spoke, her voice was also a whisper, and her eyes shone with delight: "Ah, the child is awake."

"She just came around." He moved to the night table. As he measured a spoonful of powder into a glass of water, he said in the same soft voice, "This will help alleviate any discomfort, miss." The maid joined him at the bedside. After sliding an arm beneath my shoulders, she lifted me slightly, then took the glass and held it to my lips.

The bitter-tasting potion made my mouth pucker just as biting into a fresh lemon would. "Fortunately you suffered no broken bones," the man said as the maid settled me on the pillows and smoothed my thick, unbound hair in a curtain about my shoulders. "Can you remember what happened to you?"

I drew a shallow breath, then responded with a slight nod.

"And who you are?"

"Yes." The word was little more than a raspy whisper, and my eyelids had grown so heavy it was a struggle to keep them open.

"She'll be fine," the man said to the maid.

"Thank the Lord, the child is so young and pretty."

"That she is," he murmured.

Those were the last words I heard before drifting off. Each time I awakened from the sleep that freed me of pain, someone was nearby. Occasionally it was the tall, dark-haired man, who leaned near once and asked my name. I tried to say Alexandra, but all that came out was "An."

"Ann," he'd repeated in a whisper, as if he liked the sound of what he assumed was my name. In that lucid moment I had thought to ask where I was and to say that I'd been headed for Belle Haven, but the drowsiness once again overcame me.

Most often, though, when I opened my eyes, the ample maid was hovering near. She chattered good-naturedly as she straightened the bedclothes, wiped my brow, and offered liquids.

Once I saw a beautiful chestnut-haired woman with sapphire-blue eyes staring down at me with open curiosity. She was dressed in an exquisite, low-cut shimmering silk gown over a wide crinoline. The woman, who didn't appear to be much older than I, hadn't said a word, and when she left the room, it was as if she hadn't really been there. Yet I knew, from the lingering fragrance of my favorite French perfume, I hadn't been dreaming.

Finally the gauzy webs of sleep receded. I felt wonderfully clear-headed and, except for stiffness in my body, almost free of pain. I was still in the canopied bed, and the room was bright with sunlight. How I had come to be in this place was no mystery. The miserable carriage driver was responsible! But who lived here? And for how long had I been asleep? As those questions raced through my mind, the memory of Charlotte swept back.

I swallowed the constricting lump that came to my throat, then fixed my attention on the door across the way and scanned left. The walls of the spacious and airy room were a pleasant pale green, the color repeated in the floral upholstered chairs and chaise, accented in the soft shade of apricot which matched the bed canopy. Gleaming mahogany furniture highlighted the chalk-white woodwork, ceiling moldings, and fireplace mantel with fluted pilasters. Other than the ticking of the mantel clock, which indicated it was 2:15, the room was quiet.

I rose up on one arm. Just as I was about to survey the other side of the room, a man said quietly from there, "It's good to see you looking alert."

My head jerked up, a sharp pain shooting through it.

"I'm sorry, I didn't mean to startle you."

Even before I saw the man standing before the curtained French doors, I knew him by his voice. He was the one who had come to my aid on the road, and later was at my bedside, offering words of comfort and reassurance. His compassion convinced me I need not fear being alone with him.

As he crossed slowly to my side, I saw his face clearly. My throat tightened again, only this time at his bold good looks and intense black eyes. "Have you any discomfort?" he asked, gazing down at me from beneath dark dramatic brows.

Only when I look at you, I thought wryly and scolded myself for practically gaping. "No, not really." The words croaked out when I realized I was in a nightdress. If he saw the flush of embarrassment I felt surface, he didn't let it show in his face.

"Would you like some water?" He gestured to the crystal pitcher on the night table.

Afraid my voice might crack again, I answered with a slight

inclination of my head. He poured water into a glass. Instead of handing it over, as I had expected, he slid an arm beneath my shoulders, and when he eased me up to sip the liquid, I felt a momentary surge of breathtaking current flow between us. My heart leaped out of rhythm at his nearness and enticing masculine scent, and it was a struggle to drink without choking. As he settled me on propped-up pillows, I noticed how his thick hair tapered neatly to his collar. For one pulse-pounding moment his dark gaze met my hazel eyes and the light-headedness returned, scattering my thoughts like dry leaves in an October wind. All I could think to say was "Have I been here long?" Thank God my voice didn't betray my agitation.

Apparently he, too, was having some difficulty, because I heard him swallow before he answered. "Almost twenty-four hours. Did it seem longer?" He straightened and put aside the glass.

Now that he wasn't so close, my mind began to clear. However, my heart still palpitated as he regarded me through appreciative eyes. Had he looked at me this way the other times he'd been in here? "I feared it was longer," I responded, wondering if he was married to the beautiful woman I'd seen.

"I saw your driver run off after the axle on your carriage broke and it went over. The man should be horsewhipped for leaving you!"

The oaf should be flogged for driving like a maniac, I thought, absently massaging the arm that had been pinned beneath me after the accident.

He glanced at my arm. "Does it hurt much?"

"No, it's just a little stiff."

"We have some liniment for that."

I expressed appreciation, then added, "I can't thank you enough for coming back to help me."

"Coming back?" he said slowly. "I'm afraid I don't understand."

Hesitating, I searched his face. "Didn't you and another man pass by my carriage just seconds before the accident?"

"No." He shook his head. "I was on my way home alone from Charleston when I came upon you." He inhaled a deep breath and abruptly changed the subject. "It's stuffy in here." He excused himself and turned on his heel.

As he crossed to the French doors and opened them onto an upper-level veranda, my mind flashed back to the accident. Even as groggy as I was then, I'd heard him call out to someone, for there was no mistaking this man's clear, slightly accented tones.

On his return to the bed I paid particular attention to his fine gray suit and silk waistcoat, which fit his lean frame to perfection. What a contrast these garments were to the coarse apparel he'd had on yesterday, when he'd come to my aid. Those clothes, along with his hat pulled low, were identical to the ones worn by the second rider who sped past.

"I hope you'll pardon us for going through your bags," he said. "We were trying to find out who you are. Don't you carry any papers?"

"Yes, of course, in my reticule."

"We found no reticule."

"But I had it with me, on my lap."

"It must have been thrown out of the carriage. I'll send someone back to look for it."

"I'd appreciate that, Mr.—ah—"

"Steele. Dr. Matthew Steele."

2

My mouth fell open. "You're him?"

"Yes, if the him you're referring to is Matthew Steele."

A soft breath escaped my lips as I closed them. I should have guessed, from the expert way in which he'd examined me right after the accident and his commanding bedside manner, that he was a doctor. And, since I was near Belle Haven, that he might be Matthew. "I should have guessed," I murmured distractedly, focusing on the profound pain my stepsister had caused this man.

"Guessed what?"

"Who you are."

"Why? I've never seen you before."

I hesitated. "Not even in a daguerreotype with Charlotte?"

A nerve at the corner of his mouth quirked, and he viewed me sharply. "Alexandra?"

"Yes."

He took a sudden step back, as if he'd just been burned by a scorching fire. "I had no idea you were on your way here."

"I wrote Charlotte that I was."

"Charlotte? But she's—" He broke off abruptly, then continued with caution. "Did you get my letter?"

"Yes," I replied quietly, my insides shriveling at the memory of the day I'd received his message in Paris. That horrible dark day. By then my stepsister had already been gone almost eight weeks. Now it had been four months. "It arrived right after I'd booked passage," I explained, "and had written Charlotte I was on my way to Belle Haven for a visit. There wasn't time to drop you a note before my ship sailed, and I had hoped you'd read the one I'd penned to her."

He shook his head. "It was put aside unopened with her belongings."

"Then I'm here unannounced. And like this." Glumly I stared down at myself in the bed. "I'm sorry."

He waved aside the apology. "You were on your way here even before you'd heard about Charlotte?" His dark brows V'd over the bridge of his nose.

As I answered with another quiet yes, it struck me that I was no longer self-conscious in the nightdress. But then, I shouldn't be. Matthew was a doctor. A very tall, good-looking one, just as Charlotte had written and had hoped to point out with the wedding picture she'd forwarded to Paris. But it had arrived practically in shreds, and she'd never bothered to send another. In any case, Matthew was used to seeing women in nightclothes, and without any apparel at all. Had he seen me so? I wondered on a burst of unexpected heat.

Thank goodness his cool-eyed gaze doused the warmth before it reddened my face. "It was my understanding," he said, "that you still had several months left on your apprenticeship, or whatever you call it."

Privilege was the word I used to describe the great honor of studying under Madame Fontaine. But this wasn't the time to go into that. Nor was it the time to explain, if there would ever be one, that I'd been returning earlier than originally planned to try and help my distraught stepsister straighten out the shambles she'd made of the marriage. Instead, I simply said, and in all truth, "I was going to stay another six months, but there really was no need. I was eager to be home, to see Rory and—" My voice dropped on a sad note. "Now I hope to carry out his mother's last wish."

Surprise flickered over the set masculine features. "You've been over her will already?"

"No." I didn't have to look over the document I knew by heart. Except for the request regarding Rory, it was identical to my own. Through an iron-clad stipulation in Father's will, the wealth he'd amassed as a Boston merchant and land speculator had been left equally to me and Charlotte and would always be in our control. Moreover, the estate could only be passed on to direct heirs. Rory alone had inherited from his mother, and I had been named trustee until he came of age. What an awkward situation that could be for me and Matthew! "Charlotte sent me a miniature of Rory right after he was born," I went on, "and asked if I would help care for him if anything were to happen to her."

"She had no right to make such arrangements without con-sulting me," Matthew said sharply.

"I'm sorry, I had no idea."

"And what about you? Didn't you have any reservations about putting aside your plans for the future to try and fulfill her re-quest?"

He made it sound as if I'd taken the request lightly and leaped to an impulsive decision. "Of course I had reservations," I told him flatly. "I've worked hard to get where I am."

"Exactly where is that?"

"Opening my own salon."

"Do you think you'll have clientele?"

Briefly I shut my eyes against a sudden pain. This interroga-tion was bringing on another headache. Where was the compas-sion and friendliness this man had displayed earlier? Had I merely dreamt them? I lifted my chin. When I spoke again, I managed to keep out even a hint of my burning irritation. Heaven knew, I had no wish to be at odds with the little boy's father. "I believe I have a start. A number of American women who bought the gowns I fashioned in Paris gave me their cards to contact them when I returned home."

"Then that's what you must do," he insisted. "Don't give up your plans for the future, especially when there is no need."

"I don't intend to give up one for the other."

"You can't do both."

"I can try."

"If I let you!"

I expelled a deep breath, feeling as if I'd just run up against a solid, immovable object and all the air was knocked out of me. Clearly this man did not want me here. Was he going to make it impossible for me even to try to carry out my stepsister's final wish? Unfortunately, there was nothing legally binding about it. Charlotte had simply asked that I help raise Rory, at least in his formative years, or until Matthew remarried. But whether or not I stayed on at the plantation was up to him, and he seemed deter-mined to send me packing. In a way I sympathized with his posi-tion. In his place I probably wouldn't want a stranger poking a nose into the rearing of my child, either, even if that stranger was family. Still, I had made a promise to Charlotte, and I in-tended to keep it! Just as I also intended to continue with the work I loved. Deciding now was not the time to press this issue, I sidestepped it by asking instead, "When may I see Rory?"

Matthew clamped his jaw tight, and seconds passed before he said in a grudging tone, "Tomorrow." His gaze dropped to my injured arm, which I'd absently begun to massage again. "I'll get the liniment." He brought his voice under control. He crossed to the medical bag atop the chest of drawers, lifted out a small bottle, and returned to set it on the bedside table. "A maid will be in shortly to apply this to your arm. Now, before I leave . . . I need to examine your eyes."

Before I could comment, he leaned near, and the instant his searching gaze met mine, my heartbeat accelerated. I was drowning in the black pools of his eyes. I'd never been affected by a man like this before and certainly not by a doctor. There should be a law against physicians with seductive eyes, I thought.

Matthew's attention dropped to my mouth and lingered for pulse-pounding seconds in which his respiration grew as ragged as my own. He straightened and said, after inhaling what sounded like a calming breath, "You can get up whenever you're ready, but stay inside and rest for the balance of today."

"I will." The moment he left the room, I, too, inhaled a settling breath.

Later, as I half-listened to the warbling of birds beyond the open French doors, I reflected on the pain I'd seen in Matthew's face when he learned who I was. Clearly my relationship to Charlotte had engulfed him with hurtful memories. Would this always be so?

My heart was leaden with memories of my own. Would I ever forget how stunned I had been when Charlotte wrote of her marriage to Matthew? Just mere weeks before, she had been jilted by her fiancé, whom she had loved deeply. Unfortunately, in time, he'd decided she was the only one for him and had set out to win her back.

The bedroom door opened and the middle-aged Negro maid peered in. Her face lit with obvious delight. "You is awake, child, and lookin' jest as good as Dr. Matthew say. Why didn't you tell us sooner you is Miss Alexandra?" She swept to the foot of the bed.

Now that my head was clear, I knew in an instant who this cheerful woman was. Recalling all of the wonderful things I'd heard about her, I said on a rush of warmth, "I tried to, Lizzie."

"You know who I is? Ah, Dr. Matthew must have told you."

"No, Charlotte wrote very fondly of you."

"I so sorry she be gone. I saved all of her things, in case you wants any of 'em."

"That was very thoughtful of you, thank you." For at least the hundredth time I wondered how my stepsister had died. Matthew had simply written that there was an accident. I'd thought to question him about it, but the hurt on his face had prompted me to wait for another time. For a moment I was tempted to ask this trusted servant, but it really wasn't her place to explain.

"Did Miss Charlotte tell you about Eustace and Zalea, too?"

"She praised your husband and daughter almost as much as you." I smiled at the family pride that returned the brightness to Lizzie's eyes, then inquired about the rest of the Steeles, who also lived at Belle Haven.

"Oh, they is fine. Dr. Matthew is gonna be tellin' them all you is here."

The *all*, I knew, was Matthew's brother, Tyler, who at thirty-one was a year older than Matthew, their widowed sister-in-law, Felicity, and Grandmother Hester, the matriarch of the family. "And Rory," I asked, turning my thoughts to the little boy I could hardly wait to see, "how is he?"

"Oh, you is gonna love him, miss, he be a beautiful boy babe and so good, hardly ever causes a ruckus. Me and Zalea been carin' for him. Dr. Matthew wanted to bring in a nursemaid, but I say no. Ain't no stranger gonna care for that precious child."

I bit my inner lip, suppressing a grin. This was indeed the direct and endearing Lizzie I'd come to know through my stepsister's weekly letters. According to Charlotte, this woman was the backbone of the household—everyone depended on her. She'd been born and reared at Belle Haven and through the years had worked up to chief housekeeper. Now she and the handful of others who had stayed on after the plantation suffered financial ruin three years before were free. Matthew had taken care of that when he and Charlotte returned from their honeymoon. Prior to their courtship and marriage, he'd been in Edinburgh, Scotland, completing medical studies.

"Now you is here to help us see to the babe," Lizzie continued as she straightened the bedclothes, "just like Miss Charlotte wanted."

"Caring for Rory is my hope," I murmured, thinking once again of the huge responsibility I had inherited. My stepsister had always seemed so indestructible that it had never occurred to me that her life might be cut short. It had also never occurred to me that she might betray her husband.

"Is there anything I can do for you, miss?" Lizzie was asking.

I blinked, throwing off the melancholy that had settled over me. "Hot water for a bath would be nice."

"Yes'm, I'll have Zalea bring it right up. Then I'll see to unpacking your bags. Is that all you has?" She pointed to the two pieces on the chaise, just this side of the intricately carved twin armoires in the dressing alcove.

"The rest are in Charleston, waiting to be picked up."

"I'll have Eustace fetch 'em in the mornin'. He's gone now to look for your reticule. What's this?" She lifted the bottle from the bedside table.

"Liniment for my arm. I wrenched it in the accident."

"I'll rub some on you after you washes up. Then you is just to rest like Dr. Matthew say."

As the housekeeper left the room, I closed my eyes and breathed in the sweet aroma of spring flowers that wafted in on the pleasant breeze. The headache that had begun with Matthew's interrogation had subsided shortly after he'd left my side.

Overhead, the prisms of the crystal chandelier tinkled on a gust of wind. Charlotte had loved this chiming, which occurred throughout the house when the air was briskly stirred. Actually, she'd loved everything about this twenty-room mansion she had described to me in great detail. I doubted if I would ever understand how she could have even considered sacrificing everything good that she seemed to have had here.

Scowling, I threw back the covers. Lying around brooding over the past couldn't change it. I eased myself from the bed, grimacing at the stiffness in my body and the tingling in my feet. As I longingly eyed the bottle of liniment, a knock sounded on the door. "Come in." I bit back a groan as I reached for the wrapper on the nearby chair.

A pretty, young Negro girl, carrying a heavy-looking pail, entered and bobbed her head in polite greeting. "I brung hot water, Miss Alexandra." She moved to the dressing alcove.

Thanking her, I slipped on the wrapper. "You must be Zalea," I said as the girl emptied steaming water into the tub concealed behind the ornate screen.

"Yes'm, I is Zalea," she answered brightly as she rounded the screen.

I remembered Lizzie's daughter was in her seventeenth year.

She was dressed like her mother, in the black servant's costume trimmed with white, and had the same warm face. The resemblance stopped there; this girl was small and slim. "I'm pleased to meet you, Zalea." I smiled.

She returned the friendly expression. "Can I gets you anything else before I fetches up more water, miss?"

"Nothing, thank you." Gingerly I moved to the brocade chair near the open French doors curtained in delicate Belgian lace and sat down before my wobbly legs gave way. The aroma of flowers was even sweeter here, and the breeze sensuously caressed my face and the sensitive flesh at the hollow of my throat.

While Zalea and a kitchen maid finished filling the ample porcelain tub, Lizzie returned and chatted gaily about Rory as she unpacked the two bags. Then she turned the subject to Matthew's grandmother. "You should have seen Miss Hester's face when Dr. Matthew told her you is here. She be overjoyed and wanted to get right up out of bed to come and see you. But he say no."

"Is she still feeling poorly?" I asked, genuinely concerned about the aged woman Charlotte had admired and respected.

"Yes'm, that's why Dr. Matthew tells her no. She's been especially low since Miss Charlotte gone—they got on right well. It just ain't the same with Miss Felicity. She's a nice lady and tries hard to be closer, but she just ain't got the patience for sick old folk."

I supposed Felicity was the beautiful woman who had stood at my bedside.

"And the men be gone away to the city most times." Lizzie crossed the room and closed the French doors. "So it lonely these days for Miss Hester."

"I'm looking forward to spending time with her," I said in all truth and was grateful that someone in the family was eager to see me. Would Tyler and Felicity share in a bit of Hester Steele's enthusiasm?

Later, when I was alone luxuriating in the soothing jasmine-scented bath that was gradually relieving the stiffness in my body, the longing to be back home in Boston, with dear friends, nudged the selfish side of me. And I clung to the secret hope that the family would be as keen on sending me packing, as Matthew clearly was, and I could get on with my own life. Just the thought of trying to establish a salon in an unfamiliar city, where I didn't know a soul and where the way of life was so different from what

I'd known, was more intimidating than I dared even admit to myself. Most of all, however, I questioned if I could live in a region that embraced slavery. Heaven knew, I could never reside in a house where one man owned another.

After bathing, I toweled dry and put on the delicate silk nightdress that had been laid out. As I bent to lift the matching empire-style wrapper, a twinge in my arm reminded me of the liniment. I opened the bottle and my nose involuntarily wrinkled at the putrid smell that assaulted my nostrils. Only excruciating pain could compel me to rub on this stuff! Considering Matthew's coolness, I just imagined that he'd probably taken pure delight in handing over this malodorous concoction.

3

As I glanced around the lavish room, the overwhelming emptiness once again gripped me. I was in Charlotte's home and she was gone. Really gone! The truth of her death, which I hadn't fully accepted until this moment, struck me like a thunderbolt. Chills raced over my flesh, and the heaviness that weighted my heart brought scalding tears to my eyes.

For the first time since I'd received Matthew's letter, I cried without restraint, cradling myself as the compelling need overcame me to visit the place where my stepsister now lay, in the family cemetery out back. Just beyond it was the river. I shuddered at the mere thought of it.

Stifling the sob that burned in the back of my throat, I wiped away the tears. With no more than passing consideration to Matthew's order to stay inside and rest, I changed into a simple spring dress and shoes. Then I brushed my ebony hair, scarcely aware of the bruise on my temple, and moved out onto the rear second-floor gallery.

A look around brought chills anew to my flesh, only this time they stemmed from the feeling that I'd seen this place before. In a way I had, through Charlotte's keen eyes. The immense entrance salon below was just as she had described, with its three tiers of encircling balconies and huge Waterford chandelier suspended above the round Moorfield carpet on the lustrous oak floor.

Charlotte's love of this house strummed a reverent chord in me. As I slowly descended the freestanding wood staircase, my own eyes took in the blue walls, highlighted by white woodwork and soft-textured, imported French paper, its simple pattern executed in gold leaf. To each side of the entrance salon were lavishly appointed twin drawing rooms, visible through wide doorways.

The robust wail of an infant brought me to a sudden stop on the bottom step. Charlotte's baby! My heart lurched, and my gaze flew up to the front second-floor gallery. Three doors faced it. My stepsister had occupied the middle room, with Rory's adjoining on the left. If she'd said which one Matthew had moved into after he'd found Charlotte with her one and only love, a little over a year ago, I did not remember.

The crying stopped almost as quickly as it had begun. Still I hesitated, longing to go to my nephew and hold him close, just as his mother would have done. At the moment, though, the need to be near Charlotte was the most compelling. Besides, I reminded myself, Matthew had specified that I wait until tomorrow to see Rory.

I left the house by way of the arched front door and crossed the impressive Doric-columned veranda. Like the two above, it also ran the full width of the three-storied, white clapboard structure, flanked by single-floor wings. Rattan furniture, which matched the color of the house, graced the veranda. In front of me was the half-mile-long drive, shaded by a thick tunnel of gnarled live oak trees, dripping with gray Spanish moss. Spacious lawns rayed out from the private avenue, bordering formal gardens, outbuildings, and the nearby aggregate of small cabins. I assumed they were the abandoned slave quarters Charlotte had once mentioned.

The pleasantly warm late-afternoon sun spread its golden halo over the magnificent vista, and I heaved a small sigh of relief when I saw that no one else was around. For now, all I wanted was to be alone with Charlotte.

As I rounded the house, the wrought-iron-fenced cemetery in the immediate distance on the right came into view, and I stopped short, my throat constricting. Thinking of my stepsister there was one thing. To actually see the place jolted my senses. For timeless seconds I stared numbly, then continued forward. As I passed the kitchen, separated from the house by a covered walkway, I braced for the moment when Charlotte's name would leap out at me from one of the numerous headstones.

The chest-high cemetery gate opened without a sound. As I moved solemnly among the well-maintained graves, I kept my gaze from gravitating to the nearby grassy slope I knew ended at the river. In time I would have to face it, but not now.

In less than a minute my searching eyes found the place where my once vibrant stepsister lay, beneath the shade of a sprawling, ancient oak. My pulse slowed and I felt as if the very life were draining from me. Despite my resolve to be brave, a fresh flood of tears came with the memories that swept forward. For as long as I could remember, Charlotte and I had been steadfast friends. Not even the occasional petty jealousies and arguments had lessened the closeness, the sharing of dreams and hopes and sorrows. We had called ourselves "kindred spirits," and through Charlotte's persuasive and devilish ways, we'd even been comrades in a number of pranks on classmates at Miss Bronson's Academy for Fine Young Women in Boston. I was the quiet one, who'd made friends slowly. My stepsister, on the other hand, had been blessed with the enviable effervescence that drew people to her.

The smell of water drifted up from the river, but I was too engrossed in the past to be aware of my surroundings. In Boston Charlotte had reigned supreme among the elite, and Matthew had indicated that the same would be true in Charleston. But when he brought her home to Belle Haven, they were stunned to find that while he was in Scotland, and Tyler was at Harvard studying law, their oldest brother, Brit, had lost the family fortune. Through the combination of mismanagement and adverse weather, which destroyed the rice crop, he'd very nearly also lost the plantation. With the fortune exhausted, the Steele's social prominence fell. To make matters even more distressing for Charlotte, Matthew vehemently refused to accept any of the money she put at his disposal. She was free to use her inheritance on her personal needs, but he insisted that they manage on his income.

I had admired and respected Matthew's independence. In the beginning Charlotte had felt the same. In time, however, she'd grown tired of living on what she had called "the fringes of poverty," and the complaints began. Not that Matthew's family had ever heard them, for she'd wisely concluded that the matter had to be worked out between husband and wife. If only she'd been as prudent in regard to her former fiancé. But he'd come back into her life during a particularly low period, with words of love and the promise to take her home to Boston, where she longed to be.

I blinked and glared at the headstone. I could have understood Charlotte's death if she had succumbed to an illness, or even in childbirth, as my own mother had done. But the river?

Curling my fingers into tight fists, I forced myself to look at the water that had claimed my stepsister's life, wishing to God

I could take out my anger and frustration on it. How dare it look so peaceful and innocent, moving placidly between high banks dotted with pungent pines, great oaks, and fan-leafed palmettos.

Fresh tears spilled from my eyes as I stared at the dock a short distance downstream. I was so overcome with emotion that I didn't hear the approaching footfalls from behind and wasn't aware another soul was around until an unfamiliar masculine voice said, "Alexandra."

I whirled with a start, nearly strangling on a sharp inhalation of breath. The quickened movement brought with it a wave of dizziness, and I teetered a little.

Strong, steadying hands grasped me by the shoulders. "Are you all right?" the man asked, his Southern accent nearly as slight as Matthew's.

I nodded as I breathed in fresh air that cleared my head, then looked up at him. He was tall and handsome, with fair hair and blue eyes that held a soft look.

Releasing my shoulders, he said gently, "I didn't mean to startle you. I'm Tyler. Lizzie said she saw you coming out here." He dropped a look at Charlotte's grave. "I hope I'm not intruding."

"No." I felt instantly comfortable with this man who had become a dear friend to Charlotte, as well as her attorney for local business affairs. According to her, he had understood her better than she'd felt Matthew ever would. "I just can't believe she's truly gone." My voice was little more than a whisper.

Tyler tipped back his head and exhaled slowly. "It's been hard for all of us to accept."

"Matthew didn't mention how the accident happened, only that Charlotte drowned in the river."

"I'm afraid we don't really know how it happened. She was alone at the time. We all thought she was in her room napping, and it wasn't until Lizzie went to call Charlotte for supper that we discovered she'd left the house. We can only assume that she slipped on the rain-slickened grass and fell in."

"The water seems so calm. She must have panicked."

"I expect anyone would in a rain-swollen river."

"Rain-swollen?"

"The worst I'd ever seen. We'd warned Charlotte to stay away, but for some reason she chose not to listen."

Heeding sound advice hadn't been one of my stepsister's virtues, I reminded myself grimly.

Tyler glanced at a passing sloop on the water. "She might have wandered down without even thinking. She'd been very distracted that last week or so and unusually quiet. Whatever was on Charlotte's mind, she'd kept it to herself. Did she mention any particular concern to you in her letters, something that might have recently come up?"

All that came to mind was the large sum of money my stepsister had angrily mentioned was missing from the account she'd made available to her husband, the account she told him she was going to close. That was right after Matthew had once again denied her repeated pleas to return to Boston with their son. "I know he took the money," she had insisted in her last letter. "And probably just to get even with me for what I did. I'll wager he's using my funds to start his free clinic. Heaven knows, he doesn't have enough capital of his own." From all that I had heard about Matthew, he did not impress me as one who would act out of spite. Nor could I imagine that after three years of refusing to touch a cent of his wife's inheritance, he would suddenly, and without a word, dip into her funds. If anything, it seemed more likely that Charlotte, with her poor head for figures, had probably misread the account. "I can't recall any particular concern," I lied, deciding it would be wise to review the account before discussing it.

As I glanced back at the placid water, my heart lurched at the grisly vision my mind conjured of Charlotte struggling in vain against swift currents. All the blood in my head seemed to drain away and my legs grew rubbery. Just as I swayed helplessly against Tyler, his brother snapped, from beyond the cemetery fence, "Alexandra, I told you to stay inside and rest."

Tyler drew me into his strong embrace. "I think she's going to faint," he called to Matthew.

"I'm not surprised," he shot back. "She's overdone it."

"I'll be all right," I murmured, forcing strength into my voice. With my head still against Tyler's chest, I saw Matthew push open the gate. He came toward us in long, purposeful strides, which reminded me that Charlotte had mentioned her husband was not particularly tolerant of patients who disobeyed his instructions. His look of exasperation, as he came to a stop beside us, confirmed that statement. What a devil of a situation I'd gotten myself into, I thought in despair. This was not the way to win Matthew's approval so that I could stay on at Belle

Haven. Biting my lower lip, I willed the haziness from my brain. "I'm fine," I insisted, stretching the truth more than a fraction.

Matthew's exasperation deepened. "Fine is not pale and leaning on another for support."

He reached out to take my pulse. As his fingers came down over the soft and sensitive flesh of my wrist, my heartbeat quickened. For one breathtaking instant our gazes met and held, and I felt uncomfortably hot when I noticed the glow of awareness in his eyes. Could he see the same glow in mine?

"Is she all right?" Tyler's concerned tone held no hint he noticed the attraction between his brother and me.

Matthew's lips thinned, and he released my arm abruptly, as if he had been suddenly reminded that I was the enemy. "She's fine, but that could change without adequate rest."

I didn't doubt the validity of his statement. Still, I hesitated to speak up in agreement for fear my voice might reveal the lingering thrill of his touch. Instead, as I responded with a slight nod, I compared the cool expression that now darkened his eyes to the flicker of desire I'd seen just moments ago. Those same compelling emotions had whispered over every sensitive nerve in my body. Had my thundering pulse been as revealing as the burning expression in his eyes? The heat of embarrassment washed through me.

"I suggest you go now and rest," Matthew said.

I swallowed and diverted my attention to Charlotte's grave. "In a few minutes."

I heard him shift at my side. "Only a few minutes," he insisted, a trace of understanding in his voice.

"Would you like me to stay with you, Alexandra?" Tyler offered.

"Thank you, but I'd really like to be alone."

"I'll see you at supper, then," he returned softly.

"I'm sorry, but not tonight," Matthew said. "She'll be taking that meal in her room."

"Tomorrow," Tyler persisted.

I smiled at his genuine warmth. "I'll look forward to it."

As the men turned away, I noticed that Matthew had shed the coat, cravat, and waistcoat he'd worn earlier. And his crisp white shirt was now open at the throat. I also noted that the brothers were about the same height and build, although Tyler's shoulders seemed a bit broader. But then, perhaps his well-fitting cashmere suit coat accounted for the difference.

Without thought my attention shifted back to Matthew, and I remembered that Charlotte had admitted he'd been good to her. How could she, on the other hand, have been so unfair and even cruel in return? That just wasn't like the stepsister I'd grown up with.

The bickering of nearby jays nudged me back to the present. I knelt briefly at Charlotte's grave, then left the cemetery and returned to the house.

As I moved up the entrance salon stairs, I hoped I might catch at least a glimpse of my nephew. But with no one around, it didn't appear that would be the case. Disappointed, I continued up the stairs. By the time I reached my room, I felt as if I'd walked ten miles, and I winced at the dull ache that had begun to lurk again at the back of my head. Matthew was right, I had overexerted myself.

I sank down into the nearby chair, tipped back my head, and closed my eyes. The chattering of birds and the rustle of leaves blowing in the spring breeze came to me from beyond the glass doors. This place was indeed a haven. But my home was in Boston. All my hopes and dreams for the future had always centered on that city. Abruptly I broke off those thoughts. No more self-pity! I set my mouth in a resolute line.

As I came to my feet, I noticed that one of the doors on the right-hand armoire was slightly ajar. Hadn't I closed it when I'd changed before going outside? A shooting pain in my head erased the question. On my way to lie down on the bed, I spotted my reticule atop the night table. Thank goodness, Eustace had found my bag, and I wouldn't have to go through all the trouble of re-placing my papers.

As I lifted the reticule, I noticed that it, too, was partially open. Had someone looked in it? Or perhaps even taken some-thing? Quickly I turned it upside down, spilling out keys, a lace handkerchief, my papers, and a tapestry coin purse, which ap-peared untouched. Everything was here, everything except the last letter Charlotte had written to me.

I sat down on the bed and stared at the bag. Its drawstrings had been tightly closed before the accident. It didn't seem likely that the letter might have just fallen out, and I couldn't imagine that anyone would have wanted to take it.

The only other person, besides myself, that the letter might be of significance to was Matthew because of Charlotte's accusa-tion about the money. But even if it was true that he'd helped himself to the funds, it didn't make sense that he would go to the trouble of stealing the letter I'd already read. There had to be some other explanation for its disappearance, but what?

Pondering that question, I returned my belongings to the reticule and had scarcely put it away when Lizzie came in. "Dr. Matthew sent me to see if you is still fine after that spell outside, Miss Alexandra."

My aching head conveyed the opposite. But I wasn't about to give Matthew the satisfaction of knowing I'd had a slight relapse, one that might well have been avoided if I'd followed his instructions to stay inside and rest. Unfortunately, heeding sound advice wasn't always one of my virtues, either. I'd never admit that to Matthew Steele, though, not if I could help it. "I'm fine, Lizzie," I lied. "It was thoughtful of the doctor to inquire about me."

The housekeeper's eyes narrowed and worry came into her voice. "Your color ain't what it should be."

"I'm just a little tired and was about to take a nap." Before another word could be said on the subject, I changed it. "Please express my appreciation to Eustace for finding my reticule, Lizzie. It's a relief to have it back."

"Yes'm, I'll tells him." She moved to the bed. As she straightened the covers and fluffed the pillows, I considered mentioning the missing letter. But on the chance that her husband might have, out of sheer curiosity, emptied the reticule when he found it on the road and had simply forgotten to return the letter, I remained silent. It wasn't worth making a fuss over.

As I changed back into the silk nightdress and topped it with the matching empire-style wrapper, Lizzie lit the lamps against the approaching dusk. "Can I gets you anything before I leaves, miss?" she asked, concern still in her voice.

A head that didn't ache, I thought wryly, and declined the offer with a polite "No, thank you." After the housekeeper left the room, I stretched out on the bed and rested until the pain subsided. Then I gathered writing materials from the desk, made myself comfortable on the chaise, and had just begun a letter to Madame Fontaine when someone rapped on the door. Lizzie's worried face flashed across my mind, and I hoped that she hadn't sent Matthew to look in on me. He'd upset my senses enough for one day.

4

AFTER inhaling a small breath, I called, "Come in," and was relieved when chestnut-haired Felicity entered. She still wore the beautiful, shimmering, low-cut gown she'd had on when she'd stood at my bedside earlier in the day. The friendly smile she flashed shone in her sapphire-blue eyes. I returned the smile and greeted her by name, before she had the chance to introduce herself.

Felicity's *moue* drew down the corners of her full lips in an appealing pout. "I hope that your knowing me by sight, Alexandra, doesn't mean Charlotte wrote you *all* about me," she teased. Unlike Tyler and Matthew, her Southern accent was pronounced. But then, she hadn't left Charleston for extended periods as the men had done in completing their studies.

The memory of Charlotte's fondness for her filled me with a warmth that made it easy for me to tease back. "She told me *all* only if you have no faults."

The pout vanished. "I think that would be unnatural, don't you agree?"

"Yes, I suppose you're right," I returned lightly as I tried in vain to read the distant look that briefly shadowed her eyes. Felicity's high-cheekboned face and stylish hairdo were faultless. She was a good three inches taller than my own five feet four, with broader shoulders that accentuated a bodice as my own had never done. "Won't you please have a seat?" I gestured to the nearby chair and set aside the letter I had begun.

Felicity responded with a polite thank you and sat down amid the rustle of select imported silk. She was as refined as I had expected. But then, Felicity, too, had been reared in a home of luxury, the daughter of a prominent Charleston banker. Her parents were also gone now, the victims a few years back of one of the miasmic fevers rampant during the sickly season. The only close

family she had left were the Steeles and an older brother, who
was a West Point graduate, currently assigned to Fort Laramie,
Wyoming. "I'm so sorry about Charlotte," Felicity said. "As you
probably know, she and I had become good friends."

"She mentioned that in her letters. Your friendship meant a
great deal to her." We talked quietly for several minutes about
my stepsister, then Felicity asked about my trip across the Atlan-
tic.

Grief had made the voyage seem endless. But I shoved that
memory to the back of my mind and simply said, "It was un-
eventful."

"By now I, too, had hoped to travel abroad." The touch of
resentment that came into Felicity's voice reminded me that her
dream to visit far-off lands had been shattered by the financial
disaster. "But one day in the near future I'll be packing my
bags," she added in what sounded like a vow, then evened out
her voice. "I mustn't keep you from your rest, Alexandra." She
rose. "I'll come back another time for a longer visit."

"I'll look forward to it." She seemed as nice as Tyler, I thought
as I watched her exit the room. How sad she'd lost the husband
I'd heard she'd loved deeply. Brit Steele, who had been in charge
of this once thriving plantation, had blamed himself solely for
the financial disaster that wiped out the family fortune, as well
as his wife's inheritance. Determined to recoup both, he had
joined the legion of men bound for the California Gold Rush last
year. Sadly, like countless others, he was stricken down by chol-
era on the treacherous Oregon Trail.

Restless, I was about to leave the chaise and gaze out on the
deepening dusk when Zalea came in with my supper.

"Dr. Matthew said it's time you had something solid on your
stomach, miss." The pretty girl set down the silver tray laden
with fine china on the nearby table and pulled up an upholstered
chair.

Until this moment I hadn't really felt hungry. But just a glance
at the tender-looking poached fish, spinach salad, and piping-hot
spoon bread made my mouth water. The black-eyed peas, however, I regarded with uncertainty. For the most part, Charlotte
had raved about Southern cooking. Black-eyed peas, though, was
one of the foods she had put at the top of her "be sure to avoid"
list. Rightfully so, I determined after one taste. Wrinkling my
nose, I pushed them aside and pretended they did not exist.

All in all, the meal, topped off by a rich chocolate-rum soufflé, was delicious. When I was finished, I moved lazily to the French doors, parted the lace curtains, and looked out on the moonlit landscape. Now that I had confronted the river, and had fairly well come to grips with the tragedy that claimed my stepsister, viewing the placid water wasn't quite as heart-wrenching as before.

A knock on the door intruded slightly on my thoughts. Trancelike, and without looking around, I once again called, "Come in." Then I murmured, after hearing someone enter, "It's a beautiful night. . . . Moonbeams are dancing like a million tiny halos. Come see."

Footsteps sounded behind me, then I felt the warmth of another body. "Isn't it lovely?" I glanced around. "Oh!" I choked, whirling with a start. "I thought you were Zalea coming for the supper tray."

"She'll be in shortly." Matthew stared down at me, his dark brows knitted in a frown. "I'm here to check on my patient." His attention flicked to the glass door behind me. I was practically pinned against it by his virile frame.

Heat rushed to my face when I realized my chest visibly rose and fell at his disturbing nearness. And I couldn't seem to concentrate on anything other than the hair-roughened opening at his collar. Unconsciously I held my breath and was about to force myself to squeeze past him, putting a comfortable distance between us, when his attention returned to me and his frown deepened. "You're flushed, Alexandra."

Flushed? Good heavens, I was about to faint. To my utter dismay, I felt the heat increase, and before I could move or speak, Matthew lifted his slim, long fingers to my face. My senses soared at his touch, and my limbs threatened to bend like wispy feathers. "Hmm, no fever," he muttered.

I moistened my lips and was struggling to summon my voice and insist that he move back when he tilted up my chin. Matthew stared into my eyes with an intensity that made my brain fuzzy and my insides feel as if they were about to melt. I assumed the visual probing was professional, but my pulses raced with uncertainty when his hand trembled. "Is something wrong?" I blurted, my brain suddenly reduced to a mass of mush.

Now Matthew moistened his lips, and when he spoke, his voice had become a trifle hoarse. "No, you seem fine. Although I wonder what brought on the flush."

Thank God, he hadn't guessed. "The room is stuffy, that's

all." I tried to mask the truth with the first words that came to my scrambled brain.

Something flashed in his eyes. Was it disappointment? Had Matthew hoped that he'd been the cause of the flush? Afraid of what he might see in my eyes, I willed strength into my legs and eased past him.

"Any more headaches?" he asked as I came to a stop beside the chaise.

"Not for a while," I said over my shoulder. That wasn't really a lie. After all, it had been a good two hours since the last bout. Turning, I saw Matthew glance at the French doors. Briefly his brows drew together again. Then he looked at me, a faraway expression shadowing his face.

In a casual tone he said, "This is a nice room, Alexandra. But I'm sure you'd be much more comfortable in a larger one overlooking the drive."

Larger? This room was huge. Just crossing to the twin armoires was a journey. "Thank you, but I'm comfortable in here."

After hesitating a moment, he shrugged and replied in the same casual tone, "As you wish." It wasn't until after he'd exited that I wondered why Matthew, who had been far from overjoyed by my presence under his roof, was suddenly concerned about my comfort.

By morning that question became even stronger in my mind when Lizzie also mentioned a larger room. She'd repeated Matthew's words on the subject almost verbatim, which left no doubt that she was carrying out her employer's instructions. Why this persistence on his part?

After Lizzie helped me dress for the day, in a gray-checked taffeta trimmed in crimson, and arranged my hair, I followed her down to the cheery, apple-green breakfast room at the rear of the house. "Can I gets you some coffee or tea?" She pointed at the silver pots on the Sheraton mahogany sideboard.

"I'll help myself, Lizzie, thank you."

"Yes'm, I'll go tell the cook you is ready for breakfast." She turned and went out through the nearby swinging door.

As I poured coffee into a delicate cup, Felicity came into the room. Again, she was fashionably attired, this time in a fawn-colored gown over billowing petticoats, and her hair was styled in cascading ringlets. We exchanged good mornings, then Felicity said, "I didn't expect to see you up and around so soon, Alexandra. My, what a lovely gown."

"A friend in Paris fashioned it for me."

"Paris . . ." She sighed. "I long to go there. Is it as exciting as I've heard?"

"It lives up to its reputation, and then some."

Felicity asked many questions about that enchanting city and current Paris fashions over breakfast. After the delicious meal of hot corn cakes and thick slices of succulent roast ham, she took me on a partial tour of the superbly appointed house. The main living area was of course on the lower floor, where the huge ballroom dominated the single-story wing adjacent to the north drawing room.

The second floor was family sleeping quarters, with the exception of the library between my room and Grandmother Hester's. On our way from the library Felicity said, "The third floor is guest accommodations. There's nothing of particular interest to see there."

"And the music room?" I glanced up the final span of free-standing stairs, which I knew terminated at the octagonal cupola atop the house.

Felicity also glanced up the stairs, her expression growing solemn. "Since it was Charlotte's favorite place, I thought you might want to see it for the first time alone, Alexandra."

"I would, thank you," I responded quietly.

"Feel free to do the same with her room. It's just as Charlotte left it."

With a lump rising to my throat, I nodded appreciation. A moment later we moved on to Hester Steele's door and entered after knocking. The room was even larger than my own and more lavishly decorated with rich woods and brocades, highlighted by soft blue-gray walls and rug, the upholstered pieces in rose and buff.

The rheumatoid, white-haired matriarch of the family was comfortably seated near the French doors, overlooking the rear veranda. She was small and, despite lines of age, still attractive and not nearly as frail-looking as I had expected. Nor was she bundled in nightclothes and draped in a lap robe as I had imagined she might be. Instead, she wore a finely cut deep-blue dress, set off by a delicate lace-edged shawl.

We smiled at each other as our eyes met across the breadth of the room, and Hester Steele gestured with a gnarled hand to the chair beside her.

The regal air she exuded evoked a sense of reverence that compelled me to greet her in a hushed tone. But she would have none of that. "You must speak right up, dear," she insisted in a strong and heavily accented voice. "I know you are not shy. Charlotte told me all about you."

I had suspected that all along. My stepsister had loved to talk. What had she said about me to Matthew? I suddenly wondered, though I certainly had nothing to hide. As I crossed to Hester Steele, her alert gray eyes went over me in approving appraisal. Felicity came forward and made the introductions.

Without preamble the older woman said, "You must call me Grandmother Hester, Alexandra."

Her forthright manner came as no surprise. Charlotte had warned me about it.

Felicity exchanged a few pleasantries with Grandmother Hester, then left us to enjoy our first visit alone. As I sat down in the proffered chair and arranged my voluminous skirts about me, Mrs. Steele said, "I love Felicity like a daughter, known her from the day she was born. But I felt closer to Charlotte." Her voice deepened with sadness. "Maybe that was because her vitality and zest for life reminded me of myself when I was young."

"She felt very close to you, too," I said warmly, recalling how relieved Charlotte had been when Matthew insisted that the family be shielded from their marital problems. "If they knew the truth," she had written, "they would turn against me, and I couldn't bear that."

"We used to talk for what seemed like hours," Grandmother Hester was saying.

"She mentioned that many times in her letters. Charlotte especially loved the adventures you told of your father and his father."

A smile lit the lined face. "Ah, yes, they were daring, exciting men. Privateers." Her chin came up with pride.

"They were pirates?"

The old woman grinned at my surprise and didn't mince words. "Yes, indeed, my dear, that's where the Steele money came from. Back then the seizing and selling of enemy goods was legal and even patriotic."

Thanks to the first Navigation Acts, I thought, reflecting on my history lessons at Miss Bronson's Academy. It was just that I'd never before met anyone, as far as I knew, whose ancestors were pirates.

Hester's attention shifted to the display of weapons above the marble mantel. Slowly she lifted a hand, grimacing in obvious pain. "That seaman's cutlass was my grandfather's," she said with continued pride. "And the English flintlock pistol belonged to my father."

A shudder coursed through me at the ghastly vision of people being struck down by those weapons, of lives coldly sacrificed for pirates' booty. The Steeles were direct descendants of men who'd had no compunction about stealing and killing. I had become so caught up in the chilling thought that I'd scarcely heard a word of what Grandmother Hester had gone on to say. And suddenly she was patting me on the arm apologetically. "I hope I haven't bored you with talk of the past, dear."

"Heavens, no," I said quickly, straining to put together the bits and pieces I had heard, so I could make an intelligent comment instead of staring dumbly. Hester had said something about her grandfather, who built this house a hundred years back, during the French and Indian War. The colonies had boiled with unrest then, but had she already mentioned that? Fortunately, she changed the subject.

"I hope you'll come in and visit with me often, Alexandra. I do enjoy company."

"I'd like to very much."

Hester smiled. "Have you seen Rory yet?"

"No, he was napping when I finished with breakfast."

"He is such a delight."

The door opened and Lizzie came in with a cup of tea for the older woman. Hester scowled at the steaming brew. "This is to wash down the foul-tasting medicine Matthew insists I take."

Involuntarily my nose wrinkled at the memory of the medication he'd given me, and of course there was the putrid-smelling liniment. Thank goodness the hot bath had eased the pain, and I hadn't been compelled to use the malodorous liquid. Didn't that man have anything pleasing to the senses in his medical bag?

"You should be resting now, Miss Hester," Lizzie was saying.

"Later, Lizzie, can't you see I'm visiting?"

"No—please." I came to my feet. "I'll come back another time."

The older woman hesitated. "This afternoon? For tea?" she pressed.

"This afternoon," I promised and headed for the door.

In the hallway I waited for Lizzie to come out, then eagerly asked her, "Is Rory awake yet, do you know?"

"Yes'm, he be awake." She smiled. "His room is jest across the way. Come, I'll show you." With rising excitement bubbling in me, I followed her along the second-floor gallery to the nursery, overlooking the tree-lined drive. As we crossed the threshold of the airy room, decorated with blue-striped wallpaper and white woodwork, I saw Zalea bent over the baby, changing him into a fresh lawn gown. My view of Rory was partially obscured by the other girl, so I couldn't really see him. But just the sound of my nephew's happy gurgling made my heart skip a beat, and I held my breath in anticipation.

Zalea glanced around. "This babe done soaked hisself again," she muttered in mild exasperation. "But I has him all dry now for you." She lifted Rory and I took a step forward. He was the image of his father, though Rory's smile was his mother's.

The air escaped from my lungs in one long exhalation, and my eyes blurred with tears. He was so handsome and, thank heaven, healthy-looking. How terrible it must have been for Matthew, wondering all through his wife's pregnancy, if the child she carried was his. Charlotte had insisted it was, that she had not allowed her love for the other man to be consummated, but Matthew hadn't believed her.

As I crossed to my nephew, taking in his dark hair and eyes and dimpled little hands, Lizzie came up behind me and said, "You can holds him if you want, Miss Alexandra."

Of course I wanted to hold the little boy. But I hadn't been near an infant in years, and a twinge of apprehension overcame me. "I don't know much about babies," I admitted. "I'm not even sure if I remember how to hold one. I wouldn't want to hurt him."

Lizzie touched my shoulder reassuringly. "There ain't no reason to fret. He be a strong babe." She took Rory from Zalea and handed him gently to me. He smiled up at me, two tiny teeth showing, and my heart felt as if it would burst with love. Hugging him close, I rained kisses on his sweet face. Now, more than ever, I understood why Matthew had refused Charlotte's pleas to return to Boston with their child.

In the hour I spent with the adorable little boy, my emotions ran the gamut from love and joy to moments of sorrow because Charlotte wasn't here to enjoy her son, and to see him grow up.

I returned Rory to Zalea's capable hands and went to my stepsister's room next to the nursery. After inhaling a fortifying breath, I entered. Charlotte's spacious quarters were decorated in her favorite shades of peach and champagne. My throat tightened as I moved slowly about. Being among my stepsister's belongings was even more heart-wrenching than I had expected.

At the Queen Anne desk I lifted the gilt-framed daguerreotype of myself and Charlotte. It had been taken in our sixteenth year, shortly before our parents died of influenza within a month of each other. Even in the picture Charlotte's eyes gleamed with devilment. My eyes were seriously dark, and the bows in my flowing hair gave me a little-girl look. If this was the only picture Matthew had seen of me, it was no wonder he hadn't recognized me.

Sighing, I sat down at the desk and without thought opened the center drawer. My pulses leaped as my gaze fell on Charlotte's dairy. As I lifted it, I spotted another volume near the back of the drawer. For as long as I could remember, my stepsister had maintained a daily dairy. However, in Boston she had kept them hidden in what she had called "the secret place." It really wasn't a secret. I smiled at the memory. A dear friend and I had found the place years before and pored over every word. If Charlotte had even suspected what we'd been up to, she would have tried to yank out our hair by the roots.

As I flipped through the pages of the diaries, the dates indicated that I'd already read all of the passages with my friend. I knew there was a recent volume, and I looked through the desk for it. It wasn't there. Frowning, I sat back. Might Charlotte have stashed the diary in a "secret place"?

5

I was staring at Charlotte's desk when Felicity asked from the threshold of the open door, "Are you all right, Alexandra?"

Still frowning, I glanced over my shoulder. Felicity's sapphire-blue eyes held the same concern I'd heard in her voice. "I'm fine," I assured her. "I was just wondering where Charlotte's latest diary might be. It's not in the desk with these earlier volumes."

Amid the rustle of imported silk, she crossed to my side and regarded the pair I'd set out. "I didn't even know she'd kept a diary."

I nodded. "These cover girlhood days. There was another she started before we both left Boston."

"It should be among her belongings, unless Charlotte disposed of it."

"She wouldn't have done that."

"Then Matthew or Lizzie might know where it is. Shall I ring for her?"

"Thank you, but there's no hurry. I'll ask later." I replaced the volumes in the desk drawer and slid it closed.

"Lizzie told me you and Rory took an immediate liking to each other."

I pictured the little boy and smiled. "He's precious."

"On that we all agree." She also smiled. "Perhaps you'd like to move into this room so you can be closer to him."

A twinge of suspicion rippled through me. Was this her own idea? Or had Matthew put her up to mentioning the move, as he'd clearly done with Lizzie? "I appreciate the suggestion," I said softly, "but there are too many memories in here for me right now."

"I felt the same at first," she admitted and moved about, looking thoughtful. "I helped Charlotte decorate this room."

"She wrote me that you had. It's beautiful." Again, I admired the splendid furnishings and the brocade draperies, swagged and bound over lace undercurtains at the French doors. Felicity opened them, admitting the mild air. It blew gently at the English chandelier, and the melodic tinkling of its prisms reminded me of the sound my stepsister had loved.

"Charlotte and I spent hours visiting together out there." Felicity gestured to the white rattan furniture on the front-facing veranda. "She talked of you so frequently and longed for your visit. She hoped that while you were here, you might even fashion a gown or two for her. Yours were the only ones that would do, Alexandra, and understandably so. You're very talented."

I inclined my head in acknowledgment of the compliment and came to my feet.

Felicity glided to the walk-in closet and withdrew a claret-colored satin evening gown, the underside of its funnel-shaped sleeves done in white tulle. Instant recognition brought a lump to my throat.

"This was Charlotte's favorite." She held up the gown.

I swallowed. "I sent that to her the first year she was here."

"I watched her unwrap it. She was so excited. Did she tell you she wore this to the very next ball and was overwhelmed with compliments?"

"She did, in a letter she wrote on the following day. She even included a list of the compliments and the names of the ladies who voiced them. I was never sure what she expected me to do with the list." My tone lightened with the memory. "But I suspected it was her way of trying to drum up clientele for me."

Felicity smiled. "That would have been like her. She was very proud of you. Why, if I were three inches shorter"—a mischievous lilt came into her voice—"and a mere wisp like you and Charlotte, I would have tried to talk her out of this gown. To be honest," she said on a more serious note, "I was hoping I might commission you to fashion one for me to wear to the fund-raising ball for Matthew's free clinic. Did Charlotte mention it?"

"Only in passing." And with vehement anger over the money she'd insisted he had taken from her account to fund the clinic. "I understand it's a new venture."

Felicity returned the satin gown to the closet. "Matthew started it just over four months ago to aid the poor. It's been a lifelong dream of his. Years ago his brothers and I pledged our help. Now there's just Tyler and me to lend a hand." Her voice dipped on a sad note.

A silent moment fell. Then I said, "The clinic sounds like a noble endeavor. It must be terribly expensive to operate, though."

"Matthew had to expand his office and purchase additional equipment just to get started."

"Was there a fund-raising ball for that, also?"

"No, he was able to manage the expense on his own."

Not according to Charlotte. But then Matthew may have secured a bank loan or even borrowed from Tyler, whom I'd heard had a successful law practice.

"I'm organizing the ball," Felicity continued. "It was scheduled for last month. But out of respect for Charlotte, we postponed it until the end of May, and we'll hold it in the city now, instead of here at Belle Haven."

"That's only about two months off," I murmured.

"Which is still too soon," she said apologetically. "But without fairly immediate funds Matthew will be forced to close the clinic doors. That would be devastating to the needy. We hope you understand, Alexandra."

"Yes, of course. Charlotte couldn't abide deep mourning and all the somber drapings any more than I."

"We feel the same," she answered on what sounded like a breath of relief. Then Felicity returned the conversation to the gown she hoped I might fashion for her. "If it wouldn't be too much of an imposition, Alexandra, I'd truly love to wear one of your creations to the ball. Remember"—the gleam of enticement came into her eyes—"it would be seen by every prominent woman in Charleston."

I smiled at the exciting prospect. "You do know how to tempt me."

"Is that a yes?"

"It would be a pleasure to do one for you, Felicity, as a gift," I insisted. Actually, now that I thought of it, the gown would give me another reason, aside from Rory, to stay on at Belle Haven longer than Matthew might like.

Beaming, Felicity placed an appreciative hand on my arm. "I have a wonderful seamstress," she said, "who can come in on almost a moment's notice. And the sewing room is full of fabrics I've purchased over the years."

Elation swept through me at the thought of being in my element again, and I lost no time arranging a tour of the sewing room for the following morning.

Felicity had scarcely left my side when Lizzie came in. I showed her the diaries and asked if she might know the whereabouts of the missing volume. She shook her head. "Miss Charlotte kept three of 'em in the desk drawer. If one be gone, I don't know where."

"Do you remember when you last saw all of them?"

She thought for a moment. "I don't recollect, but I seen Miss Charlotte writin' in one the night before she—"

"That would be the diary I'm looking for. Did you see her put it away?"

Again she shook her head. "She was still writin', there at the desk, when I tells her good night after turning down the bed. Is it somethin' important?"

"It was to Charlotte. I'd like to have it as a keepsake, for me and Rory."

"It's gotta be here somewhere. Ain't nobody touches anything, that I knows of. I can looks for it."

"That won't be necessary, Lizzie. It will probably turn up when I start packing away her belongings."

"If I can helps you with that, Miss Alexandra, jest let me know."

"I will," I returned with appreciation. After she, too, left, I surveyed the room. Since Charlotte had kept all three diaries in the desk drawer, a secret place wasn't likely. She'd only had one back home because of me and my friends, and with good reason. As I moved about, indulging in memories and trying to picture my stepsister in this room, my mind persistently fixed on the missing volume. Where could it be? Perplexed, I looked in both night table drawers, then drifted to those in the mahogany bureau. The sight of Charlotte's personal belongings tore at my heart—her exquisite silk nightdresses, lace-trimmed undergarments, and the treasured handkerchiefs her mother had embroidered. Blinking back tears, I lifted the linen square adorned with a delicate red rose, Charlotte's favorite flower. Her room in Boston had overlooked the rose garden and the gazebo in its center. As children, we'd played there with our dolls and presided like royalty over make-believe tea parties. Later, when young men came to call, the gazebo took on another significance. A challenge, actually, I remembered with a smile. Charlotte and I had frequently sneaked out on pleasant summer evenings for moments alone there with special beaus. Thank heaven, our parents had never caught us.

On a surge of loneliness I slipped the dainty handkerchief into my skirt pocket and continued the search for the diary. The more I looked, the more mystified I became and the more determined to find it. I wasn't even certain why. Its value was purely sentimental, and there were plenty of other keepsakes to cherish. Nevertheless, something drove me, a nagging that would not subside. I rechecked the desk. Still nothing. Although I did come across the letter I'd sent Charlotte from Paris, stating I was on the way to Belle Haven. It had been put aside unopened, just as Matthew said.

Being in Charlotte's room was more painful than I had expected, and by the time I left I was emotionally spent. The numbness remained with me through lunch, and I found myself apologizing to Felicity for the remoteness that engulfed me. "I understand," she said with compassion and allowed me to slip back into healing silence.

At the end of the meal I excused myself and went out for a peaceful stroll around the spacious grounds. The impeccable formal gardens complemented the splendid house, which was even more lavish than the one Charlotte and I had grown up in.

After father's death, managing our Boston home had fallen to me, for Charlotte had shunned the responsibility I rather enjoyed. From that experience I knew what it cost to maintain a place like this. To my knowledge, Tyler and Matthew did so with their own funds. Nowadays, however, there wasn't as much to care for as there had been in the past. All the brothers were able to salvage after the financial disaster was the house and five hundred acres of the original three thousand.

The bickering of jays nudged me from my thoughts. I turned and slowly headed back to the house. The front and rear facades of the magnificent white clapboard structure were identical, with three tiers of columned verandas and dark window shutters. Centered atop the roof was the multiwindowed cupola my stepsister had converted into a music room. For decades before then it had served as a lookout from which the entire plantation was visible.

A glance at my pendant watch conveyed there wasn't time to visit the music room today. In a way I was relieved. The walk had given my spirit a tremendous boost. Seeing the place Charlotte had loved the most would only send it plummeting again.

Back in my room I freshened myself, then went to Grandmother Hester's door. She responded immediately to my light tap. When I entered, she said with delight, "I've been looking forward to teatime with you, Alexandra. Come, sit by me."

Her smile was contagious, and I felt my spirits rise another degree. For the next hour we chatted amiably over refreshing mint tea. She was indeed as delightful and endearing as Charlotte had said. Before I left Hester to her afternoon nap, I promised to join her for breakfast in the morning.

Eager to see Rory again, I went to his room. But Zalea told me he was also napping. Matthew had insisted that I do the same until I was fully recovered from the carriage accident. I felt fine. Still, rather than chance overexerting myself as I had on the previous day, I obeyed the order. Heaven forbid, I should once again trigger Matthew's ire by ignoring his instructions.

Sleep eluded me, however, which was no surprise. I wasn't accustomed to napping. But at least I had rested and wouldn't face the temptation of choking out a fib if Matthew brought up the subject. After rinsing my hands and face at the washbasin, I reached into my skirt pocket and withdrew the embroidered handkerchief. I placed it in the bureau beside the half-dozen dainty squares Charlotte's mother had done for me. My favorite, with the sprinkling of fragile violets, was on top.

Zalea came in as I was changing into a sea-green silk and helped me arrange the supple fabric over a wide crinoline. "Pretty," she breathed, eyeing the creation, trimmed with puffs of box-pleated ribbon, as if it were a tempting confection.

I thanked her with a smile and resisted the urge to comment that I'd slaved over it. Initially the scoop-neck had dipped daringly, the long sleeves had needed more fullness at the shoulders, and the drape of the voluminous skirt had been reworked until I'd nearly screamed from frustration. At one point I'd even cursed this gown and abandoned it to the back of my workroom closet, vowing never to set eyes on it again. Now it was my favorite. It was comfortable, yet subtly alluring, and the vibrant color brightened my face. Zalea tied the sash, then fashioned my thick, dark hair in stylish cascading ringlets.

Minutes later I entered the north drawing room, where Tyler and Felicity greeted me before supper. "What a lovely gown," she said. "Is it your own design?"

Nodding, I praised her attractive lavender satin, adorned with blond lace.

"You look stunning, Alexandra," Tyler said as he came to his feet and offered me the seat beside him on the red velvet sofa. The effusive compliment along with his appreciative gaze brought heat to my face. Naturally I was flattered by his interest. What woman of sound mind wouldn't be? He was handsome, worldly, and exuded Southern charm and hospitality. The latter could not be said for his brother. When Matthew entered and saw me comfortably seated and chatting gaily with his family, a frown furrowed his brow. I forced down the scowl that threatened to overwhelm my smile. Couldn't that man at least try to hide his distaste at having me under his roof?

"Good evening," he said with a stiffness that only I seemed to notice. As he sat down opposite me, my gaze automatically swept over his tall good looks and the perfect fit of his well-tailored suit, with its soft velvet collar. Before I could avert my attention, his eyes met mine. Again, heat rushed to my face, only I wasn't certain if it came from having been caught admiring him or from his assessing expression. For a moment I thought his interest was personal. But when he spoke, his professional-sounding tone told me otherwise. "You're looking well, Alexandra."

"I'm fine," I muttered on a rush of disappointment.

Supper was served in the immense formal dining room at the rear of the house. "Grandmother Hester joins us when she feels up to it," Felicity told me. "Unfortunately, that isn't often."

Tyler turned gleaming eyes on me. "She's taken quite a fancy to you, Alexandra."

"And I to her." I noted that his suit also had a soft velvet collar. "She has a wonderful sense of humor and," I added, "the forthright manner I admire."

Felicity laughed. "That is a Steele family trait."

"It also runs in my family," I confessed. "Though being in the business world has forced me to curb the tendency."

Apparently, that comment reminded Felicity of the gown I'd promised to fashion for her, because she enthusiastically mentioned it to the men.

Tyler inclined his fair head. "That's very generous of you, Alexandra."

Matthew nodded politely. But the firm set of his mouth communicated deepening displeasure over what appeared to be my settling in at Belle Haven. Could he send me packing even if the rest of the family wanted me to stay?

After the delicious meal of quail in wine sauce, fresh vegetables, and pralines with raspberry whip for dessert, the men went up to visit with Grandmother Hester. Felicity and I returned to the elegantly appointed drawing room, illuminated by multicandled, crystal chandeliers. About the pale gray walls were superb oil paintings and long windows with rich hangings over lace curtains. "Tell me more about France," she urged, sitting down on the tufted-back sofa across from me.

I smiled at her eagerness. "There is so much, I'm not sure where to begin."

"Are their fashions much different from ours?"

"Their *couturières* are more progressive. I saw so many exciting and innovative creations just in the three short years I was there. In time I think Paris will be the hub of fashion."

"And you had no wish to stay and remain a part of that world?" She looked at me as if no one in their right mind should want to leave.

"I was tempted to stay," I admitted. "But America is my home, and I hope I'll be able to put all that I've learned to good creative use here."

Felicity sighed and said in a quiet tone, "I do envy you the freedom you've enjoyed and the opportunity to travel. I hate to admit it, but I'm the only one in my close group of friends who hasn't been abroad."

She made that sound as if it were a sin. Surely her friends didn't look down on her because she wasn't traveled. "If it hadn't been for my work," I said, "I probably wouldn't have left Boston."

"And I can't imagine not wanting to see other lands and cultures. Brit had promised me a European holiday, but that was before the financial problems." Felicity's lips twisted in a brief show of resentment. "I mustn't bore you with the grim details of my life, Alexandra."

The absence of travel hardly seemed grim to me. But priorities were as widely varied as hopes and dreams and disappointments.

"Did you meet any artists in Paris?" Felicity continued.

"Quite a few, yes."

"Any come to call?"

"One or two," I said lightly.

She arched a delicate eyebrow. "You must tell me about them."

"Next time," I promised, standing up.

"I'll hold you to that," she insisted with a smile and also stood. Felicity and I exchanged a few more words, then I excused myself and climbed the stairs. As I neared the second-floor landing, Rory began to cry. I went to the nursery to see if I could be of help. His door was slightly ajar, and muted lamplight slanted across the threshold. Easing open the door, I stepped in. Matthew was near the crib, his back partially toward me. "Hush, little one," he murmured soothingly to the now whimpering baby cradled in his arms. I'd never seen a man hold an infant with such gentleness and caring, and I marveled in silence over the heartwarming scene.

Matthew must have sensed my presence, because he suddenly turned. His lips parted when he saw me, and his gaze locked onto mine with an intensity that kindled a wave of breathtaking excitement. Rory was quiet now, and all I heard was the rapid beat of my heart.

I moistened my dry lips and responded to the questioning look in Matthew's eyes. "I heard Rory and came to see if there was anything I could do."

Matthew blinked but did not look away. For some inexplicable reason I couldn't, either. It was as if a powerful, unseen force had welded our spirits. "He'll be fine." His voice was a husky whisper. "He's cutting teeth."

"You're very good with him." My own voice fell to a whisper, and I was acutely aware of the gentle quality that heightened his appeal.

"Rory is my life." He glanced adoringly at his son, who had begun to doze off.

"Rory and medicine," I murmured, remembering Matthew's compassion and gentleness in caring for me right after the carriage accident.

He nodded. "Just as fashion is yours, much to Felicity's delight." He cleared his throat. "How long will it take you to finish the gown for her?"

The abruptness that came into Matthew's tone took me aback, and my mind conjured a picture of him standing before a monstrous calendar, counting off the days until he could bid me farewell. What an impossible situation ours was! Suppressing a frown, I shrugged. "It's hard to say." I refused to be pinned down. "The length of time depends on fabric and design." The truth of that statement was wafer-thin; time would only vary by a few days, not the weeks I had hoped to imply. Rather than chance being caught teetering on the brink of a lie, which would hardly endear me to this man, I said, "I'll leave you to Rory."

Matthew hesitated, his lips compressed. For a moment I thought he was going to pursue the subject. To my relief, he simply said, "Good night." As I swung back to the door, he gently laid his sleeping son in the crib.

Later, as I changed into a nightdress, I remembered the missing diary and wished I had thought to ask Matthew if he knew where it was. But there was always tomorrow.

I crawled into bed. As I reached out to extinguish the flame in the lamp, the sound of a woman crying came to me. From where, though? I rose up on one arm. My ears strained, listening. The crying was near and so pitiful. It didn't sound as if it was coming from the rooms to either side. Could it be traveling up through the fireplace? With chills dappling my flesh, I left the bed and went to the hearth. Leaning near, I listened again. It wasn't coming from there, either.

Perhaps the woman was somewhere out on the veranda, which ran the breadth of the house. As the crying persisted, I lit the small mantel lamp and carried it with me to the French doors. I inched open a glass panel and peered out, raising the light. The soft radiance only allowed me to see a few feet into the moonless night.

Urged on by the plaintive wailing, I crossed the threshold and moved the lamp from left to right. Empty rattan furniture was all that met my eyes. The crying was less pronounced beyond the door, which meant it had to be coming from somewhere in the house. Did anyone else hear it? Just as I was about to return to my room, the crying stopped. My pulse slowed and I held my breath. All I heard was what sounded like ripples on the river. The cool breeze stirring my nightdress was probably doing the same to the water.

As I lowered the lamp and moved back, the scraping of stone against stone, in the cemetery below, brought me to a dead halt.

⚛ 6

My heart leaped to my throat. What could be going on in the cemetery after dark? Brows knitted, I stepped toward the veranda railing, then pulled up short. Quickly I blew out the lamp and set it on the table just inside the door. Since I didn't know who or what was out there, the last thing I wanted was to draw attention to myself. At the railing I looked in the direction of the cemetery. With the moon and stars masked by a cloud cover, all I saw in the blackness was the ghostly outline of twisted trees. If someone was prowling the grounds, he or she would surely have a lantern or some other form of light to guide the way. There was none. The scraping, like the crying, had stopped, and the sound of the ripples on the river were fading. Odd, considering the breeze hadn't dropped. Although maybe a passing boat rather than the wind had stirred the water. Charlotte had written that traffic was heavy, with mail and staples transported upstream from Charleston to the various plantations. I turned my attention toward the river and scanned in one direction, then the other. No lights. Back in the cemetery the darkness remained absolute.

Hugging myself against the cool night air, I returned to the warmth of my room and closed the door. For a fraction of a second, utter silence made me question if I had imagined the wailing and the chilling noise that had set my teeth on edge. But the knot in my stomach confirmed the reality of both. Why hadn't anyone else in the house reacted to them?

Distractedly I turned out the night table lamp and crawled back into bed. The heart-wrenching sobs must have come from one of the rooms adjoining mine. Felicity's was to the left, the library to the other side, with Grandmother Hester's beyond. It didn't seem likely that either one of them would be in the library at this late hour, let alone shed racking tears there. Especially when the privacy of their own rooms was just a door or two away.

Tossing in bed, I focused on Felicity. She'd been widowed for less than a year, and since she'd loved her husband deeply, there were bound to still be tears. I drifted off to sleep convinced she was the woman I'd heard.

Upon awakening in the morning, I vowed not to mention the crying and risk the possibility of embarrassing Felicity. Worse yet, renew her sorrow.

With my thoughts still fixed on last night, I drew on my silk wrapper and went out to stand once again at the veranda railing. The air was a trifle biting, though the sun shining on my face was warm. Automatically my gaze dropped to the cemetery and the elaborate marble headstones. No one was in sight and nothing seemed disturbed. Even so, someone or something had caused the noise I'd heard. Still, with all appearing in order on both the grounds and the placid river, it was pointless to puzzle over the incident any longer. Shoving it to the back of my mind, I returned to my room. At the armoire I exchanged my nightdress for a spring day gown of white over mauve, then sat down at the dressing table and arranged my hair with side combs. With less than a minute left before I was expected in Grandmother Hester's room for breakfast, I put on my shoes and hurried to her door.

Again the white-haired matriarch responded immediately to my tap and beamed when I entered. She was seated near the hearth, which was aglow with the embers of a fire. To me it made the room uncomfortably warm. But she looked cozy and especially attractive in a morning dress of French cambric, topped by an embroidered lace shawl. A linen-draped table had been pulled up and set with Haviland china and gleaming silver. "You're looking well, Alexandra," Hester said, offering me the chair across from her at the table. "I trust you had a good night's sleep."

"Yes, thank you." I had, once I'd finally drifted off. I was tempted to mention the unnerving noise in the cemetery, but decided not to chance upsetting the older woman. As I sat down, I gestured to the twin pots on the table. "Shall I pour, Hester?"

"Please. I'll have tea, with two sugars."

I filled her cup and set it before her.

"Have you been up to the music room yet?" she asked.

I poured coffee for myself. "No, I plan to do so this afternoon." The reminder of Charlotte prompted me to mention the diaries, and I asked Grandmother Hester if she knew where the missing volume might be.

"No, I'm sorry," she said slowly, regarding me over the rim of her cup. "Charlotte told me she'd always kept a diary but hadn't commented beyond that. I should think it would be somewhere in her room. Matthew and Lizzie would be the ones to ask. Ah, here comes Zalea with breakfast. I hope you like corn muffins and roast ham."

"Very much."

"And grits, of course."

"Grits?" I repeated, trying to remember if my stepsister had ever commented on the dish.

"It's a favorite among us Southerners. We eat it with just about everything. Charlotte grew to like it."

Apparently, she must have, because it hadn't been on her "be sure to avoid" list of Southern foods. It didn't look particularly appealing, I determined as Zalea and another young maid set steaming plates on the snow-white tablecloth. I tasted the delicious ham and muffins, then swallowed a small helping of the grits. As I washed it down with coffee, Hester said with a laugh, "You don't like it, Alexandra."

"It's different," I admitted candidly. "But I expect I can cultivate a taste for it." Which was more than I could say for the black-eyed peas I'd pushed aside on my supper plate at my first evening meal in this house.

Over breakfast Hester told me more about the family, especially her grandfather. "He fought with General Francis Marion during the Revolutionary War." Her chin came up with pride.

"Francis Marion, the Swamp Fox?" I blurted, then wondered at my surprise. After all, the Steeles descended from pirates. Tramping in swamps and bogs to flush out the British and Tories who had overrun South Carolina was bound to appeal to such daring males.

"Ah, yes"—she sighed—"the Swamp Fox, indeed. He and his men were great patriots. Their fearless forays contributed tremendously to the British defeat in the South." We lapsed into a few moments of comfortable silence as we ate, then Hester elaborated on the building of this house and how her grandfather had supervised every phase of the construction. "This place is unique in many respects," she said.

Unique? I was as intrigued by the word as the secretive smile that touched her lips. I was about to ask in what way this house was unusual when she continued. "My grandfather saw to it that his every wish was carried out. The Steele men are a strong and determined lot," she finished pridefully.

Judging from her, I thought with admiration, the Steele women were made of the same sturdy fiber.

Lizzie came in to give Grandmother Hester her medicine, and I excused myself and went to the nursery. I helped Zalea bathe Rory, who kicked and splashed water in every direction. I laughed, caressing a soft, dimpled hand. "He's most energetic."

Zalea's warm face lit with smile. "He be a lively one," she agreed.

After the bath I dressed my cooing nephew in a fresh gown and played with him until it was time for his mid-morning feeding. Then I kissed the dark-haired little boy, handed him over to Zalea and went down to the sewing room at the rear of the house. Felicity was already there, looking over fabrics. She smiled when she saw me. If she was the one I'd heard crying last night, no lingering signs of the sorrow were in her face. "I hope I haven't kept you waiting," I said.

"I just came in myself." Felicity showed me around the spacious room, bright with sunlight spilling through large windows.

I gaped in amazement at the shelf upon shelf of sumptuous fabrics and the drawers of notions. There were exquisite imported laces of varying widths, braids, bindings, a large assortment of buttons, loop sets, dress shields, embroidery silks, and spools of thread in every conceivable color. For a moment I felt as if I had been transported back to the workroom in Madame Fontaine's salon. "This is the most well-stocked sewing room I've ever seen, Felicity. Did you select and purchase all of this yourself?"

"Most of it, yes. I haven't added anything new in the past couple of years, though," she complained, and I could only imagine how profoundly she must have been affected by the financial disaster that now placed luxuries beyond her means.

"You have excellent taste. Your gowns reflect that."

"Why, thank you, Alexandra." Her expression brightened. "It's an honor to receive such a compliment from an authority on fashion."

The flattery brought a small smile to my lips. Felicity and I spent the balance of the morning together, discussing her taste in gowns, fabric and color preferences, and taking measurements. She was a bit taller and broader-shouldered than the average woman and fortunate to be blessed with perfect proportions. "You're one of the lucky few who can wear almost everything," I said. "A dressmaker's delight."

Beaming, Felicity hauled out bolt after bolt of cloth and laces, endeavoring to make a choice. "I just wish I had some of the more vibrant shades that have come out recently," she murmured, surveying the lot. "Like the starlight blue."

For a moment her drooping lower lip reminded me of Charlotte, who'd always had the best of everything and had never been truly contented.

"If there were any more colors here," I said lightly, "a choice would be impossible. Anyway, let me do a few sketches first, then we'll consider fabrics."

Felicity agreed with a nod, though her eyes conveyed she still coveted the newer shades. "Charlotte purchased a drawing table for you, Alexandra, and some sketch pads."

I laughed. "Obviously, she did plan to put me to work."

"She could be persuasive."

Just like this woman, I thought in continued delight over her enthusiasm for my fashions.

"I'm not sure where Eustace put the table," she said, "but I'll find out. Would you like it set up in here or in your room?"

"My room, please." We had just put away the last bolt of cloth when Lizzie announced lunch. During the meal, my mind kept returning to the mountain of select yard goods I knew cost a fortune. Even I, in my infinite love of fashion, had never indulged in such an extravagance. But indulgences were human nature, I reminded myself over dessert.

After lunch Felicity invited me to accompany her on her daily ride, but I declined and went instead up to the cupola, surrounded by windows. Beyond was an encircling balustraded promenade. The room itself was larger than I had expected, and my heart felt as if it had been torn from my breast when I spotted the rosewood pianoforte. It had been handed down in my stepsister's family. Music had been her love, the pianoforte her most prized possession. Through years of dedicated practice, Charlotte had become an accomplished pianist and was pressed to entertain at every social function she attended.

The mahogany spinet on my right turned my mind back to her twelfth birthday, and I envisioned pretty, blond-haired Charlotte, in her new dotted swiss, whirling with glee after our parents

announced the spinet was hers. With a small sigh I crossed and
stroked its polished surface. I hadn't been this close to a piano
in years. But that was to the benefit of everyone, including myself. While Charlotte had played with flawless perfection, my fingers on the keys had caused listeners to wince. After two years
of struggles with lessons, I had been allowed by my wise father
to abandon the piano.

The harp in the corner caught my attention, and my throat
constricted. Charlotte had purchased it shortly after Rory was
born. Nearby was a snake-footed music stand and a mahogany
cabinet fitted with handsomely decorated rococo molding. There
was also a settee in the room and a pair of gilt banquet lamps
on dark side tables. The converted cupola had been my stepsister's haven. As far as I knew, no one other than she, and the
maid who to this day kept it spotless, ever ventured up here.

Engrossed in sweet memories I moved from window to window. Charlotte had raved about the view. It was splendid, and
I marveled over the panorama of the countryside. The entire
plantation was indeed visible, from the formal gardens and
spreading lawn below to the tree-lined river and the dense woods
edging vast fields. I paused and admired the magnolias in full
bloom on the front grounds. As my attention shifted to the long
drive shaded by a thick canopy of gnarled oak branches, I saw
a male rider on a black stallion. The man reined in at the gatehouse near the head of the drive and dismounted. Even before
he reached up and removed the medical bag from his saddle, my
pulse quickened at the identifying squared set of his shoulders.
As I watched Matthew secure the reins to the hitching post and
enter the clapboard structure, I remembered that Charlotte once
mentioned he maintained an office for neighboring patients. The
irrepressible urge to see him in his element swept through me.
After another glance around the music room, I left the house
and made my way down the avenue of trees.

Since Matthew's horse still stood alone at the hitching post,
I assumed no patients had come to call, and I mounted the three
steps to the porch. Standing before the door which bore his shingle, I moistened my suddenly dry lips, then knocked. The sound
of approaching footsteps intermingled with the chirping of birds
and the gentle rustle of leaves on the breeze that seemed to be
growing warmer by the second. Matthew opened the door, his
expression pleasant until his gaze fell on me. Surprise flickered
in his dark eyes, then the corners of his mouth turned down in

unmistakable displeasure. "I hope I haven't come at a bad time," I managed in a level voice.

His response was stiff. "Is this a professional visit, Alexandra?"

I shook my head. "I was just interested in seeing your office." He hesitated, and I rushed on, my tone becoming apologetic. "But if I'm intruding—" Of course I was, in his whole life. The tightening of his clear-cut features left no doubt of that. How foolish I'd been to come here, to risk aggravating him further. The regret that must have shown in my eyes apparently triggered the compassion I'd come to know in Matthew, because his expression softened. Although when he spoke again, his manner remained stiff.

"I can spare a few minutes." He stepped aside, allowing me to enter. "But I doubt you'll find anything of interest in here."

He was of interest. The moment the unbidden thought leaped forward, I scolded myself for succumbing once more to the intimate feelings I couldn't seem to stem. I'd never been this consumed by a man before. Why, even with my back toward Matthew, I sensed his commanding presence and felt the warmth radiating from his strong body.

Praying the rising heat within me wasn't evident in my face, I forced my attention on the office. We were in the reception room, which looked like all the others I'd ever seen. There were a few chairs, a desk, and a bank of cabinets. The white walls were unadorned. Beyond, through open doors, was an examining room and a small pharmacy. "Do you see many patients here?" I turned abruptly and my heart fluttered when I caught Matthew watching me with what appeared more than casual interest. On top of that he'd closed the outside door. I had expected to find it still open and his hand on the knob in a blunt reminder to keep my visit short.

Matthew's lips compressed. "I see quite a few patients here, especially during the sickly season. And always, throughout the year, a certain number of plantation workers."

His clipped tone confirmed my suspicion that he was annoyed with himself over that momentary lapse into warm regard. The twinge of excitement he'd inspired in me was overwhelmed by disappointment. I struggled to keep that emotion from my voice. "I'd heard you care for a great many of them."

"I care for everyone who comes to me," he said matter-of-factly.

"I guessed that."

"How? From what Charlotte wrote?" A hint of resentment came into his voice.

"No." In truth, the only times she'd mentioned Matthew's practice was in complaint about the free clinic and the pittance he earned as a physician. "The sensitive way in which you cared for me conveyed your dedication, and Felicity told me about your work with the poor. I admire you for the worthy undertaking, Matthew."

Again surprise came into his eyes, and I wondered if he had expected to receive the same negative response from me, in regard to the clinic, as he had from Charlotte. "Admiration is not what I'm striving for," he said flatly.

He was clearly wary of my praise. Did he think I was just trying to gain his approval so that I might stay on at Belle Haven? His skepticism was understandable. Nevertheless, I was not about to let him to think, even for a moment, that I would stoop to conniving.

I returned in the same flat tone, "I hadn't meant to imply that it was. Your work is important. I believe in it wholeheartedly."

For timeless seconds Matthew's gaze held mine, and I had the feeling he was trying to read my mind. Was I as much of an enigma to him as he was to me? In the end my sincerity must have shown through, because he replied in a soft, almost apologetic voice, "I shouldn't have jumped to conclusions." He paused, then offered me the chair in front of his desk.

Surprise mixed with delight coursed through me. Maybe in time he and I could be friends, perhaps even—I broke off the thought, refusing to let my heart rule my brain. As I sat down, I said, "Felicity mentioned you've been planning the clinic for a long time."

"Since the day I knew I wanted to be a doctor." He also sat down. As Matthew clasped his hands before him on the desk, I noticed how long and slim his fingers were.

"When was that?" I swallowed, simply recalling how his touch had quickened my pulse.

A slight smile played at the corners of his mouth. "I was about six."

"Really? At that age all I thought of was playing with dolls and growing up to be a mother."

"Instead, you're throwing yourself into the business world."

Most men, and even many women, regarded my professional

pursuit in a negative light. There was no hint of this in Matthew's face or voice.

"I prefer to think of it as following my dream," I said softly, "just as you're following yours. In time I hope to be a mother also." Of course, if Matthew allowed me to carry out Charlotte's last wish, I would be a surrogate mother to Rory until his father remarried. Prudently I did not comment on that explosive subject. Instead, I asked, "Is your clinic open on a weekly basis?"

"Every Tuesday afternoon, though I hope to expand to a full day soon."

"I'd like to help in some way," I volunteered. "Maybe with the fund-raising."

His eyes brightened at my offer. Nevertheless, he hesitated, then answered in an evasive tone, "Perhaps. In any case, I appreciate your interest and enthusiasm."

Despite the note of sincerity that seeped in, the underlying message in Matthew's voice left no doubt that he did not expect me to be here long enough to lend a hand. Frustration combined with disappointment brought me to my feet. "Thank you for your time, Matthew." I forced a pleasant smile. "And for showing me your office. I'll see myself out." He stood as I turned away.

I was so consumed by the fact that Matthew and I were still at loggerheads that I wasn't aware he'd followed me to the door. And when I pulled up short, whirled, and said on a sudden thought, "Oh, one more thing," he collided with me. I was knocked off-balance. Automatically his steadying hands gripped me by the shoulders. His touch was lightning to my senses, and I swayed against him on a dizzying wave.

"I'm sorry," Matthew rasped, pulling me into a protective embrace.

Sorry for almost knocking me down? Or for holding me close? I wondered, drugged by his strength and fresh masculine scent. I felt my blood surge when I realized his heart was beating as rapidly as my own. My mind ordered me to twist free, to spare myself from the possibility of being hurt by this man who didn't even want me under his roof, but every sensitive nerve countermanded the order. Matthew tightened his embrace, and I melted against him when he huskily murmured, "Alexandra." We were pressed so close that I felt the heat of his body, just as I knew he felt mine. His warm breath in my hair was enticing. My own breathing grew even more erratic as he entwined deft fingers in my cascading curls and rained kisses on my temple. All thought escaped me, though I sensed Matthew willing me to lift my face to his. With delirious abandon I obeyed the silent message, and my lips parted in acceptance as Matthew's mouth claimed mine in a fevered kiss that stopped time. Sensations such as I'd never known fueled the fire of urgency that made me tremble. As Matthew's persuasive lips moved on mine with wanton splendor, he, too, trembled. And I gloried in the knowledge that he was as much in my power as I was in his.

The timeless moments passed too quickly, and when Matthew lifted his head, the yearning within me demanded that I rise up on my toes and return my mouth to his. But pride and the dictates of propriety kept me from being so bold. Matthew stared deeply into my eyes, and for one heart-stopping second I thought he was going to kiss me again. Then I saw a flash of regret, and I knew the moments of bliss were over. "I'm sorry, Alexandra," he said softly as he released me and stepped back, "I shouldn't have let that happen."

His words stung, though I didn't let the hurt show. "It's all right," I insisted, struggling to preserve shredded pride.

Matthew took another step back as if he couldn't trust himself to stand near. "I believe there was something you were about to ask before we—"

"Ask?" I murmured dully. I couldn't focus on anything but the kiss. Then I remembered. "Oh, yes"—my voice sounded faraway—"I wondered if you might know where Charlotte's latest diary is. It's not in her room."

He paused. "Why would you want it?"

Why should he care? "I'd like it as a keepsake."

He expelled a slow breath. "I have no idea where it might be." Before I could utter another word, he said, "If you'll excuse me, I have work." As Matthew turned back to his desk, I saw the muscles of his face tighten.

7

THROUGHOUT the balance of the day my mind dreamily relived the passion with Matthew, then drifted to the tension I had seen in his face after I'd asked about the diary. Did he know where it was and simply did not want me to have it? I could understand if he didn't want me or anyone else to read the volume pertaining to his marriage with Charlotte. And if I thought for one moment that she had written anything of an intimate nature, I would not read it. But my stepsister hadn't been one to commit highly personal facts to paper. Maybe Matthew didn't know that, though. Or maybe he just didn't want her views of him, and the hurt and humiliation she'd caused, laid open to others. That was also understandable. In my case, however, Charlotte had already poured out her heart in our exchange of weekly letters. Had Matthew assumed as much? I wondered, recalling the resentment I'd heard in his voice when he referred to her letters during our conversation in his office.

As I eyed Matthew furtively over supper, it struck me that perhaps the tension had nothing to do with the diary, but rather anger over our kiss. After all, in the heat of desire he'd lost sight of the fact that to him I was an intruder in his life and Rory's. Matthew had kissed me in a moment of weakness, and I couldn't imagine he would ever permit that to happen again. And I didn't want it to, I firmly resolved. Not as long as he regarded me as the enemy.

As I climbed into bed that night and reached out to turn off the lamp, I automatically paused and listened. Thank heaven, there was no crying or unsettling noises. I slept soundly, and in the morning my eyes fluttered open just as the sun was coming up. I felt wonderfully refreshed and eager to get on with the day.

I slipped into a simple muslin gown, made fast work of my toilette, then went downstairs. As I entered the apple-green morning room, Tyler looked up from the table in surprise. "Well, good morning," he said. As he stood, I noticed how particularly appealing he was in the vested, blue serge suit. "You're up bright and early, Alexandra, and looking as lovely as ever."

He had a way of always making me feel attractive, and his smile was so infectious, I couldn't resist teasing, "You do know how to charm a lady, sir."

His smile broadened at my feigned Southern drawl, and he took my hand and bowed over it with an exaggerated flourish. "Beautiful belles turn my head." The words rolled off his tongue with practiced ease, and I wondered how many heads *he* had turned with his Southern charm. He was too effusive for my tastes, but amusing. Tyler pulled out the chair beside him. After seating me, he rang for Lizzie. "Are you generally up and about at this ungodly hour?" he inquired as the ample-figured house-keeper entered.

"Not as a rule." I requested a small serving of the same break-fast Tyler had before him, biscuits and eggs smothered with rich gravy and succulent sausages on the side. Nodding, Lizzie filled my cup with coffee, then returned to the kitchen. "Do you always get up at the break of dawn?" I asked, adding cream to the fra-grant brew.

A pretended frown drew Tyler's brows together. "Unfortu-nately, yes. Matthew usually joins me for breakfast, but Lizzie told me he was summoned on an emergency over an hour ago."

My mind conveyed relief that I wouldn't be seeing Matthew until this evening, though my heart sent out an altogether differ-ent message. "And Felicity?" I lifted my cup.

"She enjoys the luxury of sleeping in. And there's no reason why she shouldn't," he added in swift defense. The affection be-tween Tyler and his sister-in-law had shone through almost from the moment I'd first seen them together. If I hadn't heard that they were just close friends, I would have suspected a deeper rela-tionship. "You should indulge in the same luxury, Alexandra," he suggested.

Between following my dream to open a salon and the time I hoped to devote to Rory, sleeping in didn't seem possible. Either Tyler hadn't considered that, or he shared his brother's view about keeping my stay at Belle Haven short. On that glum thought I said simply, "I might, from time to time." Then I urged Tyler to continue with his breakfast. Being a true Southern gentlemen, he hesitated.

"Please," I insisted. After a moment he reluctantly raised his fork.

Within minutes Lizzie served my meal, and Tyler kept me company while I ate. He told me a bit about Charleston, touched on a few Southern customs, and suggested I try a mint julep before supper tonight. Then he came to his feet. "I must be on the way to my office, Alexandra. I'll see you at supper."

I wished Tyler a pleasant day and watched him move away. At the threshold he paused and said, "Felicity and I would enjoy having you ride with us this weekend."

"I'd love to, thank you." After Tyler exited, I wondered why he hadn't also invited me to his office to review my stepsister's accounts. As trustee for the substantial estate her son inherited, it was imperative that I be kept abreast. Along with that, I was curious about what Charlotte might have seen in the books that convinced her Matthew had dipped into her funds. In any case, if Tyler didn't ask me to his office soon, I would invite myself.

I drained my cup, then went up to the nursery. "Rory be done with his feeding and ready for the day," Zalea told me as I reached out and took the adorable little boy in my arms. His dark eyes sparkled as he looked up into my face and flashed a melting smile.

I kissed his dimpled cheeks. "I'd like to take him out for some fresh air and sunshine, Zalea."

"Yes'm, Miss Alexandra. We has a big quilt we sets down on the grass for him to play on. Shall I fetch it and lays it out?"

"Please. Under the shade of a magnolia would be nice. I think we'll stroll the garden first, though."

"Then you'll wants the carriage. That boy babe done get mighty heavy after a spell. It's downstairs." With Rory gurgling happily in my embrace, I followed Zalea from the room and waited on the front lawn for the carriage to be brought out. A few minutes later I was wheeling my nephew through the fragrant, sun-washed gardens. Rory was fascinated by the flitting butterflies and the spouting fountain nestled among camellias and subtropical plants. As I knelt and let him splash his chubby hands in the clear water, an uncanny urge, which seemed to rise from the very depths of me, forced my gaze up to the cupola. Chills dappled my flesh, and my mouth dried on the sudden feeling that Charlotte was watching us. One part of me hoped she was observing her happy and healthy baby and was aware of the love growing between us. But the other part, which didn't believe in spirits returning from the hereafter, compelled me to shake off the eerie sensation. I hugged Rory, then wheeled him back to the house for his morning nap.

Despite the pleasant diversion of the little boy, my mind had remained on his mother, and after lunch I felt myself being help-lessly drawn up the narrow stairs to the cupola. At the door I hesitated, my imagination running wild with visions of my step-sister waiting beyond. Even though I knew those thoughts were ridiculous, every muscle in me tightened on a wave of spine-chilling anxiety. Swallowing, I eased open the door and peered in. Bright sunlight made me blink. Shading my eyes with an up-lifted hand, I scanned the octagonal room. No one was in sight, living or otherwise. I expelled the breath that had stuck in my throat and censured myself for succumbing to the ghoulish whim of a fertile imagination. Charlotte was dead! She would always be in my heart, but nothing more than the emptiness I felt at her tragic passing had urged me to her haven.

As I moved reflectively about, running my fingers over the harp and the pianoforte, I remembered I had meant to search this place for the diary during my initial visit yesterday. But I had become distracted by memories and then the desire to be near Matthew. If he truly hadn't taken the volume, it could well be in here. I looked through the side table drawers, then opened the mahogany cabinet. Sheets of music were neatly stacked on all three shelves. Involuntarily my hand came up to sort through a few, but I forced it back down. I wasn't ready to relive the memories of Charlotte's favorite pieces. Just picturing her at the piano produced stinging tears. The diary wasn't in the cabinet. Disappointed, and more puzzled than ever over its whereabouts, I reclosed the doors.

Frowning, I went down to my room. Eustace had brought in the drawing table and set it near the open French doors, where there was abundant daylight. Upon the table were two sketch pads, a large and a small. There was also a filled silver pencil container. The prospect of being in my element boosted my spir-its, and I crossed to the table and sat down in the chair that had been pulled up. It was comfortable and just the right height for work.

I lifted a pencil, and once again my imagination flowed. Only this time in a realistic and creative vein. Over the next hour I drew everything from stylish bonnets to delicate undergarments and even roses in full bloom. It was wonderful to see my hand moving deftly over paper again, to be in the spell of the artistic energy that was the heart of me. Until today Charlotte's death had sapped that energy, and I hadn't drawn even a simple line.

Humming softly, I sketched little Rory. Then, with my mind on a distant plane, I did a likeness of his father. Matthew's clear-cut features had become acutely familiar to me, and just envisioning his dramatic, mesmerizing eyes quickened my pulse. As I penciled in his mouth, I relived those thrilling moments of his sensual lips on mine, the pressure and sweet urgency. Longing surfaced, but an inner warning shook me back to my senses. Swallowing, I set aside the father and son drawings, threw away the others, and forced my full attention on Felicity's ball gown. Since I had a good idea of her favorite styles, two designs immediately came to mind. Both had bouffant skirts, which would accentuate her slender waist, and bodices with revealing décolletages.

By the time I finished with the sketches and returned the pencil to its silver holder, I was exhausted. The accident had taken more out of me than I'd realized. I rested for an hour on the chaise, then freshened myself and visited with Grandmother Hester before going to see Rory in the nursery.

Later, on the way back to my room to change for the evening meal, Felicity spotted me as she was ascending the stairs. "Alexandra," she called, "I wondered where you were."

I stopped at the second-floor landing. As I waited for Felicity to come alongside me, I commented briefly on how I'd spent the afternoon. Then, on our way along the gallery to our quarters, I mentioned the gowns I'd sketched.

"I can hardly wait to see them." Her voice held the same excitement that brightened her sapphire-blue eyes. "Can you bring them with you to the drawing room before supper, Alexandra?"

We paused at my door. "Certainly," I agreed. "I'll see you there shortly."

Felicity nodded and we went our separate ways. I'd scarcely entered my room when Zalea came in to help me change into a fresh gown. "Which one does you wants for tonight, Miss Alexandra?" She opened the armoire, and once again regarded the colorful array like a child craving sweets.

She was delightful, and I wished I could give her one of the gowns. But where on earth would she wear it? "Choose for me, would you please, Zalea?"

Her eyes widened with surprise, then doubt set in. "Oh, I don't know," she stammered. "They is all so pretty."

"Pick your favorite."

The young maid hesitated, then sorted through the garments with pride. After several moments of careful consideration she withdrew the teal brocade adorned with seed pearls and held it up for my approval.

"It's one of my favorites, too," I told her and pointed out the matching slippers.

Beaming, Zalea removed them from the armoire. Within thirty minutes I was dressed in the teal, my hair had been re-arranged with pearl-studded combs, and I was on my way down the stairs with the sketches.

I was the first one to arrive in the drawing room, though I'd barely made myself comfortable on the tufted-back sofa when Felicity entered. Her eyes sparkled when she saw the drawings on the table before me. Amid the rustle of fine silk, she swept forward and lifted them. A silent moment fell, then she murmured, "These are wonderful, Alexandra. I particularly like the off-the-shoulder look of this one." She settled next to me on the sofa and held out the more provocative of the two designs. Her choice didn't surprise me. This woman's tastes, like Charlotte's, were more daring than my own.

Fortunately, Felicity and I had a few minutes to discuss the sketches before the men came in, and they were spared from talk of feminine fashions. Although Tyler was curious about the drawings. "May I?" He gestured to them.

"Of course." Felicity happily handed them over. "Alexandra is very talented, don't you agree?" she asked him as he sat down on the opposite sofa.

I felt a flush. With me in the room what else could Tyler say but "Yes, she certainly is."

Matthew had scarcely glanced in my direction, and because he'd seemed engrossed in thought, I hadn't expected he'd heard even a word. I was surprised when his brows rose at the compliment. "May I see the drawings?" he asked his brother.

My heart palpitated, and I prayed for his approval. Seconds dragged by as he studied the designs. When at last he lifted his gaze to mine, something in his eyes communicated he was re-garding me in a different light, that there might be more to Alex-andra Chandler than he had realized. After all, hearing talk of my carefully schooled artistic ability was one thing; seeing some of my work was another. "I'm not a qualified critic, but these seem very good," he said, and the respect in his voice swelled my heart more than the praise itself. "I can understand your desire to establish a salon."

Tyler's lips parted. "A salon? I had no idea, Alexandra. That sounds like a mammoth undertaking."

"Far more than I dare let myself dwell on," I admitted. But the salon was only part of my dream; the other part I wasn't ready yet to discuss.

Especially after Matthew added in a maddeningly matter-of-fact tone, "Your chances of a large clientele would be far greater in New York than you could ever hope to have here."

"Matthew's right," Tyler said, and Felicity nodded in agreement.

For one second their rapid responses made me wonder if they, too, wanted my stay at Belle Haven limited to a brief visit. "I'm sure he is right," I replied. I struggled against the grudging tone that threatened to seep in. After all, Matthew's only interest in my potential business was to use it like a club to pressure me out of this house and, for that matter, the entire state of South Carolina. "I don't intend to make any rash professional decisions." I evened out my tone. "For now I'm perfectly happy fashioning Felicity's ball gown."

"Ah," Tyler teased, "you're going to build your business on one frock at a time."

His good-natured humor made me smile. "I hope not," I returned lightly and sensed Matthew's attention riveted on me. But I refused even to glance at him, for if that all too familiar "I wish you'd go away" expression was in his eyes, I had no desire to see it. I didn't look at him over hors d'oeuvres, either, or the mint julep Tyler insisted I try.

"Do you like the drink, Alexandra?" he asked after I'd sipped from the tall, frosty glass.

I nodded. "It's refreshing." And relaxing, I discovered as the alcohol gradually mellowed my resolve to keep my eyes off Matthew. Twice over supper he caught me watching him, and once I looked up and found him studying me. His dark brows were knitted as if he were trying to puzzle out a mystery. The only mystery in this house was him! The fact that he'd kissed me with passion, yet leaped at every opportunity to point me in the direction of the front door, defied reason. On top of that he'd lied about being one of the men who'd sped past my carriage just before it went over. Why had he lied? My lips compressed. Might he have also lied about the diary?

By the time I crawled into bed that night, the relaxing effect of the alcohol had faded, and thoughts raced through my head in mind-boggling circles. I tossed with renewed annoyance when I recalled Matthew's smooth attempt to pack me off to New York to establish my salon. True, my chances of a larger clientele would be greater there, but I also knew that Charleston was a highly social metropolis, abundant with prominent women who could well afford exclusive fashions. Matthew had never mentioned them!

After two hours of tossing, frustration propelled me from the bed. In the dark I fumbled for my wrapper, pulled it on, then made my way out to the veranda for some fresh air. Once again a cloud cover hid the moon and stars, and there was the smell of approaching rain. It was a warm evening and a bit sultry. My stepsister had loathed the humidity in this region. Would I even be here long enough to form an opinion on the climate?

In the darkness I glanced in the direction of the cemetery and choked back rising tears. I prayed Charlotte knew her son was well and that I was trying to keep my promise to help raise him. Rory needed someone other than servants to mother him. Of course, his aunt Felicity was also in the house, but she didn't seem particularly drawn to the little boy. Just the thought of leaving him made my heart heavy, and I determined to make more of an effort to win his father's approval. Maybe in a way I was misjudging Matthew. He might have suggested New York for my salon out of a genuine wish to be helpful.

As I lifted my head, a flicker of light caught the corner of my eye. Had it come from the cemetery? Or from the river?

8

THE flicker of light brought back the memory of the
chilling noise I'd heard among the headstones two nights ago,
and the hair on the back of my neck lifted. Automatically my
gaze shifted to the area of the cemetery. Once again all I saw
in the darkness was the eerie outline of gnarled trees. Positive
I'd seen the light, I turned my attention to the river and glanced
upstream, then down. Nothing! Just like before. I sucked in a
sharp breath. This place was becoming as much of a mystery to
me as Matthew clearly was. Just as I was about to mutter an
unladylike word, the sound of ripples on the river came to me,
as it had on that other night. Only this time there was no breeze
to stir the water—the cause had to be a boat, or maybe an animal.
Or someone. Doing what, though? Hurling stones or sticks? Or
perhaps even swimming? In the dead of night?

Once more I looked upstream, then down. Seconds passed. I
was about to put on some clothes and hurry out to see who or
what was generating the noise when, through a thick cluster of
trees on the riverbank, I saw the light again. From the way it
was moving slowly away from the bank, I knew it had to be on
a boat. Had the vessel pulled in at the secluded spot, just east
of the cemetery? Or at the dock a few feet downstream and for
some reason followed the river's edge before heading into its center? Why would a boat even stop here at this hour?

Puzzled, I felt my way back into my darkened room, removed
my wrapper, and slid beneath the bedclothes. At least I had seen
the light again and knew I hadn't just imagined it.

I snuggled down, and after tossing and turning I finally dozed
off. I dreamed of Matthew that night and the kiss that had set
us atremble, and when I opened my eyes in the morning I was
surprised to find it was well past the hour I usually awakened.
But that didn't matter nearly as much as the fact that even in

sleep, Matthew dominated my thoughts. Frowning, I sat up and brushed back my tumbled hair. The day was gray, with dreary shadows falling across the room and darkening corners. If it weren't for precious Rory and my work on Felicity's gown, I might have succumbed to the urge to lie back down, tug the covers over my head, and remain in bed for a while longer. But those two brightening aspects brought me to my feet.

The room was a trifle chilly, though not enough to warrant a fire in the grate. At the French doors I moved aside the lace curtains and gazed out. Moisture dripped from the trees. Clearly it had rained during the night.

Since today was far from springlike, I selected the vibrant, pink striped gown, which would give me the look and feel of the season, and fashioned my dark hair with delicate rosettes. Then I went down to the morning room to have breakfast with Felicity, who entered a few minutes after I'd sat down at the table. Over feather-light hotcakes, served with fresh-churned butter and maple syrup, I mentioned the boat I'd seen on the river during the night.

A shadow fell over Felicity's face but only for an instant. "Oh, dear, did it wake you up?"

"No."

"That's good. You didn't hear anything, then?"

It almost sounded as if she was afraid that I had. "Just ripples on the water," I said.

She expelled a slow breath. "Probably from oars. Riverboats come and go around the clock."

"The one I saw appeared to have stopped along the bank."

"You must mean the dock, Alexandra. Supplies were probably delivered."

"In the middle of the night?" I stared at her over the rim of my china cup.

"At whatever hour supply boats happen to be passing by."

"How unusual."

"Maybe in the city, but not here in the country." She poured maple syrup over her hotcakes. "After dark deliveries are set on the dock and brought in by servants in the morning."

"Was there a delivery last night?"

"I have no idea. Is it important that you know?"

I shook my head. "I was just curious." Just as I was still curious about the cemetery noise. I was tempted to mention it to Felicity. Instead, I clung to my vow not to question her. If she had been the crying woman, I didn't want her even to suspect I might have overheard and chance the possibility of causing her embarrassment.

"If river traffic disturbs you"—she paused—"you're welcome to move to a quieter room."

I held my breath. Was she about to suggest quarters at the front of the house again? If so, that would be the fourth such suggestion since my arrival at Belle Haven less than a week ago. However, after I said, "Thank you, but my room is fine," she changed the subject.

"I appreciated having the fashion sketches to study overnight, Alexandra."

"You're welcome to hold on to them until I've completed the others I plan to do," I offered. "Then we'll discuss the designs and go over any suggestions you might have." I took another bite of the delicious hotcakes.

She flashed a grateful smile, then confessed, "I'm beginning to suffer pangs of guilt over taking up so much of your time."

"You mustn't feel that way. I'm thoroughly enjoying myself."

She sighed at my reassurance and a dreamy look came into her eyes. "And I'm going to thoroughly enjoy wearing one of your gowns. I'll be the envy of every woman at the fund-raising ball."

As attractive as Felicity was, she'd be envied even if she showed up wearing a sackcloth. Still, I appreciated the praise. It was marvelous encouragement. "I hope so," I admitted with a smile, reflecting on prospective clients. "Speaking of the ball, I'd like to help."

For some inexplicable reason my offer had a sobering effect on Felicity. She hesitated, just as Matthew had when I'd volunteered my services. Had he told her to dissuade me if I brought up the subject? Braced for that possibility, I was surprised when she said, "Well, if you wouldn't mind, there is a stack of invitations that require immediate addressing."

I shook my head. "Not at all. I can do as many as you'd like."

"Wonderful. I'll bring a batch to your room later. Hester asked to help with some, and I will give her a few. Unfortunately, the rheumatism has reduced her penmanship to scribbles. Whatever she does will have to be redone." The sympathy that came into her voice was not reflected in her eyes. But then, Lizzie had said Felicity didn't have much patience with the aged woman. That was sad, yet not so unusual. From what I'd heard, many people found it difficult to cope with the elderly, especially if they were infirm.

After breakfast Felicity went up to pay her respects to the white-haired matriarch, and I lingered over coffee. Lizzie came in, and we chatted amiably as she cleared the table. As I set aside my cup and was about to excuse myself, a feeling I didn't quite understand compelled me to ask, "Was there a delivery at the dock last night, Lizzie?"

She looked at me, taken aback. "Ain't no houseguest ever asked that question before. Is you expectin' somethin', Miss Alexandra?"

"No." I explained briefly about the boat.

"Oh, that." She smiled and tried to dismiss my concern with a wave of her hand. "Kegs of nails was left some time in the night. Eustace been grumblin' all mornin' over how heavy they was. That man of mine ain't strong like he been," she finished sadly.

My lips parted in surprise. Her husband was past his prime. Even so, his broad shoulders and heavily muscled arms made him one of the most robust men I'd ever seen. In any event, the shipment of nails solved last night's mystery. But what about the cemetery? With it in mind I questioned, "Were there any other night deliveries this past week?"

Lizzie's smile turned to a frown. "You seen more boats?"

"No, but I heard strange noises."

"There plenty of 'em in the country, but they ain't nothin' to fret over." She replaced my napkin in its silver ring.

How could she be certain when I hadn't even described them? "The sound of scraping stone well after dark is usual?" I asked bluntly.

The cup and saucer she lifted clattered, though her voice when she responded was level. "Lan' sakes, Miss Alexandra, I ain't never heard nothin' like that. Probably it was jest an animal or a night bird. I expect you ain't used to hearin' them."

True. Nevertheless, I shook my head and said with certainty, "I know the sound of stone against stone, Lizzie."

Her frown deepened. "Then maybe it came from somethin' on a passin' boat."

"Maybe," I murmured doubtfully. "But I didn't see any lights."

"Boats don't always have 'em burnin', 'specially if the moon is out full."

"It wasn't that evening."

"Hmm," she muttered. "Did anything happen when you heard the noise?"

"No."

"Then you shouldn't fret over it," she said again, only this time with more emphasis.

"I'm not worried, just mystified. Do you remember if there were any other night deliveries?"

She inhaled a long breath at my repeated question. Was she annoyed by my pressing? "I been thinkin' on that, and I can't recollect if there was others this week. But probably there was—supplies is coming in all the time." She loaded dishes onto a tray. " 'Specially now that some of the farm buildin's is gonna be repaired." She lifted the tray. "Is there anything else, Miss Alexandra?"

I shook my head. "I don't think so, Lizzie, thank you."

As she turned, she said over her shoulder, "If you hears any more strange sounds, jest call for Eustace. He'll go lookin' to see what they is."

"I will," I said appreciatively. Was she right about a boat causing the unsettling disturbance? Mulling over that possibility, I went out on the rear veranda and stared across the lawn to the treeless knoll that sloped gently to the river. There were no vessels in sight now, and I was beginning to feel foolish over my continued curiosity about the cemetery incident, apparently harmless at that! I shoved it from my mind and glanced up. Clouds still hung low, but the air was warm. On impulse I crossed the damp grass to the cemetery, opened the wrought-iron gate, and moved among the numerous marble headstones. Etched names leaped out at me, but only Charlotte's and Brit Steele's were familiar. I paused at his graveside. Which one of his younger brothers had he resembled more? I wondered. My mind flashed back to Felicity's pitiful crying, and my heart twisted. As I continued to my stepsister's monument, I tried to remember what she had written about Brit. All that came to mind was that he was inordinately handsome and, sadly, depressed most of the time because of the financial disaster he'd blamed solely on himself.

As I gazed upon Charlotte's headstone, the hollow sensation once again gripped me. Everyone I held dear, except for Rory, was gone. Would the emptiness in me fade, as it had eventually after our parents' passing within a month of each other? A vision of my distinguished-looking father pressed forward, his dark hair, gray at the temples, and trim mustache, which had heightened the ever present intriguing gleam in his eyes. He'd been a decisive man. He told me I favored him in that respect. I liked to think I inherited that quality, just as I inherited his coloring and the softer version of his well-defined features. Father had been my world. Through the years my stepsister had also come to adore him, and I'd grown to love her dear mother as if she had been my own. She'd understood my creative propensity, at times even more than Father, and had kept me supplied with pads and pencils and even shopped with me for fabrics and notions. And I would never forget the hours she kept me company while I worked with needle and thread, just as she'd sat with her daughter in the music room. My stepmother had been remarkably kind and caring, like my own mother, from what I'd heard. Now they were all together. That deep and comforting belief gave me strength. I bowed my head in silent prayer, then left the cemetery.

I wandered to the grassy knoll. As I stared down its slight incline to the water a few feet below, I recalled Tyler had said Charlotte slipped on the rain-slickened grass and had fallen into the river. Throat constricting, I looked up and down the bank. Trees loomed in both directions. This was the only grassy area. Had she stood here on that horrible day? Amid heart-stabbing pain, I stepped back on legs that threatened to buckle. Scalding tears welled. Through blurred vision I glared at the river that had claimed my stepsister. It was so sluggish I couldn't even imagine how treacherous it must have been. Yet I knew how torrential downpours could change water from calm to deadly. A shudder coursed through me, and I hugged myself against a sudden chill, which had nothing to do with the weather.

Inhaling a ragged breath, I cast out the grisly picture of Charlotte struggling in vain against swift currents and the weight of her clothing, and forced myself from the knoll. I moved cautiously downstream, along the wooded bank that dropped off sharply to the dark river. East of the cemetery I paused. The light I'd seen last night had been somewhere in this area. Without thought I scanned the lush vegetation between me and the bank. I saw nothing that indicated a boat had stopped. Oh, grasses here and there were flattened, but the rain could have done that. In any case, Lizzie had said the vessel pulled in at the dock, and kegs of nails were unloaded. Suddenly a snake slithered into view, and I shrank back as it vanished once more into the thick undergrowth. Charlotte had mentioned the vile creatures, but I couldn't recall if she had said the snakes were poisonous. Swallowing, I moved carefully to the dock, which stood in a small clearing. On the night of the cemetery noise, might stone or something that produced a similar scraping sound have been unloaded here? Or had the disturbance, as I'd been so certain then, actually come from among the headstones?

Gritting my teeth against another rush of chills, I censured myself for lapsing again to grim curiosity, then returned to my room and the sketch pad. As I worked it occurred to me that my life had begun to take on a pattern. I was settling in. Of course, Matthew, with a few simple words, could shatter my sense of belonging. But even if he pressured me into a residence of my own, it would be in Charleston, not New York, as he hoped. If he mentioned that city again, I would not hesitate to tactfully tell him I intended to remain near Rory.

I saw little of Matthew over the next two days, which was probably for the best. The less he saw of me, the less irritated he might be over my presence under his roof. On Saturday afternoon I put on my mauve riding habit and black felt hat with plumes and met Tyler and Felicity in the stables. Three sleek horses had been readied. As Tyler crossed to help me into the saddle, I saw his appreciative gaze sweep over me. "You look as lovely as this bright spring day," he said. I was flattered and felt a little heat. Primarily because I had assessed him in the same manner and wondered if he'd noticed. Snug riding breeches and tall leather boots, molded to his calves, suited him nicely.

"We're pleased you could join us, Alexandra," Felicity said.

"I've been looking forward to it." I settled on the sidesaddle and arranged my skirt about my legs. "But I must warn you I'm not an accomplished equestrienne."

"There's no need to be," Tyler assured me. As he turned and assisted Felicity to her mount, I noted how striking they were together. Which one of the Steele brothers had her departed husband resembled more? I wondered again. Handsome, fair-haired Tyler or Matthew with the dark good looks?

Tyler swung onto his spirited stallion and led the way out into the fresh air and bright sunlight. Felicity, garbed in a deep-blue habit and pert straw hat, fell in behind him, while I brought up the rear.

It was a comfortably warm day, and the air was alive with

the melodic chirp of birds, accompanied by a chorus of frogs from along the river. The trail we followed skirted the palmetto-edged bank, with its scatterings of pungent pines, then wove through woods dense with live oaks, magnolias, and weeping willows. Beards of gray Spanish moss hung from branches, and vines laced trunks. Springy ferns and tuberous runners carpeted the ground between the trees, and the deep smell of rotting wood and vegetation intermingled with the sweet scent of honeysuckle, jasmine, and oleanders. The subtropical jungle was lovely and yet almost suffocating. At times, as we moved along the narrow path, I was overwhelmed by the sense of drowning in this fragrant sea of greenery. It was dim beneath the towering trees and silent, except for our conversation and the clip-clop of hooves.

By the time we left the winding jungle trail and were headed back to Belle Haven on the main road, I had answered more of Felicity's questions about Paris. Her primary interest remained fashion, then the romantic atmosphere of the outdoor cafés and the Seine River. Tyler, on the other hand, asked about the cathedral and particularly Notre Dame. "And the Louvre. I'm eager to see it," he said, and we discussed some of the magnificent paintings that hung there.

I enjoyed relating my observations and through them reliving the three happy years I'd spent in that fabled city and the thrill of working with Madame Fontaine. "What a shame Matthew didn't visit Paris when he was in Europe," I said, then frowned at the way he was forever at the front of my mind.

"He missed a golden opportunity," Tyler agreed.

"I would have given five years of my life to go abroad in his place," Felicity added.

"Five years? That sounds a bit extreme." Tyler chuckled and I shared his sentiment. "But you've always leaned toward extremes, Felicity."

She eyed him sharply. "And in most cases they've brought rewards."

"True," Tyler conceded, then said to me in a more serious tone, "My brother is too pragmatic. He went to the finest medical school in the world to study, and *that* was his life."

"From what I've heard, Tyler," Felicity challenged, "you weren't any different at Harvard. All you did was read law."

"Oh, not quite, my lovely." He laughed with a devilish gleam. "Some things are not fit for feminine ears."

"You rogue," she tossed back with a feigned pout.

Their lighthearted banter reminded me of the fun-loving Charlotte I'd grown up with, and I wasn't sure if I would ever fully understand the change that had occurred in her during the last two years of her life. To this day it seemed unreal, yet her long list of complaints was engraved in my brain, just as I was certain they had been entered in her diary. Where was the diary? It suddenly struck me I hadn't put that question to Tyler, who had been closer to my stepsister than anyone else in the house. So I asked him if he knew where the volume was.

Tyler bit his lower lip and glanced at me sideways. "I'd heard you were looking for it, Alexandra." He shook his head. "I wish I could be of help. I'm sorry."

"It's bound to turn up one of these days," Felicity offered solicitously.

Would it? Or was it gone forever, as I assumed was the case with my stepsister's last letter to me? I was tempted to mention that disappearance to my riding companions. But I dismissed the notion. Eustace might have been the one who snooped in my bag and simply forgot to return the letter with the rest of my belongings. In the over all, it wasn't worth making a fuss about.

The afternoon ride with Felicity and Tyler was even more pleasant than I had anticipated. By the time we dismounted in the stables, I had gained better insight into the pair, and my guess that they relished the comforts of wealth was confirmed. Along with dressing well, they both planned to travel abroad in the near future, and Felicity hadn't missed a summer at Saratoga Springs in years.

"Have you ever been there, Alexandra?" she asked on our return to the house.

I'd only heard about the lavish spa in upstate New York. "No, never," I admitted.

"Everybody who is anybody holidays at Saratoga," she went on. "You're welcome to join me and a handful of friends there this summer."

"I appreciate the invitation," I said in a quiet tone. "But by then I hope to have my hands full with work." And continuing to enjoy Rory. But I didn't mention him, for an inner voice urged me not to press the issue, not even with this friendly pair. After all, everything I said could well get back to Matthew, and I was determined not to do or say anything that might further exacerbate the strain in our relationship.

Felicity acknowledged my reply with a nod and dropped the

subject of the spa. As we ascended the front veranda steps, I reflected on the lost Steele fortune and wondered how she could afford a lavish summer holiday. I knew Matthew's income wasn't up to luxuries. From what I'd heard, the only other source of funds in the family was Tyler. Charlotte had mentioned he was a successful attorney. But somehow I'd never gotten the impression that his earnings had reached the level of supporting the extravagant lifestyle he and his sister-in-law favored. How fortunate she was to have the Steeles looking after her and in a comfortable manner.

As we entered the house, Tyler said, "You're welcome to come by my office whenever you're ready, Alexandra, to review Rory's estate."

At last—the invitation I'd been waiting for. Before I could respond, he suggested, "Next Monday afternoon, perhaps?"

Once again my stubborn mind focused on Matthew. "Tuesday morning would be better, if that's convenient?"

"I'll see to it that I'm free. Now if you ladies will excuse me, I have a few business matters to attend to." At our nods Tyler bowed slightly and headed toward his study at the rear of the house.

As Felicity and I climbed the stairs to our rooms, I asked, "Do you think Matthew would mind if I were to drop in and see his free clinic when I'm in the city?"

She shook her head. "It's open to anyone who is interested. As it happens, he sees clinic patients on Tuesday afternoons."

"Yes, he told me. I'm fascinated by his work," I hurriedly explained before she guessed I was even more fascinated by Matthew.

If that thought occurred to Felicity, it wasn't evident in her face or voice. "I have a few errands to do in the city, Alexandra. If you'd like company on Tuesday, I'd be happy to show you around."

"That would be very nice." I accepted with a smile.

If Felicity had said anything to Matthew about my planned visit to the clinic, he didn't mention it over supper, and I didn't bring up the subject, lest he try to put me off. If I were anyone other than his late wife's stepsister, he would doubtless look upon me as a potential patron of his charitable work. But clearly Matthew did not want anything from me . . . except for me to leave.

Conversation over the meal was sporadic, and once when Matthew's dark and mesmerizing eyes met mine, I could have sworn

I'd seen a moment of softness. But he quickly looked away, and I wondered if I had just imagined the warm regard. As we ate, my gaze moved furtively from brother to brother, and I couldn't help comparing them. Their builds were similar, but in coloring, nature, and tastes they were complete opposites. Outgoing Tyler, who dressed impeccably in the finest imported fabrics, was dashing. Brooding and unpretentious Matthew was ruggedly virile, and trying to unravel the mystery of him was becoming an exciting challenge.

After the meal I excused myself and went up for a visit with Grandmother Hester. She was propped in bed, the covers pulled almost to her chin. For the first time since I'd met her, she looked truly frail, and her gray eyes were dulled by obvious pain. Sympathy tore at my heart. "Is there anything I can get for you?" I asked softly.

She moistened her lips. "No, dear. Matthew will be in soon with my medicine." Amazingly, her voice hadn't lost any of its vigor. "Please, sit."

I hesitated. "It might be best if I left you to rest."

"I've been doing that all day." She inhaled a short breath.

"Just until Matthew comes in, then." I sat down in the chair beside her bed.

"Felicity told me about your ride."

"I enjoyed it very much, especially going through the woods. Although the thick growth was a little smothering."

"I love the woods." Her voice took on a distant sound, and I knew she was reliving memories.

"They're beautiful beyond description. All of Belle Haven is."

The mere mention of this land she loved brought spots of color to her pale face. "I could never have lived anywhere else." A tap sounded on the door, and she murmured, "Matthew."

"I'll leave you to be with him, and come back for a visit in the morning. I hope you sleep well, Hester." I kissed her on the temple, then crossed and opened the door. Matthew towered above me.

His eyes widened. "Alexandra I had no idea you were here."

Would he have waited until I'd left if he had known? "I was just sitting with Hester until you came." I stepped out and lowered my voice. "She seems in considerable pain."

He nodded, his expression serious. "I have a new medication that should alleviate the discomfort." He held up a small container.

"If there's anything I can do—"

His lips parted, and he searched my eyes as if he was still trying to puzzle me out. Was I becoming an exciting challenge to him? "If there is," his voice was a trifle husky, "I'll let you know."

Would he really? I watched him enter his grandmother's room. "Matthew," she said, her voice still amazingly strong, "did you see Alexandra?"

Had she forgotten that I'd opened the door for him? I wondered.

"I did," he told her.

As I turned to head for my room, she added, "She's so . . . nice."

"Yes, but remember she is also—" He closed the door.

She is also what? It took iron control to resist the urge to press my ear to the dark panel. Considering the sharp edge that had altered his tone, maybe it was best that I hadn't heard the balance of his sentence.

Frowning, I entered my room and buried thoughts of Matthew in work. I sketched for about an hour, then changed into nightclothes and climbed into bed. As I snuggled down, my mind went back over the enjoyable afternoon with Tyler and Felicity. I liked the affable pair very much, yet there were times when their light outlook on life made it difficult for me to take them seriously, which was absurd. Tyler was a prominent businessman, and from what I'd heard, Felicity took charitable work to heart. But I'd often felt the same way about my stepsister and had secretly envied her carefree nature. "You are far too preoccupied with the business of life, Alexandra," she had often chided me. "You're going to have permanent frown lines before you're twenty-five." Charlotte and I had been as different from each other as silk and velvet, and yet incredibly close. I thanked God for that closeness and for the cherished memories.

I swallowed and turned onto my back, letting my mind drift to Hester. I prayed the new medication had brought her comfort. I admired Hester Steele's strength and her love of family and home. From all she'd said, I knew she had been crushed by the untimely deaths of Brit and Charlotte, just as I knew that if the Steeles had lost Belle Haven, she would have been devastated. Without a doubt that determined woman would have ruthlessly fought to the bitter end to save it, and with every means at her disposal. But had the family actually saved what was left of the plantation? I wondered, well aware of what it cost to maintain an estate like this. Or had they merely postponed what might be the inevitable? If that came to pass, would I dare offer to help? Belle Haven was so beautiful, and it was Rory's heritage. It was also a wonderful place for him to grow up. But any offer of help from me would probably increase Matthew's resentment.

I compressed my lips. I had enough concerns without adding speculation about a possible family dilemma to the list. Sighing, I closed my eyes tight and tried to force all thoughts from my mind. But the few words I'd heard Matthew say to his grandmother as he'd closed her door came back to haunt me. Actually, the more I considered those words, the more they struck me as a warning. His tone had even held that same ominous quality. My eyes flew open and I stared into the night. Was I somehow a threat to more than just Matthew?

9

ON Tuesday morning Felicity and I rode to Charleston in the liveried family carriage. The beautiful coastal city, boldly spread along the waterfront, was even more bustling than I remembered upon my arrival from Paris. But that was two weeks ago and profound grief, combined with gloomy weather, had cast a pall over my senses. In truth, the emptiness over Charlotte's passing hadn't lessened, but at least I had accepted her death, and my outlook was as bright as this sunny day.

As Felicity and I moved from one fashionable shop to another, admiring exquisite goods and making a few purchases, it seemed incredible that this splendid metropolis was only a short distance from somnolent swamps and the moss-draped jungle. As we left the milliners and made our way down the palmetto-lined sidewalk, I said on a wistful sigh, "These narrow cobbled streets and quaint shops remind me of Europe."

Felicity also sighed but in envy. "I hope to soon find that out for myself."

Coaches and omnibuses rattled by at a lax pace, and I noticed that the people who strolled past us were stylishly attired. The men touched the brims of their hats in silent but polite greeting, and the women nodded in our direction. As Felicity and I acknowledged the friendly gestures with "Good morning" or returned nods, I marveled once more over the warm Southern hospitality. Occasionally we paused when my companion spotted a friend. Invariably, as Felicity introduced us, she lifted her nose with a hint of smugness and mentioned that I was a *couturière* recently returned from Paris. Then, without fail, she also said, "Alexandra is doing a gown for me." I wasn't certain if she was endeavoring to solicit clientele on my behalf or simply trying to impress her friends. At any rate, feminine eyebrows rose and gazes automatically swept from the top of my French chip bonnet down the front of my pink and lilac promenade gown. Thank heaven, I had taken extra pains with my appearance, and I reminded myself that from now on I was a walking advertisement for the business I hoped to establish.

The more I saw of Charleston, the clearer became the vision of a salon on one of her busy cobbled streets. I loved the lively atmosphere of this prosperous city and the tangy smell of the sea that gave me the feeling of home. The churches here were as graceful as any I'd seen abroad, and the luxurious town houses held a charm that to me was unrivaled. The majority of homes were covered with oyster-shell stucco and had double balconies, adorned with iron balustrades, which faced side gardens half-hidden behind low walls. There was lush greenery and plantings in full bloom everywhere. Clearly, the semitropical air was as prevalent in the city as it was in the country.

Unfortunately, to me, there were also negative and truly disturbing aspects of this appealing setting, starting with the placards of slave auctions and raffles. It turned my stomach just to think of people being bought and sold; somehow, offering one as a prize at a dollar a chance seemed even more appalling. There were also curfew signs reminding Negroes they must be in by dark and wanted posters with rewards for runaway slaves. "Are very many captured?" I asked, pointing to the notice that guaranteed a $100 reward for the return of Jacob Turner.

Felicity glanced at the notice and shrugged. "Quite a few, from what I've heard. Bounty hunters are everywhere."

How loathesome! Did most Southerners actually accept this inhumane system? The Steeles had freed their slaves, although not until after the plantation had failed and scores of workers were no longer required. Had their release from bondage stemmed from compassion by the family or simple economics? As nice as the Steeles were, I wanted to believe the former. But until I knew them better, I could not be certain. After all, everyone I'd encountered so far was warm and friendly. Still, each time I saw a constable stop a Negro and demand to see his pass, I knew that slavery was still a widely accepted way of life in this region. Why, even Charlotte had once written that the Negroes seemed happy. Happy? As chattel?

As much as I hated to admit it even to myself, I hadn't in the past really given much thought to the issue of one person owning another. Now my heart ached at the grave injustice, and it was a struggle to keep critical comments to myself. The fact that Felicity didn't seem to notice the placards or the Negroes by no means indicated that she was particularly callous. Like everything else in this community, they were an everyday part of her life. She wasn't viewing them for the first time, through newcomer's eyes.

After Felicity and I had browsed in a dozen shops or more, we chatted over light midmorning refreshments in a cozy tearoom. Then we leisurely wandered through her favorite bookstore. I purchased two novels and a book of verse, and Felicity selected a handful of magazines and the latest edition of *Godey's Lady's Book,* the leading fashion oracle. Afterward, as we toured the city by carriage, she explained that the houses were built above elevated first floors to protect against flooding. "Through the years," she said, "the waters have risen to astounding heights."

For one chest-tightening second my mind flashed back to Charlotte and the sluggish river that had turned deadly. More painful seconds passed before I realized Felicity was still speaking. "The houses are also raised to provide greater coolness," she said. "But Charlotte must have told you about the unbearable humid heat of summer. And"—she wrinkled her nose—"the horrid mosquitoes, which particularly thrive in the country."

Before I could even nod, she rationalized. "That's why I escape to Saratoga. That is also why the majority of local planters move into their town houses every summer. The sea breezes are a godsend, and there is less chance of contracting malaria in the city." Felicity brushed at her skirts. As always, she was smartly attired, this time in a white percale dotted with black.

"Charlotte never mentioned a town house," I said. "I gather the family doesn't take up summer residence in the city."

Her lips twisted. "Unfortunately not. The Steeles' absolute devotion to Belle Haven keeps them rooted to the place year-round." I'd heard that same complaint from Charlotte many times, which made me wonder now why she hadn't also escaped to Saratoga or some other idyllic summer spot. But as my mind went back over the three years of her marriage, the answer was obvious. During her first summer here Charlotte had been a contented newlywed, the second her former fiancé had come to renew their love, and by the third she was with child. "Oh, don't get me wrong," Felicity went on, "I love Belle Haven and the South and wouldn't want to live anywhere else. It's just that for now I'm tired of seeing the same people and places year after year. Did you ever feel that way, Alexandra?"

"No, but maybe I would have if I'd remained in Boston, or even Paris."

"Oh, I can't imagine that anyone could become bored with Paris."

"The novelty of the place does wear off," I pointed out with a small smile.

"Yes, I suppose." She sighed. "In any case, you'll find the pattern of life in Carolina is the opposite of anywhere else. Instead of the city dwellers relocating to the country during the sweltering heat of summers, the rural people swarm into the city."

"That is different," I agreed, wondering how I would hold up in weeks of oppressive heat, which sounded even worse than it was in Boston. However, the mere thought of determined Matthew grimly reminded me that I would probably be living in the city beside the sea, instead of in the country. Resolutely I pushed that all too real possibility to the back of mind, which was becoming overcrowded with concerns. The list had begun with the missing letter. It hadn't just fallen out of my bag. Still, I couldn't imagine that someone would have taken it. There was also the lost diary, then Matthew's bald-faced lie about being one of the riders on the road, and his desire to oust me from the house. And I certainly could not forget the cemetery incident or the warning I had detected in Matthew's words and voice a few nights ago.

"That's Fort Sumter." Felicity gestured to the mouth of the harbor, and I recalled that Charleston was one of the federal government's strongest coastal installations. Then my mind obstinately returned to Matthew's warning, as it had so often since I'd heard it. It seemed to me that the only way in which I could be a threat to the family would relate to Rory in some way. I loved him, that had to be obvious to everyone. Just as it must also be obvious that I would never do anything to harm him. Of course, I did have a bit of control over the little boy because of his inheritance. I suspected part of Matthew's resentment was rooted in my control as trustee. Might the entire family share that feeling and also wish I would disappear from their lives? My stomach knotted on that stark possibility.

At the end of the city tour the horses were reined in before an impressive stuccoed office overlooking the water. Tyler's shingle was prominently displayed beside the door. "I'm certain Tyler will invite you to join him for lunch," Felicity said to me.

"And if you mention that you're going to the clinic afterward, I know he'll escort you there. Shall I meet you at the clinic, say around three?"

"Three will be fine," I agreed and alighted from the conveyance. The liveried driver saw me to the office door. After entering, I glanced back. Through the oval glass insert I saw the driver reboard the carriage. With a flick of the reins he urged the animals back into the heavy flow of traffic, and Felicity was on her way to attend to errands and luncheon with a friend.

As I swung back to the office, paneled in native cypress and furnished in leather, the graying man behind the desk was coming to his feet. "Good morning," he said, eyeing me expectantly.

"Good morning, I'm Alexandra Chandler. I believe Mr. Steele is expecting me."

"Oh, yes, yes, indeed. It's a pleasure to meet you, Miss Chandler." The short, darkly attired clerk introduced himself. Then, without further ado, he showed me into Tyler's private office. He, too, stood at my entrance. Tyler flashed the ready smile I'd already come to know so well. Just being near this friendly man seemed to banish my concerns. "Come, Alexandra, make yourself comfortable." He pulled out the plush chair opposite his at the mahogany desk. The walls of Tyler's office were also paneled in cypress and lined with shelves of leather-bound law books. "Did you enjoy your outing with Felicity?" he inquired.

I sat down. "Yes, very much. Charleston is one of the loveliest cities I've ever seen. And," I added with a smile, "it also has more social clubs than I've ever encountered in ône place before. If memory serves, there is a Smoking Club, a Laughing Club, Fort Jolly Volunteers, Beefsteak Club—"

"Say no more!" Tyler grinned, enjoying my teasing, "The list is longer than we Charlestonians often care to admit to. We do enjoy the pleasures of life, from clubs of every variety to Shakespearean theater companies, and what often seems like endless balls and galas right down to cockfights and horse racing."

The theater and other refined nightlife raised my interest, but the sporting events were not for me.

"I'm afraid it's been said," Tyler went on, "that Charleston is a wild place halfway on the road to purgatory. But you didn't come here to discuss our illustrious city, Alexandra." He sat down in the chair behind his desk and eyed me with the mischievous gleam I'd also come to know well. "We can do that over lunch, if you'll join me after we've finished with our business."

I nodded. "That would be very nice."

Tyler smiled at my acceptance, then regarded the two ledgers on his desk with a more serious expression. "Charlotte's accounts." He lifted the books. "One covers personal expenditures, the other encompasses a variety of local business investments, which I suggested." The hint of pride came into his voice. "At her request I have also overseen them. I think you'll agree with me that the investments have done exceedingly well." He handed over the ledgers, then added, "You're welcome to review them in here. Or if you prefer privacy, the conference room is available and quiet."

"The latter might be best. That way I won't keep you from your work."

"You're as thoughtful as Charlotte was." Sudden sadness darkened his blue eyes. Without another word he rose and showed me into the adjoining conference room. It was spacious and dominated by a large table. About it were overstuffed armchairs. Tyler withdrew one, and after I'd settled myself, he asked, "Can I get you any refreshments, Alexandra?"

"Thank you, no."

He returned to the door. "If you have any questions, I'll be in my office." After Tyler exited, I admired the gilt-framed landscapes about the paneled walls. Then I stared at the ledgers on the table. Dread welled at the thought of the personal account Charlotte had made available to her husband, the account she had told him she planned to close. As much as I wanted to believe that Matthew hadn't, against her wishes, dipped into her funds, a trace of suspicion now lurked furtively in a darkened recess of my mind. The money didn't concern me, but rather Matthew's integrity. I wouldn't even question it, if it weren't for his lie about being one of the riders who'd sped past my carriage. Maybe he had an innocent reason for lying. Then again, maybe he didn't. A shiver inched down my spine, and on a weak and cowardly impulse I bypassed the ledger pertaining to the account in question. If my stepsister's claim about Matthew and the money was valid, I didn't want to know that . . . just yet.

Swallowing, I opened the book that covered Charlotte's local business affairs. Carefully I reviewed each page and was amazed and impressed by the number of investments. My stepsister had purchased three parcels of what appeared prime city land and had put money into a hotel and two restaurants. She had also acquired control of a leading boutique. I smiled to myself. I had made several purchases there this morning. Page after page of figures confirmed what Tyler had said: The investments were generating handsome profits. Considering Charlotte's lack of interest in business, I knew she wouldn't have given a thought to investments without prodding. Tyler deserved the credit for these; he had counseled my stepsister wisely.

Noises of the thriving city drifted in through the partially open window. I gazed out on the traffic, then set aside the ledger and forced myself to lift the one I'd been avoiding. I stared at the leather cover, my pulse quickening. With a silent prayer that Charlotte had been wrong about Matthew, I eased open the book. Braced for the worst, I agonizingly scrutinized each entry. My stepsister had spent substantial sums on clothing and amusements. That was not unusual, and the expenditures were well within her yearly income. She'd also been generous with the Steele family in regard to gifts. But giving had been one of Charlotte's pleasures in life. According to these accounts, the only one she hadn't lavished with gifts was Matthew. But then, he had forbidden her to buy him luxuries. Would a man of such pride help himself to his wife's funds? Or lie, for that matter?

Grimly I continued through the figures, and when I was finished, I sat back and expelled a long breath of relief. There was no large unexplained withdrawal, as Charlotte had claimed. Or even one questionable entry. Every penny was accounted for, and I couldn't for the life of me imagine what she might have seen that had prompted the accusation about Matthew.

Puzzled, I gathered up the ledgers and returned them to Tyler. "Everything seems in order," I said, then complimented him on the excellent investments.

He smiled, pleased. "Shall I continue to oversee them?"

I saw no reason why he shouldn't. "I'd appreciate it, Tyler. However, I would like to review them with you on a monthly basis."

He inclined his head in agreement. "You plan to remain in Charleston, then?"

Something in his voice made me wonder if he, too, preferred that I make my home elsewhere. My spirits dropped. "I will be be staying," I managed in a firm tone.

A moment of dead silence fell, then the smile returned to his face. Had I simply misunderstood his tone? "With luck," he said lightly, "I'll have the pleasure of escorting you to lunch at least once a month. Perhaps, on occasion, even supper." The devilish gleam came back into his eyes. "Am I being too bold, Alexandra?"

"A little, but dining out occasionally would be pleasant." I hoped I wasn't giving Tyler the false impression that I regarded him in more than a friendly light. Just in case, I added, "Perhaps Felicity could join us once in a while."

Tyler arched an inquiring eyebrow. "Perhaps," he murmured, then once again offered me the chair before his desk. After we were both seated, he asked, "Do you have any questions about the accounts, Alexandra?"

"No, not really," I said slowly, then ventured, "I've been wondering, though, if Charlotte might have mentioned any financial concerns."

He eyed me sharply. "She expressed some to you?"

"Nothing that was crucial." My immediate reassurance was also a small lie. After all, my stepsister had thought she'd seen something in the books that struck her as crucial. Still, I wasn't even going to touch on the accusation, which appeared unfounded. "She didn't say anything to you?"

"No, nothing."

As upset as Charlotte had been about the money, why hadn't she consulted Tyler on the matter? Frowning, I said, "Maybe she just misread some figures. Arithmetic, as you may have noticed, was not her forte."

The muscles in Tyler's face relaxed. "Yes, I noticed," he admitted with a hint of amusement. "But when it came to the piano, Charlotte was incomparable."

A tap sounded on the door, and the clerk poked his graying head into the room and told his employer, "Mr. Evans would like to consult with you on an urgent matter. He says it won't take long."

Tyler stood and regarded me apologetically. "Would you mind waiting a few minutes before we go to lunch, Alexandra?"

"Not at all." I returned to the outer office and sat down as the dapper Mr. Evans entered the private office. From behind the desk the mild-mannered clerk said, "I'm so sorry about your loss, Miss Chandler. Mrs. Steele was a most gracious young woman." He shook his head sadly. "She was in here just the day before she—"

That was also the day Charlotte had written that last letter to me. My throat tightened.

"Unfortunately, just before she arrived, Mr. Steele was called out suddenly," the clerk continued. "She'd been very patient, though."

My stepsister patient? "In what way?" I asked.

He inhaled a slow breath. "I had assumed Mr. Steele wouldn't be away long, and I showed her into his office. She waited a good fifteen minutes, without complaint, before leaving."

"She didn't see Mr. Steele that day?"

"No."

That was odd. From what Charlotte had said in that final letter, I gathered she'd found the so-called financial discrepancy during her last visit to this office. "Did my stepsister perchance review her accounts while she was here?" I asked.

"No, she couldn't have, the books weren't out that day. She and Mr. Steele always went over them together."

When had she seen whatever had upset her? Why was I even dwelling on Charlotte's accusation when the accounts appeared in order? As I idly picked up a magazine, the dapper man left the inner office. A second later Tyler also came out. He thanked me for waiting, then took me by the arm and said with a small smile, "I hope you're famished, Alexandra."

I wasn't particularly hungry. Nonetheless, I nodded politely. As I glanced up at Tyler, I noted again that he was as tall and broad-shouldered as Matthew. But this man's nearness, unlike his brother's, did not excite my senses. On the other hand, Tyler was amusing and wonderfully easy to converse with. As we made our way up the sidewalk to an exclusive waterfront restaurant, I also noticed he attracted the attention of every female we passed. Inside the posh establishment we were seated at a window table. "What a spectacular view," I said, gazing out on the busy harbor and Fort Sumter, standing protectively at its entrance.

Over sumptuous seafood and fresh vegetables, Tyler told me more about Charleston. As I soaked up every word, I saw feminine eyes regarding me with envy, and I felt a rush of delight at being in the company of the handsomest man in the room. Undoubtedly, Charlotte had been right in her comment that Tyler had more than his share of lady friends. The mere thought of Matthew with close friends of the opposite gender ignited instant jealousy. How annoying! If I didn't stop regarding him in a romantic light, I was going to be hurt.

As Tyler sipped from his cup of tea, I glanced about the opulent dining room and at its fashionably attired patrons. Over the clink of silver and china I heard the women at the next table chatting about the daring exploits of a handful of abolitionists. They had recently broken into the local jail, attacked the U.S. Marshals, and freed several recaptured runaways. From the excitement in the women's voices I deduced they were delighted by the escape and were as vehemently opposed to slavery as I. Maybe the practice wasn't as widely accepted in the South as I had supposed.

On impulse my lips parted to ask Tyler about the slavery issue, but a surge of good sense warned me not to broach the topic. After all, my position in the Steele household was precarious, to say the least, and now was not the time to bring up touchy issues.

Over delicate pastries for dessert we discussed Matthew's clinic, and when I mentioned I planned to stop in this afternoon, Tyler did indeed offer to escort me. "Is the clinic far from here?" I asked, not wishing to inconvenience him.

"Two blocks up and around the corner." He signaled our waiter and asked him to summon a hackney.

Within fifteen minutes Tyler and I were standing in the reception room of Matthew's office. The place was packed with patients in patched and threadbare clothing, from babies to old people. The Negroes clustered on one side of the room, and the whites on the other side. All eyes were on us, and I could well imagine how conspicuous Tyler and I were in our stylish apparel. For the first time in my life I felt as if I were flaunting my wealth.

Tyler introduced me to the young man behind the desk, then left me to return to his office. "The doctor is with a patient, Miss Chandler," the man said. "As soon as he's free, I'll tell him you're here."

From the number of patients waiting, it looked like Matthew would be busy until well after dark. Guilt at taking up even one minute of his valuable time began to well in me, and for a moment I wondered if I should make an excuse and leave. But since I was already there, I dismissed the notion with the vow to limit my visit. Although knowing Matthew, he would probably do that himself. "Would you like to wait in the doctor's private office?" the young man asked.

Another glance about confirmed there were no available chairs. Children were even sitting on the floor, little ones with runny noses. And the old man seated nearby had a terrible, croupy-sounding cough. Concerned that I might carry home an illness, particularly to Rory and Hester, I accepted the thoughtful offer. Then I went to the room that was pointed out. I'd scarcely stepped through the open doorway when I heard the door across the the hall open. "You mustn't worry, Mrs. Winston," Matthew was saying, his voice soft and reassuring. "The inflammation is subsiding."

"I ain't worried about it, Doctor," she said. "It's my hands, they hurt so bad."

I turned and saw Matthew helping an old Negro woman from an examining room. He was looking down at her and didn't see me. A lock of hair had fallen across his temple, giving him a little boy look. But there was nothing little boyish about his well-built body and the way his dark, vested suit accentuated the breadth of his shoulders, slim hips, and long legs. "The new rheumatism medicine I gave you should ease the pain. My grandmother has been using it for the last few days, and it's done wonders for her."

"I pray it does the same for me"—her voice held the threat of tears—"but I . . . I can't pay for the medicine."

"There is no charge." The compassion in Matthew's voice reminded me of the sensitive way in which he'd cared for me after the accident, and a rush of unbidden tears came to my eyes. Quickly I lifted a hand and brushed away the moisture. Matthew must have glimpsed my sudden movement, because his head came up and our gazes locked. "Alexandra, what are you doing here?"

For an instant there was no one but Matthew and me. No sound beyond the surge of blood in my ears. Then the old woman moved and reality sped back. I swallowed. "I was in the city on business and thought I'd stop in and see the clinic. I hope you don't mind."

Matthew blinked, as if bringing himself back to reality. Then a frown furrowed his brow. That, at least, was better than the *I wish you'd go away* look. "No, I don't mind," he replied. But what else could he say with me staring him in the eyes and a patient under his nose? "I'll be right with you, Alexandra."

I nodded and turned back to the office. It was hardly more than a cubicle and uncomfortably cramped with the usual office furnishings. On the wall behind the desk was Matthew's diploma from the medical school in Edinburgh and two other official-looking documents. But what really caught my attention was the painting of Belle Haven. Amid the sprawling grounds the white clapboard house stood majestically, its Doric columns rising three floors. My gaze lingered on the glass-enclosed cupola, and in my mind's eye I saw the pianoforte and the spinet. And Charlotte! I gulped down a painful breath and shifted my thoughts to Felicity's comment about the family's devotion to the plantation. She'd made it sound as if their love of the place was a curse. How could anything so beautiful be that? Unless, of course, lack of funds kept them in constant fear of losing the beloved estate.

"The artist did the place justice, don't you think?" Matthew stopped behind me.

My heart fluttered, but I didn't look around. "Yes," I agreed. "He captured its very essence, the tranquility of the setting." Slowly I came around and looked up. Maybe Matthew was a little taller than his brother. Without a doubt the dark eyes staring deeply into mine were more intriguing and soul-searching than any I'd ever seen before. At times like this I was certain Matthew could read my thoughts, and as always, during these entrancing moments, I felt a flush. His gaze dropped and my pulse quickened. He was staring at my mouth. Involuntarily my attention went to his sensual mouth, and the memory of our fiery kiss increased the heat in my face. Embarrassed, I bit my lower lip. Too hard. It hurt. Was that amusement coming into his eyes? I looked away and forced my voice to be even. "You have so many patients waiting. I've come at a bad time . . . I'm sorry."

"I'm always busy—there is no good time." That had been amusement, and it was in his voice now. He'd perceived my thrill and the flooding embarrassment and was enjoying my discomfiture.

I lifted my chin. "Perhaps I should come back another day, Matthew."

The corner of his mouth lifted slightly at my haughtiness, and I was surprised when he didn't leap at the opportunity to show me out. "Come along, I can spare a few minutes." He stepped back into the hall. "Those three doors open into examining rooms, and this is the pharmacy." I stopped beside him and glanced into another cubicle-sized room. It was overwhelmed by a worktable. Upon it were a mortar and pestle, and implements for measuring and mixing. About the white walls were cabinets with bottles and tins behind glass doors.

"Do you perform any surgery in the office?" I asked.

"Some. Mostly on patients who can't afford the hospital. For that reason I had to add on a small operating room and purchase the necessary equipment. It's right through there." As he raised a hand and pointed to the door on the opposite pharmacy wall, his coat sleeve brushed tantalizingly against my bare arm. "Even so, space, as you've probably noticed, is tight. I don't dare expand the clinic load until we move to larger quarters."

"When do you think that might be?"

"Not until after the fund-raising ball. I only hope it brings in enough to accomplish my immediate goals."

"If not, then what?"

He expelled a long breath and brushed back the lock of hair from his forehead. "I'll have to find additional means of funding."

"You're determined to keep the clinic going?"

He nodded. "After Rory, it's my top priority."

Well, at least putting me from his house wasn't in the top two. Still, the number-three spot, which I undoubtedly held, wasn't particularly comforting. "Thank you for your time, Matthew," I said in a quiet tone as he walked me back to the door of the reception room. "I would like to help with the fund-raising any way I can."

This time as Matthew's gaze met and held mine, I wanted him to read my thoughts, to perceive my genuine interest in his valuable contribution to humanity.

"You really mean that, don't you?" he said softly, and with a hint of the same surprise I had detected when we'd discussed his clinic before. Again I wondered if he was thinking about Charlotte and her negative view of his work. Comparing us would be natural, especially when we'd been close. After all, as a rule, such a bond signified sharing the same likes and dislikes.

"Of course I meant it," I told him firmly and suppressed delight at the flicker of belief in his eyes. On that speck of encouragement, I thanked him again for his time and left the office.

On the ride back to Belle Haven, with Felicity in the family carriage, I resolved not to mention my wish to help with the fund-raising again. I'd made my desire clear. Now it was up to Matthew to decide if he wanted my help. Plainly he did need additional office space, and that reminded me of Charlotte's accusation. If Matthew had taken the substantial sum she'd claimed, it would have been more than enough to open the clinic and in a spacious, up-to-date facility. I couldn't think of anything else he might have spent such a large sum on . . . except maybe Belle Haven. The fact that he kept a painting of the place in his office confirmed his love of the family home.

As I stared unseeing at Felicity seated across the aisle glancing through a magazine, my mind focused on my stepsister's personal account. The entries had been so clear that I didn't see how she could have misread them. Yet something in the ledger had triggered her anger. What? As for the when, I could have sworn she'd said it was on the same day as her last letter to me, mere hours before her tragic death. The letter would resolve that nagging question. So would the diary. Both were gone. Chills prickled my arms and disturbing thoughts circled in my brain like birds of prey. Was the disappearance of both just a coincidence?

I gazed out at the lush landscape. Since I didn't expect to ever get the letter back, my only hope for answers was in the diary. If it was still somewhere in the house, the logical one to have it would be Matthew. True, he had denied this, but he'd lied to me before. Dare I sneak into his room and look for it?

By the time our carriage turned onto the long drive to Belle Haven, I had determined to continue the hunt for the lost volume and had laid out what seemed the perfect plan for the search.

❧ 10

LIGHTNING repeatedly split the evening sky, and rain pounded down as thunderclap after thunderclap shook the house to its very foundation. Gusting winds rattled French doors and window shutters, and though the air was fairly mild, chills dappled my flesh.

I'd retired to my room earlier than usual, to read before climbing into bed. Then I'd hoped to catch up on the sleep I had lost on the previous night, when Rory awakened crying and I'd helped Zalea comfort him. But it had been impossible to concentrate on my book with the wind sledgehammering the house; sleep would probably be just as impossible.

I was in my nightdress and matching silk wrapper, pacing restlessly, when Lizzie came in to turn down the bed. "I hope the storm won't frighten Rory awake," I said, not knowing if babies managed to sleep through such wild weather.

"He be fine when I looked in on him a minute ago," Lizzie replied, fluffing pillows. "That babe still wore out from being up most of last night. We all gonna be mighty glad when he done cuttin' them teeth."

"How long do babies generally teethe?" I winced on another vibrating rumble.

"Oh, 'bout two years."

"Two years?"

The housekeeper laughed at my startled response. "I don't expect he'll have the misery with all of 'em, though," she said in a soothing tone, then shook her head. "Dr. Matthew the one I be frettin' 'bout now. He was called to see a patient."

"He's gone out in this terrible weather?"

"Yes'm, a neighbor up the road took a turn. Dr. Matthew could be away all night."

"In this downpour it might be best if he did stay until morning."

"I suppose, if he kin get some sleep there. Most nights he don't get enough. And you gots to be gettin' your rest, too, Miss Alexandra. You shouldn't get up with the babe. Me and Zalea can cares for him. You jest enjoys him during the day."

I knew she was right, just as I also knew I had begun to take my promise to Charlotte too much to heart. Yes, I loved Rory. But I also had my work to consider, and it would suffer if I didn't get adequate rest. Still, he was so little—

"Now, you gets yourself some good sleep." Lizzie continued her motherly lecture. I appreciated her concern, though the insistence seemed a bit excessive.

"Can I gets you a glass of warm milk to helps you relax?" She stepped to the door. "Miss Charlotte used to have one before bed."

"She never liked warm milk."

"I don't know nothin' 'bout that, jest that she took to drinkin' it when she was expectin' the babe. Then she kept right on after he be born. I guess she jest got used to it."

"So it would seem." I declined the offer of the warm beverage.

After the housekeeper left, I went to the closed French doors, drew aside the lace, and glanced across the veranda. It was too dark to see the rain, except amid the frequent lightning flashes, but it pounded down harder than ever. "Matthew," I murmured and turned back to the room. Was he out on horseback or in a buggy? My concern for his safety was so strong that it hadn't immediately occurred to me that this was a good time to search his room for the lost diary. Three days had already passed since I'd decided to resume the hunt. I'd had to wait until an evening when he was out and the maids had retired. I couldn't have one of them coming in and catching me in his quarters. Yes, this was the perfect night, but the growing concern for Matthew had sapped my resolve to look for the diary. Maybe when it came right down to it, part of me really didn't want to find out if he had lied about the diary.

Halfheartedly I glanced at the clock. It was 9:30. The Steeles and their servants should all be in their rooms by now. If I didn't search tonight, another opportunity might not arise for a while.

Amid another round of lightning and thunder I drew myself up, inched open the door, and peered out. Flickering flames in the mounted oil lamps cast ominous patterns on the walls. What an eerie night. I scanned the gallery. No one was in sight. Ears and eyes alert, I stepped out and crept to Matthew's door. Rory's room was to the right, and the one his mother had occupied was just beyond.

Thunder shook the house again. I stiffened and listened. Thank goodness, still no sounds from Rory, though I wasn't even certain if one could hear anything other than the relentless storm. I was about to ease open Matthew's door when it struck me that he might have already returned to Belle Haven. After all, Lizzie really hadn't been sure how long he'd be away. Moistening my lips, I tapped on his door, my mind scrambling for an excuse for being here, just in case he was in. No answer. Of course, there was always the chance he hadn't heard my knock. With that in mind I eased open the door and peeked in. In the glow of a night table lamp I saw that his bed had been turned down and his dressing gown was laid out. Evidently he had not returned.

Again, I glanced about the gallery. Reassured I was still alone, I quickly slipped into Matthew's room and closed the door. Lightning ripped across the sky, the silver flash plainly visible through the curtains on the front-facing French doors. Braced for more thunder, I stared at the four-poster and foolishly pictured Matthew, his dark hair tousled and his eyes smoldering with an intimate invitation. The expected low rumble returned me abruptly to reality.

As I stepped farther into the room, a gust of wind shook the French doors and I started. Chills, which had nothing to do with the night air, raked my flesh. Shivering, I drew my silk wrapper more tightly about me. Over the pounding rain I heard the wild beat of my heart in my ears. Had the weather, along with my concern for Matthew, tightened my nerves? Or the fact that I was in a place where I had no right to be? A place where I might get caught and further jeopardize my already tenuous position in this house.

Quickly I looked around, trying to decide where to start my search for the diary. Matthew's quarters were larger than my own and as tastefully decorated, only in masculine blues and grays, accented with a touch of crimson. The furnishings, against cream-colored walls, were heavy.

I moved to the chest of drawers. I hadn't sneaked about like a thief in the night since girlhood days, when I'd hunted for Charlotte's secret place, then spent endless hours happily reading and rereading her diaries. Now I was looking for a particular volume, and for a depressing reason.

Quietly I slid open one bureau drawer after another and searched with great care so that nothing would look disturbed and cause Matthew to wonder. Just touching his personal apparel made me hot, as if I were under the scorching sun. The howling wind and downpour were grim reminders of quite the opposite.

The diary wasn't in the bureau. I hadn't seen any pajamas, either. Didn't Matthew wear any? Annoyance combined with disbelief coursed through me. How could I have intimate thoughts of the man, yet at the same time doubt him?

Frowning, I went to the desk, then from one night table to the other. Nothing! As I rounded the bed, I recalled that my stepsister had never slept in it. Matthew had moved into this room well over a year ago, after he'd found his wife with the other man. I couldn't even imagine the pain Matthew must have felt. Charlotte had betrayed him. Now, in a way, I was doing the same with my invasion of his private domain. My heart ordered me to leave. Gnawing suspicion canceled the order, and I forced myself to continue the hunt. I scoured the immense walk-in closet. Then on impulse I rechecked the desk. The diary wasn't anywhere in this room. Maybe Matthew hadn't lied; maybe he really had no clue to its whereabouts. On the other hand he could have hidden it elsewhere—or even destroyed it.

Just as I was about to head back to my room, a sound from beyond the gallery door caught my attention. Holding my breath, I listened, ears straining. Over the pelting rain I heard footsteps heading this way. My heart lurched and the air escaped from my lungs in a painful burst. Fervently I prayed a maid was just going to look in on Rory. Again I listened intently. Someone was coming closer and closer. The footfalls stopped, outside this door. Beads of perspiration broke out on my brow, and I almost strangled on a sharp breath of panic. Was Matthew home? My heart plummeted and my rubbery legs threatened to give way. I stared at the knob, my brain screaming the reminder that I must not be caught in here. I tried the French doors, they were locked. The closet? No, if Matthew had returned, he'd probably head for it to change out of damp clothes. The knob was being twisted. My blood surged. As the door opened, I hurled myself behind an overstuffed chair, curled into a tight ball, and once more sucked in my breath. If I moved even a fraction, the rustle of my silk nightclothes might betray me. What an unthinkable situation.

Someone entered the room. A moment later the door was shut. Silent seconds dragged by. "Damn," Matthew muttered.

My chest constricted; the pain in my lungs was excruciating. Who or what was he cursing? Matthew thumped something down on the bureau, probably his medical bag. It sounded like he was mad, or maybe just tired. He didn't move. Had he seen something amiss? He couldn't have, I'd been careful, hadn't I?

More agonizing seconds crawled by, then he started my way. My heart was beating so rapidly I was light-headed. Being caught in his room would be misery beyond comprehension, especially in this humiliating position.

Matthew stopped at the desk, less than a foot away. Thank heaven, he hadn't spotted me. But if he leaned forward, even a fraction . . . My lungs felt as if they were about to explode from the strain of the inhalation I didn't dare release. Matthew rummaged through papers on the desk, then moved toward the bed.

On a dizzying wave I exhaled slowly, then breathed in fresh air. Summoning courage, I peered around the chair. No Matthew. The closet door was ajar. I'd closed it. He had to be inside. I leaned forward, listening again. The faint rustle of fabric floated out of the closet. He was probably changing for the night. Into what? His dressing gown was still on the bed. The roar in my ears had nothing to do with the storm outside. I must escape *now*. Lightning lit the room. I waited, praying rolling thunder would overwhelm the sound of hurrying feet and the swish of silk. On the low rumble I shot another look at the closet. The way was clear. I darted forward.

"Alexandra!" Matthew boomed above the thunder just as I reached for the door. My heart and my feet stopped. "I trust you have an explanation."

I was frozen in place, my brain darkened by panic. "How did you know I was in here?" The words croaked out, and my cheeks flamed with embarrassment and guilt. I couldn't bring myself to turn and face his wrath. Somehow, being struck by the lightning that flashed seemed preferable.

"Your perfume," he flung back. "I smelled it the moment I entered. You're the only one in this house who wears that fragrance."

I grimaced at my stupidity. I should have thought to wash off the perfume. I wished I hadn't even gone in there in the first place. Obviously the muttered oath I'd heard from Matthew had been aimed at me. It was all I could do keep from muttering the same one to myself.

"Look at me," he commanded, and I knew I daren't disobey.

Salvaging what I could of my shredded dignity, I lifted my chin and came about. My heart was drumming so loudly I scarcely heard the rumble that vibrated the windows. My insides also shook, but at the sight of Matthew's angry face. His eyes were slits, his jaw rock hard. He stood just a few feet away, coatless, and his shirt open at the throat. Right behind him was the bed. What a different picture this was from the intimate one I'd envisioned upon entering his room.

In two purposeful strides Matthew was looming above me. I felt like an insect about to be squashed. "I suspected you were still in here," he said, "and I was waiting for you to try to sneak out. What in God's name are you doing in my room?"

"I . . ." I groped for an excuse, anything but the truth, which was bound to elevate his ire.

Too late, my hesitation accomplished that. I inched back. "You what?" he rasped, and his hand flashed out and captured me by the wrist.

I winced at the pain but made no protest. His anger was justified and overwhelming guilt compelled me to be honest. "I was looking for the lost diary." I almost choked on the confession.

A muscle at the corner of Matthew's mouth twitched. "I told you I don't know where it is."

"Yes, but—"

"But what? I'm a liar? That's obviously what you think—I can see it in your eyes. Would you like to know what I think?"

That sounded more like a dare than a question, and I felt like a child aching to shrink back. The cowardly side of me didn't want to know what he thought, but he told me anyway. "You are just like Charlotte, sneaky and conniving."

Stunned, I stared at him. "I am not."

"You are here, and I did not invite you," he reminded with cutting bluntness. "Although maybe I should have." His gaze dropped to my nightclothes.

My cheeks flamed anew. "Let go of me." I twisted to be free, but he tightened his hold on my wrist. Where was the gentle side of Matthew I'd seen and admired, especially now when I was really in need?

"It's too bad I can't trust you, Alexandra; things could be different between us."

"Different? I doubt it. You don't want me here, and now I know a big part of the reason—you're judging me by Charlotte. I am me!"

"I am judging you by this episode."

"Then maybe I should sum you up by your lie to me," the words tumbled out, and again I squirmed in vain against his grip.

"What lie?" He pulled me even closer and held me firmly, as if he suspected my accusation stemmed from an attempt to weasel out of my wrongdoing.

The heat of his strong body branded my flesh through the silk fabric. Why did he have to be so virile and appealing? My mind willed me to glare at him, but every sensitive nerve hungered for the thrill of his embrace. The warring contradiction increased the sharpness in my voice. "You lied about being one of the riders on the road at the time of my accident."

His lips compressed. "Even if I was one of them, that has no bearing on you."

"Of course it does. I wouldn't have come in here if you hadn't given me reason to doubt you."

"There are some things I can't talk about. Maybe one day, when we know each other better."

"At the rate we're going, that will never happen."

"If you don't stop squirming against me like that, we're going to wind up knowing each other in a way neither one of us bargained for."

I willed down the threatening flush but could not conquer the rampant beat of my heart. "It was wrong of me to steal into your room, and I apologize. Why can't you admit you lied?" I swallowed that burst of courage and shriveled a little at the grim set of Matthew's mouth.

"Yes, I lied. Now I don't want to hear another word on the subject." He shook me and my lightly pinned-up hair fell about my shoulders in what felt like wild disarray. A tremor went through Matthew, and he loosened his grip.

Even if I'd wanted to press the issue further, my fading bravery made it impossible. But Matthew didn't know that, and when I parted my lips to acknowledge his confession, he clearly misunderstood. Angrily he brought his mouth down over mine. He'd silenced me all right. But he'd also unleashed burgeoning desire, and not only in me. Matthew drew me close, his embrace crushing. As his hands moved over me, every ounce of resistance dissolved and I melted against him. The vehemence in his kiss yielded to hunger, and my lips responded to the fervent pressure. Desire spiraled to dizzying heights as Matthew's tongue dartingly explored, and doubts vanished beneath waves of urgency. His hands were in my hair, stroking. There were no yesterdays, no tomorrows, only the moment and the delicious need that set us atremble. Somewhere in all the heat Matthew scooped me up. The next thing I knew we were on the bed, and he was raining kisses on my face and the sensitive hollow of my throat. His fevered hands blazed a wanton path to my breasts, cupping, caressing, then slid lower. And I moaned softly as he inched up my nightdress. Thunder cracked overhead, but it sounded as if it were a million miles away. The house shook, though I hardly noticed over the trembling within me. One compelling sensation followed another, each promising pleasure I'd yet to taste. In Paris I'd heard women whisper about "supreme joy," and my curiosity of the ultimate intimacy had heightened. But until I'd met Matthew, I had also been a little frightened by the mere thought of it. Now I was responding with a boldness I never dreamed was in me. My mouth and tongue were as ardent as his, and I moved unabashedly against his caressing fingers, which were like velvet feathers on my yielding flesh. I felt the heat of Matthew's need and whimpered as a small thrill overwhelmed me. It was heaven, yet instinct told me pure bliss was yet to come. As I clung to him, time stopped and I knew we were on the precipice of becoming one. I couldn't think beyond the sweet urgency and my continued boldness, which brought moans of pleasure from deep within Matthew's throat. Tenderly he had dissolved my fears and restraints, and I ached to sample the unknown. "Oh, Matthew," I murmured, moving feverishly against his touch.

"Alexandra," he murmured back. Then, as if the sound of my voice had signaled a warning, he hesitated. Lightning brightened the room. Matthew looked into my eyes, and I saw a barrier go up. My heart thudded as he rolled away. "I'm sorry," he muttered, and I knew that no matter how much Matthew desired me, to him I was still the enemy.

11

In the days that followed, the hurt over Matthew's rejection deepened, and I tried to convince myself that I should be grateful I hadn't been compromised. But that was impossible, for every time I looked at him, or even gave him a thought, I was overwhelmed by yearning. I knew the clean-cut planes of his face by heart, the strength of his lean body, and the breathtaking touch of his persuasive hands. Remembrance alone quickened my pulse, and it was impossible to dismiss the thrill of his mouth on mine and the engulfing desire that had nearly brought us together as one. The power Matthew had over me was more than a trifle unsettling, and I wondered if I should remain at Belle Haven. As immense as this house was, it was not big enough for two people who were physically drawn to each other. There were bound to be times when we'd be alone, and the longing might once again overcome us.

At the moment there was no worry in that regard. Since the encounter in Matthew's room, four nights ago, he'd gone out of his way to avoid me. During supper that was impossible. Then he was stiffly polite and rarely glanced my way. What was he thinking when he did look at me? Had he deemed me brazen? Clearly I had been, yet I still felt no shame. Those wondrous minutes between us had seemed so natural, so right, and each time I gazed upon him I was certain he'd been honest about the diary. But always on reflection his lie over being one of the riders renewed doubt. Yes, he'd finally admitted he had lied, but only because I had provoked him and he'd wanted to silence me. He had accomplished that, and in an exciting way.

But I shouldn't dwell on those moments. In an effort to block them from my thoughts, I immersed myself in work. Even so, the attraction between us remained ever present in my mind. In retrospect I realized I had fallen under Matthew's spell the in-

stant I'd set eyes on him in my room after the carriage accident.
I hadn't even known who he was then.

Whether I should remain at Belle Haven or move into the city
became a plaguing question. When I was with Rory, I had no
doubt of what I wanted, except maybe during those times when
he soaked through his diapers or a bit of his feeding came up.
"I seem to be forever changing gowns," I grumbled after another
one of my nephew's mishaps.

"That's the way babies is," Zalea pointed out, plainly struggling against giggles. "Jest puts a little blanket under him when
you holds him and a diaper over your shoulder."

"A suit of armor would be more effective."

The attractive young maid laughed. "You'll needs that when
he starts throwing toys and food."

"Food?" I choked and pictured a nice, quiet town house in
Charleston. Caring for a child was more difficult than being a
couturière and required more patience, at least for me. But there
was so much love in return. If only Charlotte could be here. Despite her faults, she had loved her son. I wanted Rory to know
that, just as I wanted him to come to know his mother as I had
through our growing-up years. Matthew couldn't share those
memories, and there was always the chance that bitterness might
even prevent him from offering much about Charlotte. With all
the anger that had gone between them, I could understand, to
a small degree, why he was wary of me. How foolish I had been
to invade his privacy, to risk what little ground I might have
gained. Now I had to start anew in trying to win his friendship,
if he would even let me. The fact that he hadn't ushered me from
the house, or hinted at the possibility, gave me hope. Why hadn't
he insisted that I leave, though?

Five unseasonably hot and sultry days had now come and gone
since our heady interlude, and Matthew was still distant. From
the way Tyler and Felicity eyed us, it was apparent they were
aware of the increased strain. So I wasn't surprised when Felicity
asked, "Are you and Matthew at odds over something, Alexandra?" She lifted her gaze from the half-dozen fashion sketches
before us on the drawing room table.

Since the family still regarded me with warmth, I assumed
Matthew hadn't mentioned my transgression. I was grateful, but
also more puzzled than ever. Everyone in the household would
have sided with him and probably helped me pack. Could it be
that deep in Matthew's heart he really didn't want me to leave?

"We had a few words, but it's nothing to be concerned about," I said, then returned the conversation to the sketches. "Have you made a choice yet, Felicity?"

She pursed her lips. "They're so lovely. If your salon were already open, I'd commission you to do them all."

Could she afford them all? I watched her sort through the drawings again. "This one," she said, then instantly changed her mind. "No, no, I think this one."

Considering she'd been studying the designs for the past several days, it was hard to imagine why the final decision was so difficult. The gown she selected wasn't my favorite, but thank heaven she'd finally made up her mind. "I was wondering, though," she said, "if you could deepen the waistline V."

"Another inch, perhaps; any more would add fullness to your hips."

"An inch would be fine. And maybe the same at the scooped neck?"

"It's already risqué."

A small smile touched her lips. "I like to be a bit shocking."

"Another inch and people will stare at you through bulging eyes."

She laughed. "It wouldn't be the first time." I wondered how her husband had felt about plunging necklines. And Hester? Although as attractive and feisty as she still was, she might well have bugged out a few eyes herself, in her day.

"If that's what you want," I said slowly, "I'll make the adjustment on the sketch. You can look it over, then we can start going through fabrics."

"Tomorrow, maybe?"

"Yes, that would be fine."

"Wonderful. My seamstress is available whenever you're ready for her to come in."

"By the first of next week, I should think. Now, if you'll excuse me, I'd like to go up and kiss Rory good night." I gathered the sketches.

"I'll go with you, if you don't mind."

"I'm sure he'd like that."

On our way up the stairs she said, "I love Rory, but I'm afraid I've just never been comfortable with babies."

"I used to feel the same, but my confidence is growing."

"Babies are so constraining."

I shrugged. "I hadn't really noticed." After all, there was help in the house. In the three weeks I'd been at Belle Haven, I'd rarely seen Felicity with our nephew. Observing her now with Rory confirmed what I had suspected: Children did not appeal to her. Oh, she smiled at him warmly and talked to him, and he beamed and gurgled. But Felicity shied away from cuddling the little boy. Considering all the gowns of mine that Rory had soiled, I supposed I couldn't blame her. Still, what was a dress compared to holding him near?

Felicity stayed in the nursery for about ten minutes, then she asked, "May I take the sketch of the gown I've selected in to show Hester?"

"Certainly." I handed it over. After she left, I helped Zalea ready Rory for the night, then rocked him to sleep. As I was laying him in the crib, I heard the door open and someone enter. "Sweet dreams, darling," I murmured, then straightened and turned. My pulse quickened. Matthew stood just inside the door, the expression in his dark eyes unreadable. However, the softness about his mouth set me atingle. "Rory just dozed off." My voice was still a murmur.

"You're very good with him, Alexandra," Matthew said in a quiet voice that wouldn't disturb his son, and came forward. His white shirt accentuated his black hair and his handsomely tailored suit of the same color.

My heart swelled at the compliment, especially coming from him. "I remember telling you the same, a few weeks back." I bit my lower lip, wishing I had not reminded him of how long I'd already been at Belle Haven.

"I recall that night." He stopped beside me at the crib and gazed down on his son. Love shone in Matthew's eyes, and I suddenly knew, without a smidgen of doubt, that I wanted him to look at me in the same way.

I was in love with Matthew Steele.

Considering the affect he had on me, I shouldn't have been surprised. Nevertheless, that revelation shook me to the core. How could I have fallen in love with a man who didn't even want to be friends? "At that time you and Rory barely knew each other," he continued. "Now there appears to be an attachment."

Attachment? The word floated in my brain, and I couldn't seem to focus. "I enjoy being with him. He's a good baby, eventempered." My voice sounded faraway, as if I were in a dense fog. In a way I was.

Matthew hesitated, his eyes searching mine with an intensity that tightened my nerves. Did my feeling for him shine through? Or was he still thinking of Rory and was about to voice disapproval over the amount of time I spent with his son? Matthew parted his lips to speak but apparently decided otherwise, because he turned back to the crib. He bent, kissed the little temple, and stroked the soft hair that was as dark as his own. Then Matthew placed a hand beneath my elbow and showed me from the room. As always, his touch flip-flopped my senses. More than ever I ached to banish his resentment and build a solid foundation between us.

Outside the nursery I summoned my courage. "I am truly sorry about the other night, Matthew." Silently I prayed that reopening the subject wasn't going to bring forth a flood of words I did not want to hear.

Again he hesitated. Then to my surprise he said, "I'm sorry, too. I shouldn't have given you cause to question my integrity."

It took a moment for the full import of his words to completely register, and my knees almost buckled on a surge of relief. "Can we try to be friends?" I held my breath.

He quirked an eyebrow. "Can you keep from creeping around the house?"

After the hair-raising fright and humiliation of being caught in his room, it was easy to promise, "No more snooping."

"Then we can try." He extended his hand as one might do in calling a truce. As I placed my hand in his, I fought to keep my senses under control. As usual, they had a will of their own, and this time I feared desire was revealed in my eyes.

"You are very lovely, Alexandra," Matthew breathed, and the trace of huskiness in his voice conveyed his senses weren't behaving, either. Was he remembering our kisses, the passion?

Intoxicated, I murmured a thank-you that was little more than a whisper and struggled against the urge to lean near. Two compliments from Matthew in one evening delighted and amazed me. Until now the only favorable comment he'd expressed had pertained to my work. Matthew moistened his lips. Then with obvious reluctance, he released my hand.

Later in the quiet of my room I lay down on the bed and reflected on my feelings for him. I'd always thought love would fill me with great happiness and joy. Instead, I was in turmoil, and all because of my unrelenting suspicion. Why did it still trouble me? And why did he continue to doubt my sincerity? I'd apologized for sneaking into his room, yet he'd made me promise not to creep around the house before he'd agreed to even try to be friends. My nerves tensed on a disturbing thought. Maybe my not snooping was all he wanted. I shook my head in obstinate refusal. He was drawn to me, of that I was certain. Turning onto my back, I stared up at the ceiling and glumly reminded myself that desire had little if anything to do with love and trust.

Miserable and confused, I heaved a sigh. If I continued with the suspicion, hints of it were bound to show through and further jeopardize my chance to remain near Rory, and now, equally as important, Matthew. I must avoid giving him further reason to distrust me. No matter how strong the urge to find the diary, I would hold to my promise. That affirmation reminded me that I had not thought to look for the volume in the nursery. Charlotte might have taken it into her son's room to jot down cherished events in his life or perhaps some of their special moments together. Surely Matthew would not object if I looked in Rory's room. After all, it was hardly a private place.

IN the morning I dressed in a simple percale, had breakfast alone downstairs, then went to the nursery and helped Zalea with Rory's bath. Afterward, I took him in to see Grandmother Hester. The sight of the little boy brought instant delight to her gray eyes. "I'd like to hold him," she said.

I nodded and placed an infant blanket on her lap before settling Rory. "Protection," I said, and laughed.

She also laughed. "You seem to know babies quite well, Alexandra."

"I'm learning." I sat down in the nearby chair. "I never knew I had so much motherly instinct."

"In time you'll have little ones of your own."

"I hope so."

Hester kissed her great-grandson. "Rory looks just like his father when he was this age. Their dispositions are quite a bit different, though. Matthew wasn't so quick to smile or take to people."

Then he hasn't changed. I bit back the words. On the other hand, when Matthew did smile, my insides turned to jelly. "I think Rory will be outgoing like his mother." I only hoped he hadn't also inherited her lack of business sense.

"I think so, too." Hester gave the boy a lace handkerchief to play with. "And maybe he'll grow up to be a physician like his father. In any case, Belle Haven will one day be Rory's." Worry furrowed her brow. "I pray he'll always want to live in our home and keep it in the family."

Just the thought of anyone other than the Steeles residing here clearly distressed this woman. As I had grown to know Hester, it had become obvious that her love for Belle Haven was actually an obsession. How agonizing it must have been when the family had been forced to sell off most of the land. "This place is so beautiful," I said. "I can't imagine Rory would ever want to live anywhere else."

"What about Boston?"

The question took me by surprise. "He has no family ties in Boston."

"Yes, but the bulk of his mother's financial holdings are there."

"True, but he wouldn't have to live in that city to oversee them, any more than Charlotte and I had over the past three years."

"You wouldn't consider it essential for him to eventually make his home there?"

"Heavens, no, nothing other than an occasional business trip should ever be necessary. I have no right to try and influence him, Hester. This is Rory's home, his heritage." The look of relief that overspread her unlined face made me wonder if the entire family shared the deep concern that I might one day try to sway Rory. Had this anything to do with the warning I'd heard in Matthew's tone and words? The threat I perceived I posed to the family? If so, then I prayed that I had managed to allay the old lady's worry and that she in turn would reassure the family.

As she cuddled Rory and gave him a taste of honey from the silver bowl beside the tea service, I noticed that her hands and fingers didn't seem quite as stiff and that she was able to move them without wincing. The new rheumatism medicine was doing wonders for her. I could only hope it would also benefit some of Matthew's other patients, like the aged Negro woman I'd seen him assisting from an examining room at the clinic.

Rory began to squirm. As I lifted him, Hester complimented me on the gown I'd designed for Felicity. "Perhaps, Alexandra, when you're all settled, you might do one for me."

Settled? For the most part I felt that way here, but maybe she meant in a salon. "It would be a privilege to do one for you, Hester." We chatted briefly about Felicity's gown, and I waited for the white-haired matriarch to comment on the plunging neckline. She said nothing. Either Hester was not aware of it, or she wasn't shocked. But then, anyone who relished telling grim pirate stories, as she did, and about her own family, probably would not be shocked by a mere risqué bodice.

By the time I returned Rory to his room, he was fussy and yawning and dropped off to sleep without demanding his usual midmorning feeding. It was a pleasant spring day, and after I'd opened the French doors, allowing the comfortably warm air to circulate, I began a quiet search for the diary. As I moved down the bureau drawers, my hope for success faded, and I could hardly believe my eyes when I moved aside an infant quilt. The diary!

Quickly I lifted the volume and opened it. The sight of my stepsister's handwriting tore at my heart. In bold letters she had written *Rory Steele.* Disappointment coursed through me and settled over my spirit as I leafed through the pages. Yes, this was a diary, but it pertained solely to the first two months of Rory's life. Charlotte had eloquently written of her love for the dear baby, the friends who had come to see him, the gifts he'd received, and his first smile. It was a treasured record, to one day share with her son. Unfortunately, it didn't answer any of the nagging questions in my mind, and the hunt for Charlotte's diary had come to a dismal end.

I took the volume to my room and placed it on the desk. I'd never kept a daily journal, but I would maintain this one for Rory, as his mother would have done.

From the desk I went to the drawing table and reworked the fashion sketch. Then I took it with me to Felicity's room. She didn't respond to my tap, so I went downstairs. Lizzie was coming toward me from the back of the house. "Have you seen Felicity?" I asked.

"She gone off to the city, Miss Alexandra."

"Oh?

"Somethin' important you wants her for?"

I shrugged. "We were going to look over fabrics for her new gown."

"I sorry, but she ain't gonna be home till late afternoon. Some trouble come up with one of the charities Miss Felicity be in charge of, and she left in a terrible rush first thin' this mornin'. They keeps her plenty busy, runnin' in circles, sometimes."

As I thanked the housekeeper, I wondered if Felicity's sudden trip to Charleston had anything to do with the fund-raising ball. I'd addressed the stack of invitations she'd given me and offered to help in any other areas of need. After expressing appreciation, she'd said nothing beyond, "I'll keep you in mind, Alexandra." To volunteer further would be pushy.

With the revised fashion sketch still in hand, I continued to the sewing room to review the fabrics alone. Quietly I closed the door behind me, then moved along the shelves ladened with the wide array of exquisite materials. The multitude of colors were as pleasing to the eyes as a summer rainbow, and it still amazed me that Felicity yearned to add more shades to this collection. Why, there was enough here to clothe the entire household for years to come. For all I knew, there were even more bolts in the closet. Curiosity drew me to its door. As I opened it, a scalp-pricking sound, somewhere between a buzz and a rattle, rose from the interior right-hand corner. What was it? Hesitantly I leaned in. Just as I moved aside a roll of cotton batting, a snake coiled to strike.

⁂ 12

THE blood froze in my veins. I jerked back my hand as the snake's head shot up and a horrifying hiss combined with the heart-stopping rattles. A scream ripped from my throat, and I wheeled, sending the fashion sketch flying from my hand. In a flash I'd thrown open the hallway door and was running toward the front of the house. "Lizzie!" I shrilled, glancing over my shoulder. The snake slithered across the sewing room threshold and along the walls at the rear.

"Mercy, chil', what's all the ruckus?" Lizzie hurried my way from the entrance salon stairs.

"A snake!" I pulled up short and gestured wildly with a trembling hand. The vile reptile disappeared through the open veranda doors. "There. Did you see it?"

The ample maid stopped beside me and squinted up the hall.

"No." The word came slowly, as if she didn't understand my agitation. "Snakes be all about these parts, Miss Alexandra."

"But this one was in the sewing room, rattling and hissing. It tried to bite me."

Her mouth dropped open. "Lawdy, we ain't never had vipers in the house before." She moved to the veranda, stepped out, and looked around. "Ain't nothing here now."

"I hope there aren't any more inside, either," I gasped, still trembling. "Have Eustace check the sewing room and the others on this floor."

"Ain't no need to trouble him, I is used to snakes. I can look myself." Lizzie squared her shoulders and went bravely into the sewing room. "Where did you see it?" she called out to me.

I inched toward the door and peered in. "Coiled on the floor in the closet."

"Lan' sakes, how did it get in there?" She stepped inside, and I could hear her rummaging around.

"That's what I'd like to know." I remained rooted to the spot on the threshold, my gaze searching. "How could it have gotten into this room in the first place? The door is generally closed. And it was shut when I came in a few minutes ago," I insisted.

Lizzie reappeared, shaking her turbaned head. "I can't rightly say. 'Ceptin all the doors in the house was open during that hot spell." She picked up the sketch I'd dropped and placed it on the table by the window.

"You're right, I'd forgotten." I watched her scour the room.

"The viper must've gotten trapped when I closed the hallway door last night."

"But that doesn't explain how it got in the closet. That door was also shut when I came in."

"Hmm," she murmured, "that be a puzzle. But Miss Felicity is forever in and out of that closet and leavin' the door hangin' open for hours. Most times I has to come in and shuts it after her," she grumbled. "Anyway, there ain't nothin' to be fearin' in here now, Miss Alexandra. I'll goes have a look around the rest of the house."

"I'd appreciate that, Lizzie." After a painful swallow I stepped in, allowing her to exit. She closed the door. My heart thumped, but I gulped down the fear. After all, I had been reassured this place was safe. Even so, I moved slowly to the closet and peeked in. My attention dropped immediately to the spot where I'd seen the snake, and a shudder coursed through me.

Inhaling a deep breath, I lifted my gaze. Even though the closet was fairly deep, I was able to see into the corners and along the shelves loaded with more luxurious cloth and baskets of sewing supplies. There were several more baskets on the floor, all of which had flip-up lids that were securely in place. Nothing could have crawled into them and be laying in hiding, though I hadn't the courage at the moment to investigate.

All in all, the fright had dissolved my enthusiasm for sorting through fabrics, and I left the sewing room a few minutes later. My usual hearty appetite also suffered, and I did little more than push lunch around on my plate. I knew it was foolish to dwell on the harrowing incident, especially when Lizzie had conducted a thorough search of the main floor, but I couldn't dispel the throat-closing vision of the striking snake. If it had bitten me, would death have been instantaneous? Shivering, I left the table.

In my room a few minutes later I changed clothes, then went out to the stables. Over the past two weeks Felicity and I had spent many afternoons riding together. When Tyler was home, he usually joined us. More and more I wished Matthew would do the same. But he had so little leisure time, and he spent most of it with his son. "Besides," Matthew had said one evening when the subject of riding came up, "I'm in the saddle more than I like, looking in on patients."

Before Belle Haven, riding hadn't interested me. Now it was becoming a part of my life, a pleasant way to enjoy the lush countryside. Not only had my skill with the reins improved to where I was confident enough to venture out alone, I no longer felt suffocated beneath the towering trees. I knew every twist and turn in the trail, every moss-draped branch that formed the fragrant tunnel through the woods. It was a peaceful place where my thoughts flowed freely, and on a pleasant plane. Why, even the episode with the snake now seemed more like a horrid nightmare than reality, and I was able to push it to the back of my mind.

The encompassing serenity of the countryside stayed with me throughout the balance of the afternoon. And my spirits rose even higher when I entered the drawing room before supper and saw Grandmother Hester seated on the sofa beside Matthew. This was the first time I'd seen her out of her quarters. "You look surprised, Alexandra," she said with a smile. "Didn't anyone mention that I occasionally come down for supper?"

"Yes, Felicity did. I'm just delighted that you're joining us. You look wonderful, Hester." Her rose silk gown and light mantle of India muslin heightened the color I'd noticed in her face that morning. I sat down on the sofa beside Tyler. Felicity was in the plush chair on my right.

"I feel so much better, thanks to my grandson." Hester gave Matthew's hand an affectionate pat, then searched my face. "But how are you, dear?"

Before I could answer, Matthew spoke up, his tone serious. "We heard about the snake. We've never had anything like that happen before, Alexandra."

Felicity hugged herself as if warding off a chill. "I'm frequently in and out of that closet. Why, if I'd been home, as I'd expected, I probably would have been the one to come face to face with it."

"Thank God, you weren't harmed," Tyler said to me, and the family nodded in agreement. I drew comfort from their concern and reassurances.

With Grandmother Hester at the supper table conversation

that night revolved primarily around her love of family and home. It was heartwarming to see the younger Steeles listening attentively to the stories they must have heard a hundred times. Their indulgence was testimony to deep affection and respect. But family love wasn't the only emotion I saw and felt among the four. There was another in the air, underlying and yet very real. As I studied faces, it gradually came to me that beneath the pleasant expressions was anxiety. Nothing in the voices or the conversation gave me a clue to the cause. At one point, though, over dessert, I had the horrible sinking feeling that the uneasiness had something to do with me.

After supper the men helped Hester back to her quarters, and Felicity came to my room to see the revised fashion sketch. She beamed at the alterations I'd made. "This is perfect, Alexandra."

Perfect for those who like cleavage, I thought. "I'm glad it pleases you," I murmured. I longed to inquire about the tension I'd sensed during supper. I had to find out if it was linked to me, but I couldn't think of a tactful way to broach the subject.

"Are you free to look over fabrics in the morning?" Felicity asked, then added lightly, "I promise to be available."

I nodded. "Around ten?"

"Ten it is." After Felicity left, I roamed my room. I was too keyed-up for bed and didn't even feel like changing into night-clothes. Maybe I'd just imagined that the underlying anxiety had anything to do with me. Matthew's resentment had doubtless made me overly sensitive. Not knowing how he really felt about me was maddening. Unbidden, the thought came to me that if I were gone, Matthew would have Rory all to himself and com-plete control of the trust fund. With proper management it was more than enough to maintain Belle Haven and the free clinic indefinitely. Scowling, I tried to divert my mind from the grue-some thought by immersing myself in a good book. Unfortu-nately, the heroine in the romantic novel I'd selected was just as perplexed and agonized by the man she loved, and the tension within me doubled.

I set aside the book and returned my attention to Felicity's gown. The design was adaptable to several fabrics. I hoped it wouldn't take her as long to make a choice as it had with the design. On the chance it might, I reminded myself that it would be wise to assess the fabrics alone and be ready with suggestions at our meeting in the morning.

The mantel clock told me it was 10:05. It was a little late to be moving about, but being in the sewing room wasn't apt to disturb anyone. My stomach knotted and I forced down the renewal of fear. After all, the family had assured me that what had happened with the snake couldn't possibly occur again. Clinging to that thought, I came to my feet, smoothed my brocade skirt, and changed into soft-soled slippers, which would muffle the sound of footsteps on the wooden floors. Then I went carefully down the stairs and along the dimly illuminated hall to the rear of the house.

Outside the sewing room I inhaled a deep, fortifying breath, then eased open the door and listened. No rattle or hissing. With continued caution I lit the lamps and looked around, searching. I was alone. The closet door was closed. Tonight it would remain that way.

As the tension eased from my body, I became engrossed in the fabrics and lost sight of time. My hands moved over one bolt after another. As I made choices, I set them on the large worktable before the curtained windows. Beyond them the moonless night was black as ink. For some reason I couldn't understand, a vision of Charlotte came forward, and I ached at the thought of her out there. On impulse I drew aside the lace curtains, then wondered why I had bothered. I couldn't see the cemetery. Even the veranda just beyond the windowpanes was hidden in shadows. Yet I stared out as if hypnotized, my mind recalling pleasant childhood days with my stepsister. I saw her in our playroom, surrounded by favorite china dolls, her golden hair adorned with a bright ribbon. Then there was a vision of her as a young woman, sneaking out to the gazebo in the rose garden to meet a beau. A flash of light intruded on my reverie. I blinked. From somewhere near the river came another flicker, just like the ones I'd seen before, only this time they seemed farther upstream.

My breathing became ragged, and I stared intently. Seconds passed. No more light. Had it been on a boat? If so, maybe I could see it from the rear veranda and lay my curiosity to rest once and for all. I left the sewing room and made my way to the doors. The grandfather clock near the entrance salon stairs chimed twelve times. Midnight! Chills prickled my scalp, then shot down my spine when I opened the veranda door. Before me, at the top of the steps, was the shadowy outline of a broad-shouldered man; his back to me. His feet were wide apart, and he stood like a sentinel, straight and tall.

🌿 13

THE word *sentinel* had stuck in my mind. Was the broad-shouldered man, whom I assumed was either Tyler or Matthew, standing guard? Suddenly he wheeled as if sensing my presence. "Alexandra!"

"Tyler, you startled me." I squinted at him through the darkness and felt oddly vulnerable framed in the glow of the hallway lamps.

"How long have you been there?"

His brusque tone lifted the hair on my nape, and I was sure he noticed me flinch. "Only a minute," I said. "What are you doing out so late?"

"I was about to ask that of you." He moved to stand before me in the doorway, his powerful body a wall against the night. Tyler was dressed in the same dark suit he'd had on at supper. His face was still partially in shadows so I couldn't read his expression. But when he spoke again, his voice was casual. "I wasn't sleepy, so I came out for some fresh air. What about you?"

I felt his scrutiny and my insides shriveled a little at the sensation of being under a magnifying glass. "I couldn't sleep, either, and came down to the sewing room."

"Really? After your scare I shouldn't think you'd be eager to go there, especially in the dark."

"There's no reason for me to be frightened, is there?"

"No, but most women would probably shy away for a while. In any case, what brought you to these doors?"

Why should it matter? And why did I feel at a marked disadvantage being the only one caught in the glow of the lamps? Purposely I stepped back and held my response until after Tyler crossed the threshold. "I saw lights on the river and was curious." The look of his features was as casual as his tone, but his blue eyes held a dark emotion I couldn't define.

"You saw lights from the sewing room?"

"Yes."

"I wasn't aware the river was visible from there."

He doubted me. Why? My pulse leaped. Had Matthew, after all, mentioned my invasion of his room and asked the family to keep an eye on me? The mere thought of being watched set my teeth on edge. "It can be seen from the corner window. Look for yourself in the morning." My polite but firm tone must have been convincing because the doubt faded.

"That's not necessary," he said softly.

I was tempted to ask if my movements were indeed being policed, but I realized that would be a waste of breath. If I was under observation, Tyler wouldn't admit it. Instead, I said, "You must have also noticed the lights."

"I saw some on a passing boat, a few minutes ago."

"All I glimpsed were two flashes."

He arched an eyebrow. "Two flashes, eh? That sounds mysterious."

His sudden shift to humor took me aback, although this was the side of Tyler I'd come to know. Nevertheless, I wasn't up to teasing. "It struck me that way at first," I responded in a flat tone.

Tyler cleared the amusement from his voice. "A bit of intrigue would liven up Belle Haven, but I'm afraid such goings-on died with the Revolution."

"So Hester said."

"Unhappily, I'm certain. She would have loved to live during the days of our intrepid forebearers. In any case, I'm sure what you saw was just the boat slipping behind trees." He closed the door. "It's late, we should go up to our beds. But first, Alexandra, would you like a sip of brandy to help you sleep?"

"Thank you, no."

Tyler held out his arm. "Then allow me to show you to your room." As always, he was the true gentleman. Still, a tiny part of me wondered if his offer might have stemmed from the wish to make certain that I made no side trips on the way to my quarters. Maybe my initial impression, of generating the unease I'd perceived among the Steeles, had been well-founded.

FELICITY and I spent most of the next morning and a bit of the afternoon poring over fabrics and laces. As I had feared, once again she couldn't make up her mind. But at least she hadn't added to the bolts of cloth I'd set out the night before. "I appreciate the time you've given to narrowing down the choices," she said, shortly after we'd met in the sewing room. Much later she admitted, "I just don't have an eye for putting design and fabric together, Alexandra. Which of all these would you choose?"

After hours of shifting heavy bolts and watching her before the full-length mirror holding fabrics up to her face, I was ready to close my eyes and pick. Fortunately, in my mind, I'd narrowed the selection even more. "I'd say the white glacé for the under-dress, the overdress in blue silk, trimmed with point lace." I draped one cloth over the other, accented with the lace, and laid the sketch alongside. "What do you think?"

Felicity pressed her lips together. "That is striking."

"The blue is the exact shade of your eyes, and the texture of the fabrics would be flattering to your figure."

She considered for a moment longer, rescanning the other fab-rics. Then she expelled a long breath, as if a weight had been lifted off her. "The blue and white it is. And if I even try to change my mind," she said lightly, "please don't listen."

That was a promise I would have no trouble keeping, though I tactfully didn't come right out and say so. "I'll start drafting the pattern some time after lunch. That reminds me, is there paper to work with?"

"As I recall, Charlotte ordered the kind you use." Felicity crossed to the walk-in closet. Slowly she opened the door and peeked in. "No snakes." She laughed, but I felt a chill. "I think the paper's in here somewhere. Yes, there it is in the back." She stepped in.

I moved to the door. "What's in the baskets on the floor?"

"Baskets? Oh, just yarns for knitting and crocheting." Felicity emerged, carrying a wide roll of lightweight paper. "Where shall I put this?"

"Here, on the table by the window." I cleared a spot. "I need good light and plenty of room to work. This will be perfect."

She set down the roll. Before Felicity straightened, I saw her lean forward and glance out the corner window, the one from which I'd seen the lights last night. My jaw hardened. Had Tyler continued to doubt me after all and asked Felicity to verify if the river really was visible from the sewing room? She looked around at me, an innocent expression in her sapphire-blue eyes.

"It's going to be a lovely day, Alexandra," she commented in a casual tone.

"Just as lovely as yesterday and most of the others," I pointed out, forcing my tone to match hers. Weather, indeed! I hoped the view convinced her that I had been in here last night and she would pass that on to Tyler and the rest of the family. Clearly, I was under their watchful eyes. Considering my infringement on Matthew's privacy, I couldn't really blame them, I firmly reminded myself, or cease to be grateful that they hadn't asked me to leave.

With her chin tilted in a pleasant attitude, Felicity asked, "Charlotte told me you love to sew. Will you be doing any on my gown?"

A small sigh of resignation escaped my lips. "I do enjoy it, but my focus now is design and fit. From what I've seen of your gowns, Felicity, your seamstress is an expert. I'm sure she'll do this garment justice."

"I have complete faith in Justine's ability."

"I'm looking forward to meeting her," I said.

Immediately following lunch I took Rory for a stroll of the gardens. Afterward, I returned to the sewing room, hauled out pencils, yardstick, scissors, and Felicity's measurements, and went to work. Drafting patterns was a challenge I thrived on, not only now but also in my youth. In my sixth year I had begun fashioning clothes for the dolls Charlotte and I had called our family. By age nine I was experimenting with clothes for her and me. Of course, most of those early garments were a disaster. We'd giggled over them and agreed they weren't even fit to go into the box for the needy.

The afternoon passed quickly, and by the time I had to change for supper, I had drafted and cut the bodice and felt a great sense of accomplishment.

Once again Grandmother Hester joined the family for the evening meal. And once again, despite friendly faces and light conversation, I perceived underlying anxiety and even noticed the exchange of quick, secretive glances. Something was going on, something the Steeles did not wish to share with me. I felt isolated. I was in the family but not of it. I didn't know what to think. On the one hand they distrusted me. On the other there was a definite softening from Matthew. He smiled at me more, and earlier tonight, as he'd handed me a glass of claret, his dark eyes had met mine with a melting expression. That look and the huskiness that had come into his voice as he'd murmured, "To good health, Alexandra," communicated his mind was on more than the continued soundness of our bodies. And when he lifted his glass to mine, and our fingers brushed, the tremor of excitement I felt go through him heightened the awareness in me. For pulse-pounding moments I was immobilized and could scarcely breathe. The hum of conversation from the rest of the family returned me unhappily to reality, and I wondered if anyone had noticed the sensual attraction between Matthew and me.

The more I reflected on the positive change in him, the more it seemed that my intrusion in his room had nothing to do with the tension among the Steeles. What, then? And what about Tyler's suspicion?

Later, as I relaxed on the chaise in my quarters, struggling to concentrate on the romantic novel, I pondered Felicity's glance out the sewing room window. Might the lights I'd seen have something to do with the family's unease? Or was I simply letting my imagination run wild? Why, for all I knew the tension could simply relate to Hester. After all, it had started on her first night at the supper table. The family adored her, and there was always the possibility they worried she might overtax herself. Perhaps she even fretted a little in this regard. Plainly Hester Steele was determined to live a long life as mistress of Belle Haven. All in all, she seemed fine during the meals. But by the time they were over, fatigue had shown in her face and she was eager to return to her room.

Tonight I, too, was tired and had excused myself earlier than usual. Drafting patterns set my creative juices aflow, but it was also backbreaking, and it was heaven to stretch out on the chaise. The French doors were partially open and the scent of spring flowers floated in on a pleasant breeze. Yawning, I shut my eyes. In the distance a night bird cried, and I felt myself drifting into a dreamless void. I had no idea how long I'd slept before the sound of footsteps awakened me. Drowsily I opened my eyes and looked around. I was still alone. A maid hadn't come in, as I had thought. As my sense of awareness sharpened, I realized someone was on the veranda. I turned my head toward the doors. Moonlight fell through the opening. The footsteps were coming closer. It was only Felicity. She had exchanged her lilac gown for a shimmering pink wrapper. I reclosed my eyes, but couldn't shut out her muted footfalls. Felicity stopped just beyond my room. Was she about to enter the library next door? That question had hardly crossed my mind when she moved on. I doubted she was going to see Hester, who was bound to be asleep by now. Certainly she wouldn't be headed for Tyler's quarters at the far end. I listened like an eavesdropping schoolgirl who relished intrigue and gossip. Two or three minutes later Felicity retraced her steps. This time I didn't open my eyes and glance her way. Apparently she was simply enjoying the night air, and I chided myself for thinking she might have been on her way to a rendezvous. The sound of her footfalls faded, then it was quiet again. I assumed Felicity had returned to her room, adjacent to mine.

By now I was wide awake and had probably managed to get just enough sleep to keep me up half the night. Frowning, I glanced at the mantel clock. 10:30. Ordinarily I didn't see or hear Felicity at this late hour. Was she restless and unable to fall asleep?

The memory of the pitiful crying brought a lump to my throat. I put aside the book and went out on the veranda to see if she might have settled in one of the rattan chairs and perhaps be in need of company. But Felicity was nowhere in sight. The evening was lovely and silent. No crying, thank heaven. And no grating noise from below. Tightening my cambric wrapper, I inhaled a deep breath and crossed to the railing. The three-quarter moon was bright in the cloudless sky, and stars winked like diamonds on a carpet of black velvet. In Paris I had enjoyed the night from my small balcony, only there the hubbub of the busy city was intrusive. Boston had been the same. In a way I had taken comfort in the familiar sounds, but I didn't miss them. Here, the stillness was soothing, and I knew that if I didn't have so many concerns, I would feel complete peace and contentment.

I lowered my gaze and looked across the lawn to the grassy slope where Charlotte must have stood on that tragic day, five months ago. In the moonlight I could see the river clearly, and I stared at the water, willing away pain. What had happened to my stepsister could not be undone. For Rory's sake, more than my own, I mustn't continue to think of the river as a malevolent body. I glanced upstream, then down. If there were any boats on the water, I couldn't see them through the thick wall of trees that lined the bank to each side of narrow grassy slope.

Meditative, I meandered quietly past Hester's darkened room to the end of the veranda and stopped at the railing in front of Tyler's quarters. No lights shone behind his closed doors, either. I leaned against one of the Doric columns and gazed at the cemetery on my right. The scattering of tall oaks placed much of it in shadows, but I could see Charlotte's headstone.

"Alexandra!" Felicity called, her voice sounding loud in the still of the night. I hoped she hadn't awakened Hester and Tyler.

As I turned toward Felicity, I glimpsed something move just beyond my stepsister's grave. Startled, I swung back and scanned.

My abrupt reaction must have alarmed Felicity because apprehension sliced through her voice. "Is something wrong?" She stopped beside me.

Still scanning, I hesitated. "No . . . I thought I saw something move below. But I must have been mistaken—there are so many shadows."

"Maybe it was just a tree swaying in the breeze."

"Maybe," I murmured, noting the breeze had picked up.

"It's getting cool. Since we're both wide awake, why don't you come to my room, and we can chat for a spell?"

"That would be nice."

"I was out a few minutes ago, but you weren't around." She whirled and started up the veranda.

I dropped another glance at the cemetery, then followed after her. "What brought you back outside?"

"I'm at loose ends . . . too much on my mind, I guess." Felicity opened the French doors. A second later we were in her room, which was about the same size as my own and superbly appointed. The walls were eggshell white, the draperies, bed hangings, and upholstered pieces an attractive combination of dove gray, pink, and mauve. Twin armoires, identical to the ones that held my wardrobe, were against the wall that separated our quarters. But what I noticed most was the gilt-framed daguerreotype of Felicity and a tall, dark-haired man of sturdy build.

"That's my husband, Brit," she said, following my line of vision. Felicity lifted the picture from the night table. "We were married for seven years before he—"

Her expression and tone conveyed deep sorrow. "He was very handsome," I said. Exceedingly so, just as Charlotte had written. Nevertheless, Matthew was better-looking. However, I supposed I was a little prejudiced, particularly when the brothers bore a striking resemblance.

"Brit and I always knew we would one day marry," Felicity went on. "I'm not sure if I'll ever love again. Sometimes,

though—" Her lips compressed, and she abruptly returned the
photograph to the table. "I mustn't go on like this."

"Talking often helps," I suggested.

Felicity shook her head, her unbound chestnut hair whispering about her shoulders. "Not for me." She gestured to a pair
of matching damask chairs.

As I made myself comfortable, I tried to puzzle out her emotions. Felicity's love for Brit was easy to perceive; I'd seen it in
her eyes. But what had altered her tone and the set of her mouth?
As I watched her sit down in the other chair and arrange her
wrapper about her ankles, the answer gradually came to me.
Along with love she bore resentment. As far as I knew, the only
thing that could have generated that emotion was the loss of the
family fortune and her own inheritance. Brit had blamed himself
for both. Since the comforts of wealth were uppermost with Felicity, might she also blame him?

She straightened and changed the subject. "I fear I haven't
been a proper hostess, Alexandra. By now I should have introduced you to some of the women in the area."

Her comment gave me hope that she wanted me to remain
at Belle Haven, or at least in this region. "I met a few of your
friends in the city," I reminded her.

"True, but a tea or perhaps a luncheon in your honor, if it
isn't too soon after Charlotte—"

"An informal daytime gathering probably wouldn't be inap-
propriate, but I know how busy you are with your charitable ob-
ligations."

"They do take their toll of my time and thoughts." Felicity
elaborated on the worthy organizations she chaired and briefly
commented that the plans for the fund-raising ball were falling
nicely into place. She didn't mention my offer to help, and I
didn't bring up the subject, either.

It was well after eleven before I returned to my room and
climbed into bed. Another hour passed before my eyelids grew
heavy and I drifted off. Through most of the night I tossed and
turned on a string of nightmares. Each centered around eerie,
moving shadows in the cemetery. Twice I was startled awake,
my heart pounding so rapidly I gasped for breath, my body wet
with cold perspiration.

In the morning when I left the bed, I was still tired. There
were dark smudges under my eyes, and I went about my toilette
with scant enthusiasm. I selected a simple gown and fashioned

my thick, ebony hair just as simply, with plain combs and a few pins. To my dismay, Matthew was at the table when I went down for breakfast. "I didn't expect you'd still be home at this hour," I said, wishing I was at my best for him.

As Matthew rose from the table, he eyed me with concern. "I saw a few patients in my office out front." He paused. "You look a bit under the weather, Alexandra."

The corners of my mouth drooped, and I struggled against the impulse to admit I felt like the first garment I'd ever created, a botchery of ill-joined pieces. Instead, I said, "I didn't sleep well."

"I'm sorry." Matthew pulled out the chair beside his. "I have powders, if you ever feel the need."

I sat down. "No, thank you, I don't believe in taking anything to sleep."

He smiled. "That's good."

"You don't believe in sedatives, either?"

"Only as a last resort." That must have caused some dissension between Matthew and my stepsister, I thought. Charlotte had often relied upon the powders. But why, if he disapproved of their indiscriminate use, had he been so quick to offer them to me? Had he presumed that I was like Charlotte in this regard, too?

Just being with Matthew made me feel better. Breakfast was bliss, though I hardly knew what I ate. My concentration was on him and our conversation. For the first time since we'd met he regarded me without a trace of bitterness.

The meal ended all too soon, and Matthew came slowly to his feet. "I have patients waiting in the city." He looked and sounded as reluctant to move away as I was for him to leave. His unspoken desire to remain with me kept me on a euphoric cloud for a long time after we parted, then fatigue flowed back, with a vengeance. The nightmares of the cemetery were the cause! Scowling, I envisioned the marble tombstones standing eerily in the glow of the moon. I also saw the shadows and wondered if Felicity had been right about the movement I'd glimpsed. That it had been nothing more than a tree bending in the wind.

🌿 14

THE nightmares convinced me that I had spent too much time thinking about Charlotte and the cemetery, and I decided that packing away her personal effects might put more of the grief behind me. So late one afternoon, while Rory was asleep and I'd left the sewing room for the day, I took Lizzie up on her offer to lend a hand. "I be glad to help, Miss Alexandra," she said. "I'll have some boxes and barrels brung up."

"And a small cedar-lined chest, if you have it, for the things I'd like to keep."

"Yes'm, I think there be one in the attic."

I hadn't gone into my stepsister's room since my first week at Belle Haven, and the pain of being among her belongings swept back the instant I stepped across the threshold. As I went through bureau drawers, placing what I wanted to keep in one stack and the remainder in another, I nurtured the slim hope that I might still find the diary. Not knowing what had happened to it was more perplexing than ever.

Zalea came into the room. "If you wants, I can helps with the putting away, too, Miss Alexandra."

"I'd appreciate it," I said, eager to complete the heart-wrenching task. "Whatever I place on this pile is mine. You and your mother can pack the rest. If either of you would like to keep anything, feel free to help yourselves."

Zalea's eyes widened. "Anything we wants, Miss Alexandra?"

I nodded.

"That be nice of you." She dropped down beside the delicate nightdresses. She was about Charlotte's size, so whatever Zalea took would fit.

Lizzie smiled at me in appreciation, then turned the warm expression on her daughter. In a way I could understand why my stepsister had thought the Negroes in the region seemed happy, for these two clearly were. From what I'd seen of the others at Belle Haven, they, too, appeared contented. But, like this pair, they were also free, well cared for, and received wages, which was far from representative of the majority.

For two afternoons Lizzie, Zalea, and I worked side by side in Charlotte's room. The chest I'd filled with keepsakes held only memorable items. There were embroidered handkerchiefs, kid gloves from Father, a shawl handed down from Charlotte's grandmother, heirloom jewelry, family miniatures, and the collection of pressed flowers. My stepsister had saved every bouquet from beaus, which was well above the number I'd ever received. Understandably, her list of suitors had been almost twice as long as mine.

Lizzie kept one or two shawls for herself and asked if she might have the silver-backed set of brushes. My stepsister had loved and respected this woman. "Charlotte would have wanted you to have them, Lizzie." As I handed over the set, she blinked away tears.

Zalea was ecstatic with her mountain of garments, especially the gown I'd fashioned for my stepsister and had forwarded from Paris. She held it up, her eyes bright. "Is you sure I can have this, Miss Alexandra?"

"Yes, Zalea." Her continued delight dissolved the somber atmosphere which had prevailed. "Why don't you try it on—I'd like to see how it looks. Probably your mother would, too."

Smiling, Lizzie nodded, and her daughter darted behind the screen and quickly changed from the muslin into the sleek satin. Then Zalea glided to the middle of the room and whirled like a little girl in a new party dress. The claret color complemented her pretty face, and except for a bit of slack across the breast, the garment was a perfect fit. "Very lovely," I breathed past the lump rising in my throat. If only I could have seen Charlotte in that creation.

"It's the prettiest dress I ever saw," Zalea bubbled, whirling again.

Lizzie lifted her chin with pride and mildly insisted, "You gots to take good care of it now, chil'."

I had no doubt that the young maid would cherish the gown, though I wondered where she would ever wear it. But it hardly mattered; she was happy and that was all that counted.

Those moments of joy gradually faded, and the sadness resettled. "I'll always remember Miss Charlotte," Zalea murmured as we glanced about the room now empty of everything that had once been my stepsister's. Although her favorite shades of peach and champagne remained in the hangings and soft, upholstered pieces.

By supper that evening I was emotionally drained. The family must have noticed because they were quiet. Hester hadn't joined us for the meal, which under the circumstances was probably for the best. Both she and Felicity had asked for a small remembrance of Charlotte, and I had given them each one of the delicate handkerchiefs her mother had embroidered. Matthew and I had discussed the packing some time ago, and I sensed he was relieved that I had finally seen to it. Later that night, when he and I met briefly outside the nursery, his words confirmed that feeling. "Thank you, Alexandra, for tending to that difficult task." He gestured to Charlotte's former room.

I swallowed at the gentleness in his voice and ached to place my hand on his. "I saved a few things to share with Rory," I said in a tone that matched his.

Matthew inclined his head in approval. "Charlotte was a good mother. I want our son to know that."

It was uplifting to hear him speak of my stepsister in a positive light. I could only hope packing away her belongings would also help ease the strain between Matthew and me.

"In spite of everything," he went on, "I, too, have grieved. But mostly I think for what once was and for what could have been."

The pain that darkened his eyes twisted my heart, and I longed to hold him near and whisper words of comfort. But he moved away and the fragile moment of closeness was gone. How could Charlotte have hurt Matthew? And how could I still look upon him with even a twinge of doubt? If only I had found the diary. Now I feared it was gone forever, like my stepsister's last letter to me.

THE rest of the week passed quietly, and I was busy from the moment I awakened until I retired in the evenings. The pattern for Felicity's gown was completed, and I had begun cutting the pieces in muslin. "Why muslin?" Felicity asked when she saw me enjoying the warm night air on the veranda outside my room.

"I do all gowns in that fabric first, making certain fit and drape are perfect before I take scissors to expensive cloth. By the way, is your seamstress still coming out to the house on Monday?"

Felicity sat down in the rattan chair opposite me and smoothed out her fine lawn skirt. "Yes, and she's eager to meet you, Alexandra. Justine's never worked with a couturière before. She's excited, and I think also a little intimidated."

"As expertly as she seams," I said with a smile, "I'm the one who should probably feel that way. Can you tell me a bit about her? Is she young, middle-aged? Has she been a seamstress for a long time?"

Felicity inhaled a small breath and glanced out on the moon-dappled lawn. "Justine's in her late twenties, about my age. She's warm and bright, a bit on the plump side, but still moderately attractive. I think she said she's been sewing since she was five. She's built up a good clientele. Most of my friends do business with her, though I seem to be her favorite patron." Felicity finished on a prideful note.

"Considering she's busy, yet available whenever you need her, you must be her favorite."

"She's done the majority of my gowns, and I've sent a number of influential women her way."

"Is she married?"

"A widow." Felicity's voice grew somber. "Justine's husband and infant daughter perished in one of the horrid floods that plague the city. That was about four years ago."

"How sad."

She nodded. "I recall that day as if it just happened. Over the last few years so many people I've known have died." Felicity hugged herself. "It's getting cool. I think I'll go in. You might want to do the same, Alexandra. In this climate it's easy to catch a chill, especially at this time of the year."

"I'll bear that in mind." I watched Felicity come to her feet and move slowly away. At her door she paused and glanced back. In the light of the full moon I saw her brows knit.

"Good night," I said and felt my own brows draw together. Was she annoyed because I hadn't heeded her advice to go indoors? I saw no need; the night air was still mild, which made me wonder if the talk of death might have caused her sudden chill.

"Good night, Alexandra." She stepped into her room.

A few minutes later I strolled along the railing. Gradually I was becoming used to the shadows moving in the breeze. Thank goodness, I hadn't suffered further nightmares. Packing away Charlotte's belongings had lessened more of the sorrow. Moreover, I no longer permitted my gaze to linger on the cemetery. I glanced at it, then lifted my eyes to the moon. A billowy cloud was crossing its face. The sound of ripples floated up from the river, along with the scent of water. As I lowered my gaze and turned to look upon the river, a sudden movement just beyond Charlotte's grave caught the corner of my eye. A sharp breath lodged in my throat, and I stared intently. A shadow, tall and quick. In an instant it was gone. To where? Behind a headstone? This time I knew for certain that my eyes had not deceived me; maybe they hadn't before, either. Lizzie had said I was to summon Eustace if I saw anything that struck me as mysterious. But by the time he could respond, whoever or whatever was out there might be gone, if that wasn't already the case.

I whirled, the swish of my silk skirts loud in the night, and hurried from the veranda, and my room. I thought to tap on either Tyler or Matthew's door, but I'd lose precious moments just trying to explain. As I rushed down the stairs, I warned myself it was unwise to investigate alone. But I had to know what was happening. Besides, I had no intention of going into the cemetery, not after dark.

I pulled open the rear veranda door and went out. The cloud now obscured most of the moon, but there was ample light to guide me. Gathering up my skirts, I descended the steps. Heedless of the dew on the grass, I quickly, but quietly, moved over it, my gaze darting this way and that. Trees loomed, their network of gnarled branches like ghostly tentacles against the night sky. The closer I came to the fence-enclosed cemetery, the louder the tom-tom of my heart in my ears. An owl hooted and chills raked my flesh. Another eerie sound and I'd probably whirl in retreat. Thank goodness, snakes didn't slither about at night. At least, that's what I'd heard.

Inhaling a fortifying breath, I slowed my step as I approached a cluster of oaks, their thick trunks shrouded in weird shadows produced by the beards of moss. As I crept along, a sturdy form suddenly stepped from behind a tree. I stopped dead. A scream rose in my throat, yet I heard no sound beyond the air escaping from my lungs in a painful swoosh. I teetered, but strong hands caught me by the shoulders. "Alexandra, what are you doing out?"

My head jerked up, though Matthew's voice had brought instant relief. In the faint moonlight I saw that he was scowling down at me. I was the one who should be angry. "You scared the wits out of me," I snapped, struggling to catch my breath.

"What about your promise?"

"Promise?"

"No more prowling."

His tightening grip and dictatorial manner elevated my ire. "That pertained to the house. What were you doing hiding behind a tree?"

"Hiding? I was out for a walk and heard the rustle of your skirts. Why are you here?" he demanded again.

"I saw something from the veranda. But now that you've halted me, whoever or whatever it was is probably gone." The shadow was tall like him. Maybe—

"What are you talking about?"

"Movement in the cemetery."

"I was in there minutes ago."

"Isn't that an odd place to be after dark?"

"Only if you fear spirits will rise up out of the graves." He turned me about and with a hand beneath my elbow urged me back across the lawn.

"Most people are struck by that feeling." I tried to twist free, but he held me firmly. "Were you also in the cemetery a few nights ago?"

"Why do you want to know?"

"Can't you just answer with a simple yes or no?"

Matthew pulled up short and stared into my face. "And can't you quit poking your nose in where it doesn't belong?"

His retort bluntly reminded me of my tenuous position in this house. If I remained at Belle Haven, would it always be this way? "I'm sorry, that was not my intention. It's just that I could have sworn I'd also seen movement then."

His fingers on my bare arm loosened. "It could have been me, or even a servant out for a bit of air."

"A servant? In the family cemetery at night?" I kept my voice soft, lest I fuel his anger. Even so, a spark leaped.

"What difference does it make who it was? You know, Alexandra, if you feel some kind of a threat, you don't have to stay at Belle Haven."

His words were a saber thrust, and painful seconds passed before I could respond. "I don't feel threatened, especially now that you've explained the moving shadow. I'm just mystified and curious."

"You seem to suffer from volumes of both."

That callous remark sharpened the pain and unbidden tears surfaced. "I've overstepped bounds again—it won't happen anymore." I pulled free and whirled.

Matthew's hand flashed out, and he recaptured me by the wrist. "I'm sorry, I didn't mean to be so rude." Gently he wiped a tear from the corner of my eye. "But sometimes you are exasperating."

"Sometimes you make me feel like a naughty five-year-old," I whipped back. He was so near, his presence overwhelming.

"A child? I could never think of you in that way." He caressed my cheek and tears were forgotten as every sensitive nerve within me tingled. "Do you feel like one now?" He narrowed the distance between his mouth and mine.

"No," I whispered. I was a woman who yearned to be kissed.

Matthew gazed into my eyes with searching intensity that reached to the very depths of my soul. "For the sake of your safety," he murmured, "I'd rather you didn't venture out after dark."

His changed attitude and warm breath on my face intensified excitement, and my mind drifted on a higher plane. "What danger could there be, way out here in the country?"

He lowered his head even more, as if lured by the huskiness that had come into my voice. "Animals, and there are bounty hunters roaming everywhere. Will you do as I ask?"

Reality swept back abruptly. He hadn't used the word *promise,* but that's what he wanted. My mind balked, but I was powerless to verbally protest. I was a prisoner to Matthew's will, to the overpowering need he inspired. Did he see desire in my face, sense it from the rise and fall of my chest? I could scarcely breathe, let alone speak. My response was a short nod.

A flicker of relief touched his features, but when he spoke again, his voice was rough with longing. "You are desirable beyond words, Alexandra." Slowly Matthew slid his hand down to my shoulder, lingered, then inched along my bare arm, the soft pads of his fingers feeding the blaze deep within the heart of me. I leaned closer, the firmness of his body quickening my breath. Matthew moved to draw me into his embrace. Then, suddenly, he hesitated, as if he'd heard a shouting inner voice, and his hand dropped again to my elbow. For a moment I stood stiffly, every part of me braced for another rejection. "It's late," he murmured, and I was crushed when he quietly ushered me back into the house. Would he ever come to fully accept me, to look upon me as more than an extension of his late wife?

All the way up to the second floor I ached to know what he was thinking. I also wondered if, through his sudden change, he had manipulated me into tonight's promise. Of course, since this was his house, I'd really had no choice but to agree. Was Matthew truly concerned for my safety, though? Or was there some other reason for wanting to keep me in at night? And had he really been the one in the cemetery? At my door he simply said, "Sleep well, Alexandra." Then he moved slowly away, as if he didn't want to leave. Would I ever understand him? Should I even continue to try?

I didn't see Matthew again until supper on the following evening. Then it was agonizing to look upon the man I still doubted, the man whose interest in me was unclear. Occasionally throughout the meal our gazes locked, and once or twice I felt him watching me. But I refused to glance up, to let him search my soul.

Later, when I entered the nursery, I was dismayed to find Matthew there. He was tucking in his son.

"Is Rory asleep?" I asked in a quiet voice as I went to the crib.

"Yes." Matthew looked into my eyes, and my knees weakened.

With an effort I tore my gaze from his. I bent and kissed the little boy on the temple, then left the room with his father. I was about to bid him good night and turn away, sparing myself from the ache of his nearness, but he stayed me with his voice.

"I know how much time you spend with my son, Alexandra."

Automatically my spine stiffened. "Do you object?" I didn't know what I would do or say if he replied with a yes.

To my relief, he said, "I just thought it might be easier on you if you moved into the room on the other side of his."

Charlotte's room, he'd meant. It seemed so hard for him to even say her name. "I appreciate the thought, but I'm comfortable where I am."

His lips thinned and he regarded me as if I were an immovable object. But then, he'd offered me quarters at the front of the house before, once through Lizzie. "It would be more convenient for you here," he pointed out.

"I don't feel inconvenienced, but if I change my mind, Matthew, I'll let you know. Sleep well." I ended our conversation with the same words he'd used last night, and swung about. However, I did not move slowly away the way he had, or watch after him, as I sensed he was now doing.

Moments later I sat down at my dressing table and stared unseeing into the mirror. My mind fastened on those initial offers of another room. I'd been led to believe that they had come from Matthew's wish to upgrade my comfort. Comfort, really! At the time he'd been bent on ousting me from the house. Since I had doubted his reason then, did I dare look upon this recent one as valid?

I went to the bed. As I changed into a nightdress, I considered the family's vigilant watch over me, after dark. The first time I'd tried to leave the house in the late evening, Tyler loomed before me. On the second occasion I'd scarcely crossed a few feet of lawn before Matthew suddenly appeared. On top of that he was quick to see me back to the house. The men's reasons for being out were plausible, and I supposed there was always the chance that my coming upon them was a coincidence. Still—

I extinguished the flame in the lamp and crawled into bed. As I snuggled down, I focused on Felicity. Almost every time I relaxed on the veranda anymore, she came out and sat with me. I enjoyed company, but I wasn't like Charlotte, who had hated being alone. Might Felicity think that I was? Or be that way herself? Or was the veranda socializing actually more of the keeping an eye on me?

Those disturbing questions remained at the front of my mind, and as the days passed, I found myself watching the family. I wasn't sure what I was looking for, but I suspected there was some connection between my movements at night and the room I occupied, which overlooked the rear of the house. Were the Steeles afraid of what I might see?

15

On Saturday I took my usual afternoon break from the sewing room and went for a ride on my favorite trail through the woods. Tyler and Felicity had planned to accompany me, but at the last minute they'd become caught up in some business details and had their heads together in the study. Matthew was in his office out front. But he didn't care to ride, and I wouldn't have asked him anyway. Besides, an hour or two alone seemed wonderful.

The spring sun was warm, and I wore a comfortable, light-weight habit and complementing, wide-brimmed straw bonnet. Birds chirped merrily, and from time to time lizards scurried across the path.

I was halfway through the woods when the breeze dropped and the air became still and oppressive. For the first time in a long while I once again felt the suffocating closeness of the verdant jungle. It pressed in, cloying and drooping more heavily than usual. Constricting tightness ringed my chest and I could hardly breathe. Panic welled and I nearly cried in relief when I saw the clearing beyond the canopy of moss-hung trees.

Eagerly I urged the gelding to a canter. Leaves and twigs snapped resoundingly beneath his hooves. Then, to my horror, he stumbled, and I felt myself being thrown into a thick cushion of ferns and creepers. On impact every bone in my body shook and the wind was knocked from my lungs. Somewhere in my fright I had heard the horse cry as he'd hit the ground. In all the confusion and shooting pain, I'd also heard him scramble up and run off. I was alone, and lying in the pungent greenery like a rag doll that had been tossed aside by a disgruntled child.

Moments of dizziness came and went, and the pain gradually subsided. Gingerly I moved my legs and then my arms. Thank God, no broken bones. Just as carefully, I sat up. I winced at a twinge in my shoulder, the same one I'd injured when the carriage went over. Until I'd come to Belle Haven, I'd never been in an accident. Now there were two, in just over a month, both involving horses.

With trembling hands I straightened my straw bonnet and shoved wisps of hair from my face. A spot over my right eye felt wet. I touched the sticky moisture, then looked at my fingertips. Blood! Since it wasn't streaming down my face, I knew luck had kept me from sustaining more than a minor scratch. I dabbed at it with the handkerchief I'd pulled from my pocket, then shakily came to my feet. My habit was stained, thankfully with leaves and moss and not more blood. Without thought I brushed at my clothes. Then on uncertain legs I picked my way the few steps through the lush underbrush and back onto the trail, my ears and eyes alert for snakes and any other loathsome creatures. The birds still sang, but at a distance. It was quieter than before. The absence of the familiar breeze and the sound of hooves were the reason.

The end of the woods was mere yards away; from there the balance of the trail to the main road was in a meadowlike setting. Still, it was a long walk home, and I could only hope my horse had headed back to Belle Haven and someone would come looking for me. Or maybe a rider would happen along and give me a lift.

Rubbing my shoulder, I glanced at the area where my horse had stumbled. There were small potholes here and there, which had never troubled the animals before. This time, though, I had pressed mine faster than usual. Upon closer scrutiny, I also saw a weathered rope lying across the trail. One end was tied about the trunk of a sturdy tree; the other end lay limp between tall shrubs. The rope looked as if it had been exposed to the elements for a long time. Odd that I hadn't noticed it on my other rides through these woods, although it was the same color as the ground. In any event, the horse couldn't have tripped over the hemp line without someone having applied tension, and there was no one around but me. A sudden chill shot down my spine, and I looked about. I was alone, wasn't I?

Swallowing, I continued up the trail before my fertile imagination ran wild and before the closed-in feeling once again overcame me. As I approached the clearing, I heard pounding hooves on the road. Someone was riding hard. My mind flashed back to the carriage accident and the dark-dressed riders who had whizzed by. But that was then, and it had nothing to do with now. At the moment my primary concern was a lift home. I hurried into the clearing, my body beginning to feel a little stiff. As I lifted a hand to flag down the rider, relief caught in my throat. "Matthew!" I shouted and continued forward.

He reined in sharply. For a second, before his assessing eyes went over me in a quick sweep, I saw a shadow cross his face. Was it worry? "Alexandra, are you all right?" He swung down.

"Yes," I called back.

In four long strides he was standing before me on the trail. "What happened to you?"

"My horse stumbled and threw me into the brush."

"My God, you could have—" Matthew reached out, and for a breath-suspending moment I thought he was going to take me into his embrace. Instead, his hand went to my temple. "You have a nasty scratch."

His eyes met mine, and my mind went blank. All I could think to say was, "I'm fine. Really."

He moistened his lips. "Let me be the judge."

"What do you mean?"

"I'm a physician, remember?"

"Yes . . . of course," I murmured inanely. It had to be obvious my brain wasn't working. My eyes were functioning properly, though; I hadn't missed the nice fit of his dark suit and pin-striped shirt.

"You should be checked over."

"Oh?"

Clearly he assumed the rise in my voice came from alarm, because he added in a reassuring tone, "Just as a precaution. It won't take but a minute or two in my office."

"I don't think that's necessary."

Matthew lifted an eyebrow in exasperation. "Do you have a medical degree, Alexandra?"

I responded with a helpless-sounding "No" and followed after him. "How did you know to come looking for me?"

He hesitated. "I was leaving my office, to make a few rounds, when the gelding you always ride came galloping up the road. I caught your horse, tethered him, and mounted my own. By the way, I hope you don't mind riding double."

My pulse leaped at the suggestive picture "riding double" conjured. And I was taken aback when I heard myself saying, "No, not at all." It was as if someone else had answered for me.

"I should have had the good sense to bring a buggy," he said. "But I was in such a rush to get to you."

Rush? He had ridden at lightning speed. Dared I hope that meant he cared for me after all?

We stopped at the black stallion. Matthew transferred his medical bag from the back of the saddle to its horn. Then his hands went to my waist, to help me into the saddle, and I swayed at the tantalizing pressure of his fingers.

Matthew drew me firmly against him. "I hope you're not going to faint."

In truth I felt as if I were about to expire from suppressed longing. "No, I'm just a bit dizzy, probably from the fall." Even before he spoke again, I knew that lie was a huge mistake.

"An examination *is* in order," he insisted.

After I was settled on the stallion, Matthew swung up behind me in the saddle. He was pressed close, his arms imprisoning me as he reached for the reins. If he had shouted in my ear, I wouldn't have heard over the pounding of my blood.

He turned the sleek black horse toward home. As we moved along the rough dirt road, shaded by trees, the movement of Matthew's powerful body against mine became torture. "You must ache all over from the fall," he said after a long quiet spell, and the huskiness in his voice conveyed he, too, was in sweet torment.

My senses soared in that knowledge, and I dreaded to answer for fear my voice would be as revealing as his. But I couldn't ignore the question, and if I merely shook my head, the broad brim of my bonnet would flap in his face. I stared at his hands before me, his slim fingers skillfully working the reins. "No, not really."

Matthew's breath quickened at the sound of my voice, thick and laced with longing, and I saw tension ease in and out of his fingers. Heat surfaced in my face. Apparently, he'd also felt a burst of warmth, because he pulled at his shirt collar.

Neither one of us uttered another word until we reached his office at the base of the drive and he helped me down from the saddle. "I'll have a quick look at you," he said, his voice still husky, "then you can be on your way up to the house."

I thought to protest again, but I knew that this dedicated physician wouldn't take no for an answer, especially after my comment about the dizziness. Without a glance in my direction he secured the stallion next to my horse at the hitching post. I crossed and gently patted the gelding's nose. "Thank heaven, you weren't injured, boy," I murmured, and he tossed his head as if he understood.

A moment later I reluctantly followed Matthew into his office. He closed the door. I swallowed. As he put down his medical bag, he gestured to the lone examining room. "Make yourself comfortable, Alexandra."

That wasn't possible, not in here alone with him. At least he hadn't instructed me to undress. Heart thumping and palms wet, I went into the small room. The examining table stood before me, a medical cabinet on the left. Of all things, there was also a single bed just inside the door on the right. I hadn't noticed it the first time I'd come to this office, and I nearly blurted, "What's that for?" Fortunately, I caught myself before the words slipped out. It was a convenience for patients after minor surgery, wasn't it? I tore my gaze from the bed and perched on the corner of the examining table. Along with the anxiety I was beginning to feel excitement at seeing Matthew in his element again.

My thoughts scattered to the wind when he ordered, "Take off your hat, please." A muscle in my face flexed. If he mentioned even one article of clothing, I would insist upon being examined by another physician. "Your hat," he repeated, as if I hadn't heard. He came in and stopped before me. He was so tall, so commanding, I felt fragile in his presence.

As I reached up and untied the ribbons beneath my chin, I fought to still my trembling hands. In removing the straw bonnet a few pins came with it, and I felt hair tumble about my shoulders. Matthew's intake of breath tightened the knot of anxiety in my stomach. "I can pin it back up," I quickly offered.

He shook his dark head, and it was obvious from the firm set of his jaw that he was as keyed-up as I. "It would be best if you removed all the pins. It will make it easier for me to check for any bumps you might have suffered."

Just the thought of his fingers in my hair brought on another bout of dizziness. With my brain enveloped in the haze, I released the rest of my hair. It went every which way. A lock fell over the minor wound on my temple. Gently Matthew pushed back the stray wisps, then probed my scalp, his fingertips like tiny flames. Breathless, I stared at his slim waist and was shocked by the impulse to lower my gaze. Heaven help me if he checked my pulse or put the stethoscope to my heart.

"Luckily, no bumps." His voice wavered. Matthew hesitated,

and I wondered if he was beginning to wish he'd never started this examination.

I seized the opportunity to give him, and myself, a way out. "If you're finished, I'll—"

"No, I am not finished," he practically snapped. He lifted my chin, leaned near and stared into my eyes. At first the intensity of his gaze communicated the visual search was professional, then the gold flecks in his eyes took on a smoldering glow.

"Really, I'm fine," I gulped and tried in vain to look away.

"Yes," he murmured, "and beautiful." I heard him swallow, it sounded painful.

I forced my chin from his touch. "I'd better leave."

"I think that would be wise. Let me clean that scratch first."

"I can do it in my room."

"A cleansing extract would be more effective than soap and water." The excitement of seeing him in his element had faded as quickly as it had come, and before I could protest further, Matthew stepped to the cabinet. He moistened cotton with liquid from a bottle, then sat down beside me on the table. "This will sting a bit," he said and dabbed at the scratch.

I grimaced. "At least it doesn't smell like that horrible liniment you gave me after the carriage accident."

A slight smile lifted the corners of his mouth, though his eyes still held the smoldering expression. "It wasn't that bad. Which reminds me, how is your shoulder?"

"Fine." I'd scarcely answered when his skilled hand dropped to the spot in question, and he applied a little pressure. "Ouch!"

Matthew frowned. "You've reinjured it—why didn't you tell me?"

His thrilling nearness had overwhelmed the pain, but I wasn't about to admit to that. And I wasn't going to give him reason to detain me any longer, either. "It doesn't hurt much."

"That was a pretty emphatic *ouch.*"

"What are you doing?"

"I'm going to examine your shoulder." In an instant Matthew had unfastened the top buttons of my habit and exposed the area. I braced against his hand on my flesh. Even so a shudder of pure delight coursed through me. He felt that tremor as strongly as I, I could see it in the deepening glow of his eyes and detect it in the tensing of his hand. Neither one of us moved for a second. It was as if we'd been caught and held in a sensual current, and instinct conveyed there was but a single means of release. My heart palpitated erratically. Without thought I moistened my upper lip with the tip of my tongue. Matthew noticed and his gaze was devouring. "Alexandra," he breathed as his eyes slid closed, and he lowered his mouth to mine in an evocative kiss that stoked passion's fire. My mind shouted to push him away, but the hunger he kindled shouted even louder.

Matthew eased his hand down from my shoulder, branding my flesh on his way to the scooped-neck of my camisole and the hollow between my breasts. He teased the sensitive flesh with featherlike strokes, then tormentingly inched to the tip of a breast. A moan of pleasure rose in my throat, and I encircled his neck and buried my fingers in the hair that tapered neatly to his shirt collar.

As Matthew lay me back, he looked into my eyes. My insides melted from the inferno I saw in those deep pools. Then his mouth was back on mine. Time slipped away and nothing but the need we inspired mattered. We were in a world where doubts and fears were overwhelmed by sensations and responses I could never have imagined.

Somewhere in all the pleasure and headiness, Matthew had briefly left my side. He'd locked the outside office door, then scooped me up and placed me on the bed. I had no recollection of when he'd relieved me of my clothes and shed his own. But in a small corner of my mind I saw myself unbuttoning his trousers, as I must have done in reality. I had never thought myself capable of such boldness, yet where Matthew was concerned, I had no reserve, no inhibitions. But then I had never known a man so patient and gentle, just as I hadn't known there was such a wealth of sensitive places. One by one Matthew revealed them as he lifted me higher and higher on the plane of ecstasy. With tenderness that brought tears to my eyes, he swept me to the world of utter joy and contentment.

✤ 16

THE rest of the afternoon was a blur. All I could think of was the joy of complete surrender and the wonder of fulfillment. I'd never felt such utter contentment. From the sweet words Matthew had murmured, I knew it had been the same for him. "You were made for love," he'd breathed near my mouth, and I reveled in his praise. If only he'd said he loved me, though. Surely Matthew wouldn't have taken me to bed, and even risked my honor, if he didn't truly care. Again and again, he'd kissed me deeply as we'd lain in an ardent embrace, then we'd reluctantly dressed and gone our separate ways.

With Matthew foremost in my mind, I took particular pains with my appearance before joining the family in the parlour prior to supper. Everyone, including Grandmother Hester, was there, everyone but Matthew. "He hasn't returned yet from looking in on a few patients," Tyler told me as he stood and offered me the seat next to him on the sofa.

Apparently, Felicity saw the glow I felt because she said, "You look very relaxed, Alexandra. You must have had an exceptionally satisfying afternoon."

My heart fluttered and a tingle teased sensitive nerve endings.

"Satisfying and also frightening," Matthew said as he entered the room. The tingle deepened and I longed to meet his eyes. But I knew my own would be all revealing, and I feared the family would guess the intimacy we'd shared. Luckily, there was nothing in his voice or expression that would raise suspicion. "Alexandra was thrown from her horse in the woods," he finished in a level tone.

"Oh, dear," Grandmother Hester gasped, and concerned gazes fastened on me. "I trust you weren't seriously injured, Alexandra."

"Nothing more than wounded dignity."

"I wondered about that scratch on your temple," Tyler said.

"Thank heaven, you didn't suffer anything worse." This from Felicity.

"She did reinjure her shoulder," Matthew volunteered, sitting down beside his grandmother on the sofa across from me. There was no way I could avoid his eyes now, though I met them only for an instant. They were bright, with a meaning I prayed was unreadable to everyone but me. "With a little liniment, though, Alexandra will be as good as new."

Liniment? My nose automatically wrinkled. Matthew regarded me teasingly, and I couldn't resist a small smile. Felicity noticed the playful exchange and arched an inquiring eyebrow. "So you looked her over, then?" she asked Matthew.

I felt a flush, which I hoped didn't show.

Matthew cleared his throat and regained the casual expression and tone. "Yes." As I stared at the glass of wine Tyler had graciously handed over, Matthew explained how he'd gone out looking for me after my riderless horse returned home.

"We've never had any trouble on the wooded trail before," Tyler commented, and Felicity nodded in agreement.

Or snakes in the house until I came along, I thought.

Matthew poured himself a glass of wine from the decanter on the table between us. "I've instructed the stable hands to inspect the trail and repair potholes."

The glow within me deepened, and I inclined my head in appreciation.

Conversation over supper was more animated than usual, though perhaps it just seemed that way because of my delicious mood. I loved Matthew, and I wanted to believe that the new light I saw in his eyes was love in return. He had given me pleasure beyond compare. Would he have even tried to satisfy my desire if I were nothing more than an amusement?

Apparently, my mind had lingered too long on our intimacy, because near the end of the meal, Tyler said, "You've grown very quiet, Alexandra. I hope nothing is troubling you."

"Just daydreaming," I admitted, and Matthew viewed me with a small, knowing smile. I had become too caught up in his expression to notice if anyone else had observed it.

Hester Steele touched on the fund-raising ball. "I do wish I could attend," she said, her eyes pleading.

Matthew shook his head. "I'm sorry, Grandmother, but it would be too tiring."

"I'm much stronger these days, dear."

"I know, but the ride to the city could cause a setback." Hester's lower lip drooped, and by the time the mocha meringue was served for dessert, she, too, had fallen quiet.

After supper I excused myself and went to the sewing room. I didn't really feel like working on Felicity's gown, but I needed something to divert my mind. If I didn't come down from the euphoric cloud soon, the family would surely guess what had transpired in Matthew's office.

I picked up the scissors and had just begun to cut the last pattern piece from muslin when I heard the door open. "May I come in?"

A shiver of excitement coursed through me, and I looked around quickly. Matthew stood on the threshold, his well-built body filling the doorway. "Please." My voice wavered on a whisper.

He crossed to stand before me. "You've seen me at my work, Alexandra. Now, if I may, I'd like to see you at yours." A boyish smile spread across his lips. "You look surprised."

Actually, I was delighted. I swallowed and regained control of my voice. "I didn't think fashion design would be of interest to you or any other male."

"You mustn't underestimate me," he teased, and I thrilled to this new side of him. "Your work is a challenge, and that element always attracts me." He paused, and his eyes told me that my artistic flair wasn't all that had drawn him to this room. "So does determination, which you seem to have in abundance." He lifted the sketch, studied it for a few seconds, then glanced at the muslin pieces I'd stacked neatly at the end of the worktable. His dramatic brows knitted. "It looks as if you've created a puzzle. A complex one, at that."

His genuine interest and respect for my profession deepened the love in my heart, and when he asked about the different steps of fashion design, I explained briefly. Then he frowned at the muslin pieces again. "Will Felicity's gown be ready in time for the fund-raising ball?" He replaced the sketch on the table.

"With long hours and plenty of hard work."

"Is that why you're laboring this evening?"

He met my gaze, and my pulse quickened in response. The flicker in his eyes conveyed a similar reaction, and my legs felt like wispy feathers. Heart racing, I took a step back. A hint of amusement touched his tempting mouth, and I just couldn't bring myself to admit that I'd come in here to take my mind off him and the intimacy. So I told a small lie with the word "Yes." Then I added, "The seamstress will be here Monday morning." In truth, I could have finished the cutting then.

"Once she starts on the gown, will your work be completed?"

The amusement had faded from Matthew's face, and I couldn't read his expression. But I knew that If he had asked that question before the sweet lovemaking, I would have suspected his motive. Now I refused to consider, even for a moment, that he could still want me to leave Belle Haven. So I wasn't the least bit evasive. "With the gown in capable hands, I'll have the option of stepping aside. But I prefer to oversee every phase of the construction."

"You make it sound as if you're building a bridge."

The extra separation I'd managed to put between us eased the heady strain on my senses, and I replied in a lighter tone, "In a way that might be easier. Women are extremely particular and often difficult when it comes to fashion."

"Among a few other things." He laughed. It was such a nice sound, one I'd heard far more often from his brother than him, that I couldn't be offended by Matthew's words.

After a silent moment I said, "I've been thinking about something, Matthew."

"Oh?" He quirked an eyebrow.

A suffocating flush rose. "Regarding the ball," I clarified. "And your grandmother. She seemed so disappointed that she won't be able to attend."

"Yes, and I hated to deny her. She's very social and always thrived on such functions."

"What if it were held here, as originally planned, instead of in the city?"

"Then there would be no problem. I just don't want her undertaking the carriage ride. But it's too soon for a large, social function here, don't you think?"

"Well, yes, except this one's for a worthy cause. Don't you suppose that should make a difference?"

"I hadn't thought of it that way, but you've raised a good point."

"Could it be transferred back, for Hester's sake?"

The tenderness I was coming to know in Matthew shown once

more in his face, and my breathing grew ragged when he stepped near, dissolving the gap I'd placed between us, and ran a gentle finger over my cheek. "You are very thoughtful and giving, Alexandra. I've never met anyone quite like you before."

And I'd never met anyone who made me feel more feminine and alive. "I think the world of your grandmother, Matthew, and if I can, I'd like to help bring happiness into her life."

"She has few pleasures, I know. Still, the work of switching the ball back to Belle Haven—"

"I'd be willing to do whatever is necessary."

"That's very generous, but it seems to me you already have your hands full."

Was that why he hadn't taken me up on my offer to help with the ball? "I can manage," I assured him.

Matthew hesitated, then a slow, appealing grin spread across his lips. "I expect you can."

"Is that a yes?"

"Having the ball here is fine with me. But Felicity is in charge. The decision is hers to make."

"May I discuss the possibility with her?"

He nodded, his eyes holding mine. The familiar sensual surge leaped between us, and I yearned to feel his arms about me, his mouth on mine. But something deep within held me in check. Was it the old doubt, or the fact that Matthew didn't reach for me? And what was that emotion coming into his dark eyes? Caution? That word stuck in my mind and I found myself asking, "Have you had other fund-raisers before?"

"No." His answer was the same as Felicity's when I'd put that question to her. "Two of my friends from medical school helped with the initial investment of the clinic."

"How generous." I hesitated. "I don't think Charlotte was aware of your friend's financial support."

"Charlotte wasn't interested in my work," Matthew said flatly, and I knew the truth of his statement. "In any case," his voice softened, "thanks for sharing your work with me."

"I appreciate your interest," I murmured and watched him turn away. At the door Matthew looked at me over his shoulder. "I'll be making rounds of neighboring plantations soon, to examine any workers requiring attention and to pass out advice on health care. Would you like to come along one day, Alexandra?"

My heart skipped a beat. "I would, very much." At this rate I would never come down from the clouds.

I was still floating on air when I looked in on Rory a short time later, then went to my room. I was too happy and excited to sleep and certainly not up to concentrating on a book. Dreamily I sat down at the dressing table. I removed the combs from my ebony hair and hummed to myself as I brushed it into a silken sheen. Then I crossed to the open French doors and peered out. No Felicity. Maybe for a change I could enjoy the night air alone. Although I did need to discuss the ball with her, but tomorrow morning would be soon enough. I only hoped she wouldn't think it was presumptuous of me to make such a suggestion.

Quietly I moved to the railing, scanned the landscape, then lifted my eyes to the silvery moon. It seemed brighter here than anywhere else I'd ever been. But there again maybe my sense of euphoria painted an overall rosy glow. Was that why I hadn't perceived the tension among the family and the quick glances, as I had over the past several evenings? Or had whatever was disturbing them finally been resolved? I leaned against a Doric column, lay back my head, and shut my eyes. The scented breeze and blissful silence soothed my keyed senses. For timeless minutes my thoughts flowed freely, then fastened on my work in Paris and the wonderful friends I'd made there. Had I really been in that exciting, historic city? Sometimes it almost seemed a dream. Sighing, I opened my eyes, then started slowly back across the veranda.

"Alexandra."

The familiar masculine voice caught me by surprise, and I whirled toward Tyler's room. Squinting, I saw him rise from one of the chairs in the shadows. How long had he been there? "I didn't see you when I came out," I said, wondering if this was more of the watching over me.

As Tyler came forward, I noticed he'd shed his suit coat, and his imported French lawn shirt was open at the throat. Seeing him in a casual mode was something new, an added dimension to his good looks. "I saw you step out," he said, "but you seemed preoccupied, and I didn't want to disturb you."

"That was very thoughtful. I've had quite a bit on my mind lately."

"Nothing troubling, I hope?"

This was the second time Tyler had asked me that very question this evening, and it made me wonder if he sensed my suspicion and was endeavoring to find out what I might know. In truth, I wasn't even certain what lay behind the doubt. "No,"

I murmured, still aglow from the intimacy. How long had Matthew and I been in his office? An hour? Whatever it was, it had passed too quickly.

"That's good." Tyler inclined his head and gazed at me as if trying to read my thoughts. Thank goodness, the moonlight wasn't slanting across my face. Even so, I schooled my features in a casual expression. "Matthew told me about your suggestion to return the ball to Belle Haven. I'm all for it, Alexandra. God knows, I spend enough time on the road to the city. One less trip will be a blessing. More important, Grandmother will be delighted. Would you sit me with me for a while? You and I haven't visited alone in some time."

That was true and I did enjoy his company. I nodded, and we settled across from each other in the rattan chairs. Tyler and I talked about the ball a bit more, then I asked, "Did Matthew mention my suggestion to Felicity, do you know?"

He stared appreciatively at my hair, and I remembered he'd only seen it down one other time, at our initial meeting in the cemetery, of all places. "I would doubt it," he said. "He and I discussed the ball over plantation business in the study. We've been having a devil of a time getting in supplies to begin the repairs on some of the outbuildings."

That reminded me of the grating sound I'd thought had come from the cemetery. "Lizzie told me about the kegs of nails."

"Nails?"

"The ones that arrived a few weeks back." ·

"Oh, yes, yes, I've been so busy they slipped my mind." Tyler tried to laugh off this lapse of memory, but the sound held a hollow ring. Had there really been a shipment of nails? If not, what had I heard that night? "Now we're waiting on lumber and shingles," he continued and told me a little about the work to be done. Afterward, I commented that Matthew had invited me to make rounds with him one day. "Really?" Tyler's eyebrows shot up. "He's never asked anyone to accompany him before."

"Never? Not even Charlotte?" The lights on a boat passing the grassy slope caught my attention.

"Not that I'm aware of. In any case, she had no interest in plantation workers."

Or Matthew's profession, I reminded myself as I watched the vessel disappear behind the trees.

"You seem intrigued."

"In what way?" I returned my attention to Tyler and was taken aback by his intense gaze on me.

"The boat—do you often watch them?" He blinked and glanced casually into the darkness.

Did it matter? When it came right down to it, Felicity could answer that question almost as well as I. After all, she seemed to always be on the veranda with me. Now Tyler was at my side. Was that a mere coincidence? Or did the boats have something to do with the family tension? "No," I said. "That was the first one I've actually seen at night."

"River traffic has dropped off lately," he explained in the continued casual tone. "So tell me, did you accept my brother's invitation to make rounds with him?"

"Yes, I think it would be interesting and certainly give me the chance to see more of the area. Does Matthew visit the plantations on a regular basis?"

"Several times a year, for which the owners pay him a nominal annual fee."

I hesitated. "The owners care about their help, then?"

Tyler's lips compressed. "They can get more work out of healthy slaves." His expression and dose of sarcasm indicated he opposed human bondage. But from the way he abruptly switched the conversation to travel abroad, it was obvious he had no desire to discuss the volatile issue. And my precarious position at Belle Haven hardly gave me the confidence to pursue the touchy subject.

Unfortunately, I may have already struck an explosive match in regard to the ball. Yes, the men were amenable to the possible move back to Belle Haven, but what about Felicity? She'd done all the planning, the work, and I could well imagine what a monumental endeavor it was. Just putting my suggestion to her might trigger anger. That dismal thought dissolved the lingering euphoria. Tyler and I spoke for a few minutes longer, and after we retired to our rooms, my mind focused on Felicity. She'd been most pleasant and hospitable, and the last thing I wanted was to trod on her toes.

IN the morning Matthew was the first person I thought of, and I wished he were at my side. I yearned for his warmth pressed near, his caresses, and the heady sensations his hands and mouth evoked. But even if he tried to bed me again, my strict moral upbringing told me that I must not yield. Willpower had always been one of my strong suits, and where he was concerned, I must exercise every shred I possessed.

I clung to that resolve as I left the bed. It was only eight o'clock, but the sun was already throwing out fiery rays. I dressed in a cool, sprigged percale, its cap sleeves edged with delicate lace, and swept up my hair to keep it off my neck through the heat of the day. Then I went down to the morning room. Lizzie greeted me with a bright smile. "My, my, Miss Alexandra, you done looks like summer in that pretty lavender gown."

I acknowledged the compliment with a returned smile. "It feels like summer, Lizzie."

She laughed, shaking her head. "Lawdy, no, summer be much hotter."

Hotter? Would I survive? I slipped into my seat at the table. Ordinarily, the family, with the exception of Hester, enjoyed Sunday breakfast together. But there were only two place settings on the crisp linen cloth, mine and Felicity's. "Have the men already eaten?" I asked.

"Yes'm, they been up since dawn. They's out ridin' the land, lookin' to see what work needs to be done. But Miss Felicity be down soon." Lizzie filled my coffee cup, then went to the kitchen to inform the cook I was ready for breakfast. Within minutes a golden waffle, topped with fresh strawberries, was placed before me. I was nearly finished with the delicious meal by the time Felicity came in.

"I'm afraid I overslept," she said apologetically and sat down at the table. She, too, was dressed in a cool gown, cut more deeply than my own, and her hair was also swept up. We exchanged pleasantries, and I waited until she was nearly finished with breakfast before I cautiously, and with all the tact I could summon, brought up the ball.

Felicity's sapphire-blue eyes narrowed, and the sharpness that edged her tone tightened the knot of anxiety in my stomach. "Do you realize how much work that would entail, Alexandra?"

"Volumes, I'm sure. But I'd be glad to do whatever is necessary," I offered quickly.

"You'd put yourself through all that for Hester?" She viewed me with suspicion, as if I had an ulterior motive. Like what, trying to win my way into the family by impressing Hester? Or maybe Matthew?

"Yes," I said with quiet emphasis. "And for Charlotte's memory. She loved Hester and wouldn't have wanted to stand in the way of her happiness. Had I known sooner that the ball was important to her, I would have spoken up immediately. But if returning it to Belle Haven would be an impossible undertaking—"

"It wouldn't be impossible." The hardness eased from her eyes but not completely from her voice. "It would be much easier on me to have it here, and, of course, would also be nice for Hester. She gets lonely."

"She doesn't appear to have anyone but the family to keep her company."

"Her friends are all gone now."

"Then the social event would be doubly wonderful for her."

"Yes, but there are so many people to notify, and time is running out."

"Perhaps if you drafted a list of what has to be done, I could start on it tomorrow."

"Tomorrow? Justine is arriving then. I don't want the work on my gown delayed."

"It won't be," I promised. "I'll consult with her before I leave—she shouldn't require close supervision. I only hope that relocating the ball won't inconvenience any of the guests and prompt them to drop it from their social calendar."

"That won't happen. If anything, the change will probably increase attendance and even the amount of contributions. Most of the invited would prefer to come to Belle Haven instead of a hall in the city. Have you seen our ballroom yet, Alexandra?" Her spark of enthusiasm lessened the tension in my stomach.

"No. You mentioned some time back, though, that it's in the wing next to the north drawing room."

"If you have time, I'll take you there."

At my nod Felicity finished her coffee, then we went to the ballroom. It was huge and even more grand than the one back home in Boston. But Charlotte had told me that, though she hadn't gone into detail. Elaborate crystal chandeliers were gracefully suspended from the ornate plasterwork ceiling. Rich brocades draped the front-facing windows and the bank of French doors overlooking the rear veranda. The same fabric was on the chairs arranged in cozy groupings on an immense Aubusson carpet. Long tables for food and drink were near the entrance, and the walls at both ends were lined with multicolored glass, which I knew would reflect a kaleidoscope of color as dancers glided past. As I looked around, I could almost hear the strains of a waltz and see myself being whirled about the room in Matthew's arms. That picture was almost as evocative as the more intimate one that repeatedly swept forward, and I feared my willpower with Matthew was going to be strained to the limit, and probably well beyond.

🌱 17

TEARS sprang to Hester's gray eyes when Felicity and I told her that the ball was going to be held at Belle Haven after all. "In your honor," Felicity said as the old woman gave us each an appreciative kiss on the cheek.

"I haven't been to a ball since Matthew and Charlotte's wedding," Hester murmured, her mind clearly on that night three years ago. "You must send Lizzie right up so that I can give her instructions on preparing the ballroom, the decorations, and the refreshments."

"You mustn't concern yourself with any of that," Felicity insisted in a soft voice, "and chance overtiring. Alexandra and I can handle the preparations, and help will be coming in to lend the household staff a hand."

"She's right," I said in support. "We want nothing more than for you to be at your best on that night, Hester."

"A few instructions won't lay me low," she persisted.

"Matthew might not agree," Felicity warned. "You know how strict he can be when it comes to your well-being."

"Yes, yes, you all fuss over me," the old woman grumbled, then after a quiet second, she admitted with a small smile, "I do thrive on it, though. Thank you, my dears, for putting yourselves to so much trouble. You've made me very happy."

"Then that makes us happy." I gave her hand a gentle pat. We visited with Hester for a while longer, then Felicity and I took Rory for a stroll of the grounds.

The rest of that Sunday passed quietly, and early on the following morning the seamstress arrived at Belle Haven. Felicity introduced us, then left for business appointments in the city. "I've been admiring your work on Mrs. Steele's gowns," I said as I showed Justine into the sewing room. She was dressed in a simple but well-crafted pink percale that flattered her full figure and heightened the color in her pleasant face.

She blushed and returned almost apologetically, "I don't have any special training, just what I learned from my mother."

"She was an excellent teacher." Justine and I spent an hour going over the pattern and muslin pieces. She was warm and friendly, as Felicity had said, and sharp of mind. I had no doubt that the capable seamstress and I could work harmoniously together.

After I left her side, I put on my bonnet, caught up the list Felicity had compiled for relocating the ball, and set out for the city in one of the liveried family carriages. It was a sultry gray day, and my clothes clung uncomfortably.

As we entered the city, a noisy gathering of well-dressed men on a street corner caught my attention. Curious, I craned my neck. They were calling out sums of money as they scrutinized a handful of half-naked Negro girls who were lined up like merchandise on the sidewalk. My mouth dropped open, and all the life seemed to drain from me. I'd heard of slave auctions, but somehow in my sheltered world I'd never been able to make myself believe such atrocities actually existed. Outrage boiled in me, and the fear I'd seen in the young faces weighted my senses with a pall that made me feel even gloomier than this sullen day.

My first stop was at the printer's shop, where I placed an order for change-of-location cards Felicity and I would send out to the invited guests. From there I had a light lunch at an outdoor café, which brought back happy memories of Paris. I had thought to invite Matthew to join me, but I firmly reminded myself that his days were a steady stream of patients, and he generally ate the midday meal in his office. After lunch I continued down the list. My last call was at the hall, where I canceled the reservation. "It's against policy to refund deposits," the man in the office told me, but I would make up that loss from my own funds. By now the afternoon was almost over, and I was tired and ready for a cool drink. Tyler's office was just a few doors up, and I stopped in to see if he was free to join me. His clerk wasn't at his desk when I entered. I waited a few minutes, and when he still hadn't returned, I began to wonder if Tyler was about. I went to his door and tapped lightly. "Yes, come in."

I eased open the door, hoping I wasn't intruding on him and another client. Tyler was alone at his desk, his fair head bent and eyes intent on the open law book before him. How clearly

I recalled that day when I had sat in the chair across from Tyler as he and I discussed Charlotte's accounts. "Good afternoon." I sounded more cheerful than I felt. The gloom of the slave auction hadn't completely subsided, and the heat had also taken its toll.

Tyler's head shot up, and a startled look crossed his face. "Alexandra, what a surprise." He came slowly to his feet. "To what do I owe this pleasure?"

The smile he now flashed seemed genuine, but his initial expression had not instilled a sense of welcome. "If I've caught you at a bad time—"

"No, not at all." He was quick to assure me. "How may I help you?"

His tone and demeanor were so businesslike that I felt a bit frivolous. "It's nothing important," I said hesitantly. "I just came in to invite you to join me for light refreshment, if you can spare the time."

"For you, always." His smile broadened. "It was thoughtful of you to think of me, Alexandra." He pulled on his suit coat, then crossed and offered me his arm. "What brought you to the city today?"

As I told him about the list, the middle-aged clerk stepped in from the sidewalk, and we exchanged a few words before Tyler and I left the office. On our way up the street to a small tearoom, he asked, "Have you completed your list of errands?"

"Yes, though it took me a bit longer than I'd expected. I wanted to make certain everything was just right and not undo any of Felicity's good work. She's seeing to the orchestra and one or two other items herself."

As Tyler and I chatted amiably over delicate pastries and tall glasses of refreshing lemonade, the weariness eased from my body. But my soul still ached from the memory of the Negro girls being auctioned. On top of that was another memory, one that had swept forward in Tyler's office, and had to do with Charlotte's accounts. I hadn't given them much thought since that day I had reviewed them and deemed them in order. Now, for some reason I didn't understand, I found myself once again trying to puzzle out what my stepsister might have seen that triggered her accusation about Matthew and the missing money.

That rekindled question whirled in my mind as if an unseen force had gained control over it. As Tyler and I left the tearoom, it was that force that compelled me to say, "I'd like to look over Charlotte's accounts again, Tyler."

He arched a questioning eyebrow. "Of course," he said slowly. "Any particular reason, Alexandra?"

I had no idea, and I couldn't even begin to explain this odd feeling that controlled me. So I simply said, and with a grain of truth, "I just realized this might be the only time I'll have free to do my monthly review before the ball."

"Yes, I guess you will be busy between now and then."

Back in Tyler's office, he showed me into the conference room. "I'll get the ledgers," he said and moved away. A minute or so later he returned with the pair of books. Alone at the long table, I once more pored over the accounts. There were a few recent entries, but still I saw nothing out of the ordinary.

Frowning, I sat back and stared unseeing out the window overlooking the sidewalk. Charlotte had been wrong, I told myself again. If I continued to wonder otherwise, I would have to suspect Tyler of wrongdoing. But he had been my stepsister's dearest friend in this city. She had admired and respected him. More to the point, he was the brother of the man I loved, the one Charlotte had accused of stealing.

HEAVY thunderstorms plagued the region over the next two days, and the river rose alarmingly, flooding rice fields. Fortunately, the water hadn't gone over the banks behind the house, although I hadn't ventured out to see the swirling currents for myself. That would have been an agonizing reminder of that horrible day in January. As the rain pelted, the house seemed uncomfortably cool. Since I was the only one who appeared to feel the penetrating chill, that made me suspect it stemmed more from the grim memory of Charlotte's death than the foul weather. All about the grounds the trees drooped beneath the weight of the downpour, and I felt a great burst of relief when the sun at last reappeared. For a change I didn't even mind the accompanying humidity.

By the end of the week the floodwaters had subsided, and the roads had dried enough for carriage travel without the threat of bogging down in mud. "I hope a full day on the road won't be too tiring for you, Alexandra," Matthew said as we set out in the buggy one pleasant morning on his rounds of scattered, neighboring plantations.

With him I could only be exhilarated. "I'll be fine," I assured him with a smile. As we moved along the rough road, canopied by oaks and pungent pines, Matthew told me a little of his boyhood days at Belle Haven. "I hated to leave for medical school abroad," he said. "Now I feel as if I've never been away." He glanced beyond the trees and tangled underbrush to the endless expanses of prosperous rice fields. "I can't picture myself living anywhere else."

Recently I had begun to feel the same, but I knew that was primarily because of Matthew and little Rory. "It's so beautiful and unspoiled here, I've come to love it myself."

Matthew gave me a sideways look, his dark eyes questioning. "You don't miss Boston, or wish you were back in Paris?"

I met his eyes squarely, though every inch of his lean body was engraved in my mind. Today Matthew wore a smart, lightweight charcoal suit and shiny, black leather boots. "No, I don't miss Boston anymore, although I'd like to go back occasionally to visit old friends, and I have business investments to oversee. As for Paris, it was a wonderful and exciting experience. But I don't plan to return, at least not for many years to come. I have my work, and one day I hope to marry and have a family."

A slight frown touched Matthew's brow, and he shifted his attention to the pair of bays. Had my mention of a family reminded him that I might have conceived? That thought had worriedly crossed my mind, but I had no regrets. If I was with child, I knew that Matthew, with his proper upbringing, would do the honorable thing. Of course I wouldn't want a husband who didn't love me. But I reminded myself that Matthew wouldn't have bedded me if he didn't care.

We turned onto a long drive that led to an exquisite columned mansion, surrounded by immaculate grounds. Beyond were miles of rice fields, submerged in ankle-deep irrigation water, and hundreds of slaves toiling beneath the sun. A vision of the girls being auctioned rushed back. A lump came to my throat, and my heart plummeted as we pulled up in front of windowless slave quarters and I saw toddlers wearing clothes that couldn't even be called rags.

Matthew helped me down from the buggy, then gathered the children about us as he gave them small confections that brought smiles to their sweet faces. He examined one after the other in the airy cabin that had been readied for him, and the workers were called in from the fields. As Matthew talked with the large gathering, the pain within me deepened at the sight of their sweating bodies and the scars and angry welts from untold beatings. Once again outrage welled, only this time even greater than before. Aching to do something for these people, I asked Matthew, as he began examining those who required medical attention, "May I help?"

Matthew looked at me in surprise. "Well, yes, if you'd like, you can keep the line of patients moving and hand me medical records from that cabinet in the corner."

I nodded and followed his instructions. Matthew and I worked wonderfully together, as if we'd been doing it for a long while. And when our gazes occasionally met, I saw admiration in the deep pools of his eyes. By the time we'd gotten halfway through the line of patients, I was assisting him with cleansing and bandaging wounds. At least in a small way I was easing some suffering. When we were finished and Matthew closed his medical bag and helped me back into the buggy, he gave my hand a gentle squeeze. "You're the best assistant I've ever had, Alexandra." His tone matched his touch. "And by far the prettiest."

At any other time I would have been elated by his praise, but being among these people and their misery had numbed my heart, and it was all I could do to manage a small smile in reply. At the next plantation I automatically fell in at Matthew's side and set to work.

The morning passed quickly. As we once again made our way up the road on the rounds, Matthew shook his head in wonder. "It amazes me, Alexandra, that you aren't squeamish. Some of the wounds we treated were pretty severe."

"I'm amazed, too," I returned quietly. "Ordinarily, the sight of blood makes me nauseated. But I can't think of myself when those people live under such deplorable conditions." The critical words poured out, but with Matthew, and the compassion I'd seen in him for the Negroes, I knew I could bear my heart. And I wasn't surprised when his view was the same as mine.

"I know," he murmured. "Slavery is morally wrong."

"It's a grave injustice."

"And now in the wave of industrialization, it's also obsolete. Unfortunately, it's still central to the Southern economy and won't be abolished overnight. I do what I can to ease the misery, just as countless others do the same, in their own way."

"And unscrupulous men are probably still smuggling Negroes into the country," I bit out. A muscle at the corner of Matthew's mouth quirked, but he didn't voice an opinion. Did he know for certain that illegal slave trade was still a fact of life?

Matthew maneuvered the horses onto a narrow side road, and we wound through a deep meadow. "Is our next call down here somewhere?" I asked, seeing nothing ahead but woods.

He flashed a boyish smile that gave my spirits a lift. "No, I just thought my able assistant might enjoy a picnic lunch alongside the river."

"I'd love it." I smiled back. Matthew Steele was the most thoughtful man I'd ever met. He reined in near the sluggish water, caught up the picnic hamper Lizzie had packed, then came around and helped me down. As always, his touch set me aglow. Matthew laid a cloth beneath a spreading oak on the bank, and we sat down facing each other. It was a small cloth, and he was temptingly near. Birds sang in the trees, and though the air this day was pleasant, it was delightfully cooler in this peaceful spot. It was also isolated, and I felt as if we'd stepped into another world.

As Matthew removed his coat and set it aside, I reached into the hamper and lifted out a feast of roasted ham, thick slices of bread, fresh fruit, and a container of lemonade, which had once been ice cold. But even tepid the tangy beverage was refreshing. "We could have had lunch at our last stop," Matthew confessed with a devilish grin, "but I thought this might be nicer."

"It's perfect." Heaven couldn't be better.

He gave my hand another gentle squeeze, and the light in his eyes made my heart palpitate. For several minutes we enjoyed the meal and the serenity in contented silence, then Matthew asked, "How is Felicity's gown coming along?"

"Very well, thank you. Justine will have the muslin finished today, and tomorrow I'll corner Felicity for a fitting. She's such a busy person."

"The same can be said of you," he pointed out. "Although the reasons for what you both do seem to be very different."

"How is that?"

"Felicity is motivated by the sense of power and authority, and there is nothing wrong with that. She accomplishes a great deal of valuable work through the charities."

"And me?"

The light in Matthew's dark eyes brightened. "I suspect you're driven as I am, from the feeling of self-satisfaction."

"Yes," I admitted, delighted that here again he and I were much alike.

"Do you still intend to open a salon?"

I nodded, lifting my glass of lemonade.

"And after you accomplish that?"

"After?"

"I get the feeling you have something else you want to do, besides the salon and being a wife and mother." He leaned near, immobilizing me with his virility and intoxicating masculine scent.

"You're very perceptive." I put aside the glass before my trembling hand revealed his powerful effect on me.

"I think I'm coming to know you quite well." His gaze clung to mine, and I felt as if I were being caressed. "Would you share that other dream with me?"

Could he see that I wanted to share the rest of my life with him? I cleared my throat. Nevertheless, my voice sounded a little raspy, and I tried to distract my mind by busily clearing the cloth. "One day I hope to create and produce patterns for the average woman, who cannot afford seamstresses or tailors."

"Really? Although I shouldn't be surprised. Anyone who is as determined as you can do anything she wants. But is there a demand for such patterns?"

"Oh, yes, I've studied the need for the past several years. There are no patterns for the home seamstress, and most of them simply haven't the skill to devise their own." Matthew's devastating presence was fire on my senses, and I didn't know how I was managing to speak coherently, let alone with a degree of intelligence.

"How would you sell those patterns?"

"In catalogs and ladies' magazines."

"You've obviously thought this out well." His gaze dropped to my mouth. *His* mouth held a passionate message.

"I'd like to think so." I could scarcely hear over the hammering of my heart. "My primary goal is to produce patterns that will be inexpensive and easy to use."

"You're very bright," he murmured. "I realized that the first time I looked into your eyes."

And he was so near, his breath warm and tantalizing on my face. "I've worked hard for I want, like you." Helplessly I leaned closer still, my body aching for his touch.

"And when do you suppose, with all you hope to accomplish, you'll even have time for a husband and family?"

The huskiness in his voice strummed over sensitive nerves like a warm velvety stroke, and sparks danced down my spine as Matthew let his fingertips gently graze the side of my throat. "A husband and family would be my first priority." My chest rose and fell in heady anticipation.

"You're sure of that?"

"Positive."

"You're an exciting woman, Alexandra." He traced my mouth with a gentle thumb. "What if I were to kiss you?" He lowered his provocative mouth to within a breath of mine.

My brain reeled and every ounce of willpower had long ago melted. "I'd kiss you back."

"Promise?"

"Put me to the test."

FOR a fractional second Matthew hesitated, and I stiffened. Was he having second thoughts? Heaven knew, we shouldn't let this happen. One kiss wouldn't be enough, and try as I might, I hadn't the strength to resist him. His hesitation seemed endless, and a thrill spiraled in me as his eyes closed and his mouth at last came down on mine, and with an urgency that nearly darkened my brain. Every nerve ending was ablaze and the sensitive places that had been revealed through his tender lovemaking, mere days ago, pleaded for his touch. As Matthew's mouth moved feverishly on mine, I looped my arms about his neck and strained against him as my lips parted effortlessly beneath his demanding pressure.

With a moan of pure delight, Matthew slipped his tongue between my teeth, and the provocative darting rocked my senses with explosive magic. My fingers tunneled through his thick hair as he gently laid me back. Without lifting his head and missing one deliberate stroke in my accepting mouth, Matthew removed my bonnet and buried his long fingers in my upswept curls. The heat of his touch on my scalp sent teasing shock waves to the very core of me.

Matthew nibbled at my ear and whispered unintelligible words before trailing moist kisses to the hollow of my throat. I whimpered his name repeatedly as my hands slid down to his back, and I thrilled to the muscles that tautened beneath the pressure of my touch. Matthew's mouth went to the V at my bodice, and I arched as he unbuttoned my shirtwaist and released my breasts from the constraints of fabric. They swelled at the joy of his tongue. "Beautiful," he rasped as he tormented one after the other, then lingered in the valley between as he cupped and massaged. In the delirium of swirling sensations, I was vaguely aware of the gentle breeze and the birds still chirping in the trees. Enticingly Matthew's mouth returned to one rosy tip, then the other, loving each with quick, circling motions that sent excitement shooting ever higher. Once more I was in the world where my mind was free, and I was bold beyond all that was proper.

Somewhere in the midst of the excitement Matthew and I had shed our clothes. How rapidly that must have happened. We were two people driven by the madness of sweet release.

My body was hot, yet the air beneath the trees was pleasantly cool and I knew we were safely hidden from the outside world by tall grasses and lush undergrowth. I listened to the lilting of birds and the ripples on the river as Matthew caressed the soft inner flesh of my thighs. My chest rose and fell with the tantalizing featherings, and my eyes slid closed against reality. I hovered in that blissful, far-off space that held the promise of the joy I ached to taste again. Until Matthew I'd never known such pleasure, such tenderness and caring. How could I not love this man who pleased me in every respect?

My mind relayed sensual messages, and the thrills were heavenly torture, almost more than my brain could comprehend. On a burst of ecstasy I lifted to meet Matthew as he poised above me, to thrill him as he was thrilling me, but he hovered, teasing us both with the strength and heat of his own need. My breathing was a drum in my ears, and visions that sharpened arousal flashed in my mind. I'd never had such imaginings before, and at any other time they would surely stain my cheeks red. Swallowing, I looked into Matthew's face; his lips were parted and his head back. Higher up were aged branches heavy with spring foliage. There were trees in heaven after all. My eyes slid shut as he began his entry, and I wondered if he also saw provoking pictures in his mind.

Matthew's mouth returning to mine was fierce, his tongue an exciting whip on my reeling senses. Were other women this fired in the heat of passion? Did they feel as if they were about to faint from pent-up excitement? Twisting and turning, we clung greedily to each other. And a whimper of pure bliss escaped my lips as I achieved the crest of joy, and Matthew and I sailed the tidal wave of ecstasy together.

THE next two weeks passed far too quickly and it was a race to finish Felicity's gown. Justine put in long hours with needle and thread and without complaint. "I really appreciate all your efforts," I told her for at least the tenth time.

She lifted her pleasant face from the last seam she was completing. "I've never minded hard work. It's been wonderful doing this gown with you, Miss Chandler."

"Alexandra, remember?" I reminded her lightly.

"Alexandra. I've learned so much from you. I hope I'll have the chance to work with you again one day."

"Actually, if all goes well and I open my salon in the city soon, I'll need an expert seamstress or two."

Justine's eyes widened. "Are you saying you might hire me?"

"If you're available. I know you have a large clientele of your own."

"Well, yes, but once they see this gown you've fashioned for Mrs. Steele, I'm sure they'll be your clientele, too."

"I hope so. If that's the case, will you consider my offer, Justine?"

"There is nothing to consider, the answer is yes."

Smiling, I held out my hand, and we sealed our verbal commitment with a firm shake. "Now, with luck, this gown will be a huge success, and you and I will be busy for a long time to come." She bobbed her fair head in silent agreement, and I felt a moment of panic at the realization that I'd probably just hired my first employee. The mere thought of opening a salon still overwhelmed me, and here I'd taken the initial step. Thank goodness, it was a sound one. Justine was supremely capable, diligent, and easy to get along with. I respected her work, and she respected mine. There were, of course, two things that could delay my business venture. First, if the gown I fashioned wasn't well received and I found it necessary to do several more before gaining commissions. Second, if I was with child. Yes, I wanted one of my own, and as much as I enjoyed Rory, perhaps even several. But I wasn't ready yet to be a full-fledged mother. How could I have even put myself at risk? Still, I had only to think of Matthew to know that if I had the choices to make again, they would be the same. He was on my mind day and night, and I yearned to be a permanent part of his life. We complemented each other in every way, and from the words he'd said here and there, I knew that what we'd shared in those treasured minutes was beyond anything he, too, had ever known before. I longed to spend the rest of my life pleasing him. But more than anything, I yearned to hear Matthew say, "I love you, Alexandra." If that emotion was in his heart, wouldn't he have confessed his love during our heady intimacies?

Maybe I would never hear those words from him, I told myself that night as I lay in bed. Maybe I was a blind fool who couldn't see that all he might want from me was the ecstasy which came from our bodies entwined. Maybe he thought that was all I wanted, at least for now. I'd placed such heavy emphasis on establishing the salon that it would be reasonable for him to assume a husband and family were not in my plans for the immediate future. Until Matthew, that had been true. Yes, I'd told him of my hope to have both one day. But I had said *one day,* not tomorrow or next week or even next month. Even to me one day sounded far off.

I tossed in bed and hugged the pillow, wishing it were Matthew and remembering that afternoon by the river. Just thinking about my boldness made me blush. With him I was a different person, a seductress I'd never known existed. I liked that other side of me, the compelling audacity, the way I drove Matthew mad with wanting. He'd called me a temptress at the zenith of passion, and I'd thrilled at the praise. Still, was it normal for a woman of strict upbringing and refinement to be so wanton? Wasn't that for harlots? Despair tensed my stomach muscles. Might Matthew think that in a way that's what I was, or had become, especially after three years of living in the romantic and risqué city of Paris? Several men there had made flagrant advances, and an overzealous artist from New York had cornered me in his garret. I had escaped from each pursuit with my virtue unscathed. Matthew knew he was the only who had bedded me; the momentary pain I'd felt the first time had conveyed that truth. Unless he thought I had simply pretended the pain.

My eyes widened at the horror of that possibility, and I rolled abruptly onto my back and stared into the darkness. Matthew and I hadn't seen much of each other since that afternoon at the river. But then, he'd been away for several days completing his rounds of the plantations, and I'd been busy with Rory and the gown. However, on the occasions when he'd joined the family for supper, there had been a special glow between us. I'd felt it in every fiber, seen it in his eyes. And I knew that he'd seen it in mine. Once when we'd met outside his son's door, I'd spotted longing in Matthew's eyes, and I knew he ached to bed me, just as I ached to do the same with him. But we'd gone our separate ways, and in my mind I was grateful. I'd tempted fate enough, though my heart and my body were not concerned with fate.

From the pointed glances Felicity and Tyler had cast our way,

I was positive they were now aware of the attraction between Matthew and me. But I couldn't tell if they were pleased.

However, I did know for certain that Felicity was more than pleased with the gown. "It's exquisite, Alexandra," she bubbled when she tried it on and Justine pinned the hem.

"It's a perfect fit," I said, scrutinizing the drape, "and very flattering."

"In a most provocative way," Felicity added, admiring the daring neckline. The majority of her creamy breasts were scandalously revealed, and the delicate ruffled lace heightened the allure. Wider point lace was at the softly draped short sleeves of the blue silk overdress. It dipped generously over the white glacé underdress, also trimmed with the point lace. The gown billowed over a bouffant crinoline and rustled with almost every breath she inhaled. Felicity ran a hand over the form-fitting bodice that ended in a deep V below her slender waist. "I shall raise eyebrows!" she exclaimed with delight, her eyes aglow with anticipation. In her own way Felicity was a seductress.

"Hester is eager to see the gown," I reminded Felicity.

She shook her chestnut head. "No one outside the three of us is going to see me in this until I come down the stairs tomorrow night to greet our guests." She sounded like a bride, savoring the cherished promenade down the church aisle. In any case, she was planning a grand entrance, and I certainly didn't mind. Such a show would bring more attention to the gown, though I was more than a little nervous about that neckline.

ON the night of the ball Felicity's entrance was indeed grand and precisely timed. She glided down the stairs, in a silken rustle, just as the first of a long line of carriages rattled up the drive and merry guests spilled into the entrance salon. As I stood in the reception line with Matthew and Tyler, my heart lurched when all gazes riveted upon Felicity and muted gasps of shock abounded. Seconds dragged by and I felt the misery that tightened my face ease as murmurs of delight penetrated the dull roar in my ears. "What a stunning gown," a nearby middle-aged woman said to her balding husband.

"Quite, quite," he breathed, his wide eyes on the décolletage.

The compliments made me heady, and standing beside Matthew as we continued to greet guests intensified that feeling. He was more striking and virile than ever. Just looking at him in the impeccable evening clothes did strange things to my heart and my breathing. The lapels of his black coat were silk, and his snow-white shirt was studded with pearl buttons down the front and at the cuffs. And I wasn't the only female admiring him. Tyler also had a wealth of feminine gazes on him, for he, too, was outstanding in his evening attire of select imported cloth. To me, however, Matthew was the handsomest male at the ball, and probably in the entire state of South Carolina. The sparkle in his dark eyes as he looked at me made me feel as if I were a raving beauty. The satin gown I wore was of my own design, in my favorite shade of blue with matching ruffles, and worn over a sweeping crinoline. The neckline was modestly scooped, with just a hint of cleavage. And my ebony hair was upswept in soft curls and adorned with diamond-studded combs that my step-mother had given me on my sixteenth birthday. "You're beautiful," Matthew had leaned near and whispered during a quiet moment, and I'd felt a provocative tingle. His effect upon me was growing stronger with each passing day, and I repeatedly prayed that I was more than an amusement to him.

After the majority of the guests had arrived, Matthew and Tyler assisted their grandmother down to the ballroom. Her white hair shone with lights from attentive brushing and was swept up in a style similar to my own. Hester's unlined face was wreathed in a bright smile, which made all the work of switching the ball back to Belle Haven worth the effort. I gave her hand a gentle squeeze after she was comfortably settled in one of the chairs grouped cozily on the Aubusson carpet. Overhead, the crystal chandeliers were alight with flickering white candles that cast a romantic glow. "You look lovely, Hester," I said, and she truly was radiant in a pale green taffeta and mantelet of embroidered lace.

"You are the beauty," she complimented with obvious affection, her shining eyes moving from me to Matthew as if she had guessed the truth of our relationship.

A touch of heat rose to my cheeks, and I felt even warmer when the orchestra began the first waltz and Matthew took my hand in his and led me onto the dance floor. To my delight, he had written his name several times in my dance card, beginning with the opening waltz.

I'd never been the first one out on the floor, and I was self-conscious under the gazes of the guests who filled the room to capacity. They were a sea of happy faces, dark evening suits and splendid gowns of every color. Matthew took me in his arms, and we circled the immense room before others came out to join us. He moved with superb grace, and I felt as if we were floating over the lustrous oak floor. I was so keenly aware of him, of his sparkling eyes holding mine, that I scarcely heard the music, saw the lovely decorations, or smelled the abundant floral arrangements. It was a perfect moonlit, spring night and the doors and windows were open wide. "Judging from the large number of guests," I said to Matthew as he drew me even closer, "the fundraiser is a tremendous success."

His gaze was on my mouth, but I could tell from the gleam coming into his eyes that his mind was on our bodies swaying together in perfect rhythm. He swallowed before answering. "Thanks to Felicity and her hard work, and to you for suggesting we return the ball to Belle Haven."

"Having it here has made your grandmother very happy."

"Yes, and in case you hadn't noticed, Alexandra, she's come to love you very much."

"And I her."

The light in the dark pools intensified, and for a spellbinding moment I had the sensation that Matthew was about to whisper the words I longed to hear. Unhappily, he merely said, "There's another big success this night, the gown you fashioned for Felicity. You must have seen the women swarming around her. What is it about women and fashion?" he asked with a small laugh that sounded as if he was trying to divert his mind. From what or who? From me?

Despite disappointment, I managed a smile. "I'm not sure, but whatever it is, I'm grateful." As Matthew whirled me past the walls of reflecting glass, I reminded myself that he was a private person, and it would not be like him to express the depth of his heart in a crowded place. Matthew would choose a romantic spot, with the moon and stars as a backdrop.

After the dance he returned me to his grandmother's side. A pair of matronly women were conversing with her, and Hester introduced us. As Matthew excused himself to chat with a colleague, the women and I exchanged a few pleasantries, then they went in search of their husbands. "Where is Felicity?" Hester asked with a note of asperity. "I haven't seen the gown yet, and she knows how eager I am to look over your creation."

"Maybe she's been detained by friends," I said in swift defense, for surely that must be the case. It wasn't like Felicity to be thoughtless, especially with the aged woman. "I'll go look for her, Hester. I won't be long."

I glanced around the room. Felicity was nowhere in sight. The second waltz was about to begin, and some man I'd scarcely met would be coming to claim his dance. Not wanting to keep him waiting, I hurriedly wove my way through the crowd and back to the entrance salon. Felicity stood in its center, soaking up compliments from the gathering of well-dressed women about her. As I approached the group, I heard the one in lavender ask, "Will Miss Chandler be opening her salon in Charleston?"

Felicity shrugged. "I'm not sure, but business-wise, New York would be a better choice."

Of course Felicity was right. But from the sound of her voice, I gained the sinking impression she preferred that I move to that other city. Did the rest of the family feel the same? Glancing around, Felicity saw me and flashed a sweet smile. "Alexandra, do come over. My friends are eager to hear more about your salon." With a heavy heart I continued to the gathering. I answered a few questions, promised to meet with each of the ladies individually over the next two weeks, then asked them to please excuse Felicity and me.

A few seconds later Felicity was showing off the gown to Grandmother Hester. "Oh, my, it is lovely," she breathed. "You must do one for me, Alexandra, but with a more conservative neckline." She laughed. "I haven't worn anything that revealing in more years than I care to remember."

So Hester had also dressed scandalously, I thought during the next dance. Somehow I had the feeling that if she had lived at the time of her grandfather, she, too, would have been a pirate.

The next dance was with Tyler. Afterward, I was back in Matthew's arms, and when the orchestra took a brief intermission, he and I moved to the long tables of food. Upon crisp linen were canapés, imported cheeses, succulent roasted ham, tender barbecued beef, breads, pastries, and confections. The beverage table was ladened with liquor decanters and immense crystal bowls brimming with champagne, rum, Madeira, claret, and exotic fruit punches. I helped myself to the food and drink, while Matthew prepared a plate for his grandmother, then returned to serve himself.

After the refreshments Matthew insisted that Hester call it a night. "I'm not tired," she protested, but the pinched look about her mouth conveyed otherwise. Matthew tilted his chin in a determined attitude, and when she saw that he was not going to relent, she grudgingly succumbed to his benevolent order. I bent and kissed her good night. As Matthew helped his grandmother up to her room, Tyler led me back onto the floor for our second dance of the evening together.

"You are stunning, Alexandra," he said. "What a shame you haven't eyes for me."

I looked at him in surprise. He'd never given me any reason to think he wanted me to regard him in an amorous light. Surely he was teasing. Assuming he was, I teased back, "There are plenty of women here who have eyes for you, Tyler Steele."

"Perhaps, but none are as lovely as you."

"Quite true," Matthew said, claiming me for the next waltz. My heart swelled at his very presence, and I was hardly even aware that his brother had bowed slightly and moved away. As Matthew whirled me about the room once more, I felt the familiar powerful current arcing between us. He was devouring me with his eyes, caressing me with the pressure of his hand at my waist. The strains of the music feathered my senses, and I tingled in all the sensitive places. I fought against temptation, but of course that was silly. In this crowd I had no worry.

To my dismay, however, Matthew danced me onto the veranda and into a shadowed corner, away from the lights of the decorative lanterns that had been strung up between the graceful white columns. Before I could even think to protest, he imprisoned me against the house with his powerful body. Matthew's mouth came down on mine, and my lips parted as if they had a will of their own. His heat was engulfing, his pillaging tongue lightning and thunder on my senses. Every thought coming into my head was focused, and I yearned to ride the tidal wave of desire to its shuddering conclusion.

As Matthew's mouth and tongue worked their magic, the evocative pictures floated teasingly in my mind. With a mammoth effort I forced them out. I would not put myself at risk again, especially without the words of love I longed to hear. I had thought they would spill from Matthew's mouth that day at the river. Even after we'd finally parted and were freshening ourselves in the sluggish water, I had clung to the hope that he would take me back into his embrace and whisper near my ear. Gently he had washed away all traces of the lovemaking from my flesh and just as gently he had helped me dress. But such thoughtfulness and caring weren't necessarily testimony to a deeper emotion. For all I knew, Matthew was nothing more than a consummate lover, and maybe I wasn't the only one he'd recently bedded.

My heart turned to ice on that thought. I didn't really believe it, but at least it cooled my senses, and I was able to jerk my mouth away from his. "Alexandra," he murmured, cupping my chin and forcing my face back to his. "Let me come to you later."

It was torture to resist, but I had to. "No." To my dismay, my voice lacked conviction.

A laughing couple emerged from the ballroom. Matthew and I held our voices until they descended the veranda steps and started up the now torch-lined path that led to the rose garden. Then he said in a husky tone, "Your body is pulsing with desire, just like mine."

"Not true," I lied, struggling more than ever against the very desire I was trying to deny. "What I feel is anger. I am not yours to play with!"

"What?"

"Let go of me."

Instantly Matthew removed his hands, as if I'd just hurled an insult of the worst kind. "How could you think that, Alexandra?"

"How can I not think it? I'm a single woman, whose reputation has fallen under a cloud."

His lips twisted, though he pointed out with blunt, but quiet control. "I am not the only one responsible. Nor am I the only one who reaped the pleasure."

Heat flooded to my face, but I lifted my chin with what little dignity I had left. "You are no gentleman, Matthew Steele."

"I want to be much more than that with you," he murmured as I pushed past him and returned to the crowded ballroom.

Much more? The words played over and over in mind during the rest of the evening. What had Matthew meant by them? If I hadn't lost my temper, might he have voiced his love? Or would he have simply continued with his attempt to persuade me to bed? I wasn't going to let that happen again, not without the sanctity of marriage. No matter what my body demanded.

After the ball I retired to my room and paced for the better part of the night and for the next three nights. Matthew and I hadn't said more than a dozen words since I'd rebuffed him. Somehow we managed to be pleasant enough to each other, but with an underlying coolness that only he and I appeared to be aware of. If he loved me, wouldn't he at least try to convince me that I wasn't just an amusement? Plainly I'd been a fool. Now I could only hope I wasn't a pregnant one.

⚘ *19*

COMMISSIONS began to come in for my gowns, and Justine worked feverishly in her home to finish the garments she'd promised to her patrons. "Another week and I'll be available to work with you again," she said on the afternoon I stopped by her modest, but charming residence in the city.

Justine was up to her eyebrows in silks and brocades, and I was up to mine in sketches and lists of feminine measurements. "With so many women coming to call," I commented to Hester one morning over breakfast, "I'm beginning to feel like a celebrity in the community."

"Well, dear, you are exceptionally talented," she replied with a prideful smile, "and I'm sure that the women for miles around are delighted to have a *couturière* straight from Paris, under their noses so to speak, and catering to their fashion whims."

Her enthusiasm added to my own excitement. Unfortunately, Felicity's zeal for my work had waned, but for a specific reason. "There seems to be a steady stream of women in and out of the house these days," she complained, looking over the sketches on my drawing table.

Her annoyance was justified; the family privacy had been invaded. Even the men, who were away at their own work six days a week, seemed irritated. Or at least I assumed that was the reason for the tight expressions I'd seen over supper of late. "I'm sorry for the inconvenience," I said to Felicity. "I never expected anything like this to come from the ball—one, maybe two commissions at the most. Justine has offered her home for our place of business until I can find a suitable vacant shop and decorate appropriately. I'll talk with her tomorrow."

"You will be settling in this region, then?" Felicity's tone and expression had softened. Still, there was an underlying emotion I couldn't fathom.

"Yes, I'll be staying. I like it here very much."

She moved around my room, thoughtful. "You might feel differently once the heat of summer takes hold. Charlotte did. She despised our weather and even living in the country."

"It is a different way of life," I agreed, one my stepsister had never accepted. I could only assume that it was the strain of being where she didn't want to be, and living on Matthew's modest income, which had changed her from the lighthearted girl I'd grown up with to the unhappy and complaining woman she'd become. "But I think I'm fairly adaptable," I added. "And it would be hard for me to leave Rory, if not impossible." In spite of everything the same still applied to Matthew. He was as strongly entrenched in my mind and my heart as ever, and I doubted that would ever change, or that my hope to hear a declaration of love would fade. With each passing day such an outpouring seemed less likely, and while that realization deepened the ever-present ache within me, there was also immense relief. I was not with child. There would be no forced marriage, with a one-sided love. Sharing my life with a man whose sole interest in me was physical would be the ultimate agony.

Felicity didn't say another word about my resolve to remain in the area, and I hoped my feeling that she wanted me to leave was unfounded. For the most part she and I got on well, and I had no reason to believe her friendship wasn't genuine.

When Felicity and I went riding on the following afternoon, she was once again the warm and friendly woman I'd come to know over the past two months. We reminisced about the ball and delighted over the generous contributions that were coming in for Matthew's free clinic. Then Felicity asked, "Did you and Justine discuss conducting business from her place during your meeting this morning?" We continued up the wooded trail. The potholes had been repaired, and even the weathered rope that had been lying across the trail was gone.

"Yes, her offer was still open and I accepted." The look of relief altered Felicity's features. I saw that same expression briefly touch the masculine faces when she mentioned over supper that my clientele would no longer be calling at Belle Haven.

"You're off to a sound start with your business, then?" Matthew asked me in a polite but distant tone. Clearly whatever was on his mind had nothing to do with my work.

"It is," I responded, wondering if my words had even registered. Actually, all three of the Steeles were preoccupied and conversation was sporadic. However, I noticed an instant alertness when a frowning Lizzie came in and whispered something in Matthew's ear. Once again there were quick, secretive glances, and the feeling of isolation crept back through me. If the family didn't trust me enough by now to take me into their confidence, I couldn't imagine they ever would. On the dismal thought that I should move into the city, I excused myself and went to the sewing room.

What had Lizzie said to Matthew? I wondered as I tried burying my troubled thoughts in the pattern I was drafting for the gown I'd promised Hester. The aged woman was the only one in the family who truly regarded me without reserve. Even the servants of late seemed a bit distant.

I worked for about an hour, then left the sewing room. On my way to the stairs I heard tense masculine voices behind the study door. I couldn't make out what Matthew and Tyler were saying, which was none of my business anyway. But I stopped dead, startled, when the door was jerked open. Matthew stood just beyond the threshold, with his hand on the knob and face turned away from me. "I'm the master," he bit out in an undertone to his brother. "It's my neck at stake."

His neck? Had he meant that literally, or simply as a figure of speech? Matthew swung about and his eyes narrowed to slits when he saw me. "Eavesdropping, are you?" he bit out again.

My chin shot up and anger coiled in my stomach. "No! I was passing by, and you startled me. Must I defend everything I do and say in this house?" Without waiting for a response, I whirled and continued to the stairs. After what Matthew and I had shared, how could he still distrust me?

"Alexandra." He came alongside and halted me with a gentle hand on my arm. "I'm sorry, my accusation was uncalled for."

"I'm sorry, too, Matthew, for many things." I'd managed a civil tone. Even so, my words clearly pained him, and his lips compressed as if I had just dealt him a terrible blow. Still, he couldn't possibly hurt as much as I. Twisting free of his grip, I hurried away.

In the privacy of my room I flung myself down on the bed and let the tears flow. All the endearments he'd whispered had been for the single purpose of insuring continued romps with me, I told myself bitterly. How long I lay sobbing there was unclear, and I didn't even remember changing into my nightdress and turning down the lamps. Every move I made was mechanical, every breath mired in misery.

In the slant of moonlight that fell into the room, shadowing corners, I crawled into bed. One hour dragged by and then another. Too wrought-up to sleep I left the bed, tugged on my wrapper, and went out on the veranda. The moon was full and stars winked in the cloudless black sky. I glanced around and inhaled a grateful breath when I saw that I was alone. But then who in their right mind would be up after midnight?

Before the railing I stared glumly at the grassy slope that dipped gently to the river. There was no breeze, and the air was heavy with sticky heat. Tomorrow I would go into the city and hunt for a place of my own, I decided. I could no longer stay at Belle Haven, where I didn't truly feel welcome, or continue to torture myself with the hopeless love for Matthew. I would miss him terribly, as I would miss being with Rory daily. The little boy was creeping now, and the new discovery thrilled him as much as it did me. Another rush of tears surfaced, and I sank down on a rattan chair. I was mopping my eyes with the hand-kerchief I'd pulled from my wrapper pocket when a sudden sound snaked chills along my spine. My head came up and I stiffened, listening. There it was again. Grating! Just like I'd heard on that night a few weeks back.

Holding my breath, I continued to listen, my ears straining. The sound was below, on my right. The cemetery! My flesh crawled. Quietly I slid forward in the chair. I peered over the railing and scanned. My throat constricted, and the startling sight I saw made me light-headed. This couldn't be real. I blinked, clearing my vision, and looked once more into the moonlit cemetery. My eyes had not deceived me. A marble head-stone beyond Charlotte's had been moved aside, and Negroes were coming up out of the grave. My ears drummed as I watched four men, two women, one carrying an infant, and three children dart to the far fence and an open gate. I'd never even noticed there was one there, but I'd never wandered to that side of the cemetery. The small group passed through the gate and ran to someone signaling them forward with his arm from the shadows on the tree-lined bank. The Negroes ducked into the trees and vanished. Where were they going, across the river? Upstream or maybe down? Swimming? No, not with a baby. There had to be a boat. If there were lights, they weren't visible through the thick growth. But the moon was full, and Lizzie had said there weren't always lights on bright nights.

Cautiously I moved to a white column, hid behind it, and peered around at the river just beyond the grassy slope. Seconds passed; it was unusually quiet. If a boat was out there, wouldn't I hear ripples from the oars in the water? Nothing. More seconds passed, then my heart skipped a beat as a sloop headed upstream came into view. Squinting, I saw two dark-dressed men maneuvering the vessel with slender poles which, unlike oars, were noiseless in the calm water. The Negroes had to be on that boat. Where were they being taken and for what reason?

Movement from the trees downstream caught the corner of my eye, and I looked around. A broad-shouldered man was crossing to the open gate. As he stepped from the shadows, my lips parted. Matthew! He went into the cemetery, closing the gate behind him. As he wove among the tombstones to the opposite gate, the grating sounded again, and I saw the marble headstone moving slowly back over the false grave, sealing it shut. No one other than Matthew was in sight. Who had slid the stone back into place and by what means? What was below? A room? A passageway? From where, the house? I shivered at the thought and resisted the impulse to hug myself against the chill that had nothing to do with the weather.

Quietly Matthew left the cemetery. As he crossed the lawn to the house, he glanced up at the veranda before my room. Instinctively I pressed against the column and prayed he hadn't spotted me. Was he checking to make certain that I hadn't seen his late-night activity?

Back in my room a minute later I paced, trying to piece together what I had observed. Whatever Matthew and maybe his whole family were up to had to be illegal, or they wouldn't be doing it furtively, and in the dead of night. They wouldn't be policing my movements, either. But what were they doing? The word *illegal* stuck in my mind. When I associated it with the Negroes being sneaked from Belle Haven and transported silently upstream, my first thought was—slave trade.

I shook my head at the absurd guess. The Steeles had freed their slaves and were good to those who had remained at Belle Haven. Added to that, Matthew oversaw the health of hundreds of Negroes in bondage, and with great compassion. Would he do so if he were trading others for profit? Besides, he'd told me himself that slavery was morally wrong. But—my mind raced on—he'd also said it was still central to the Southern economy.

I crawled back into bed, my head awhirl with questions and contradictions. Charleston had been a mainland port to which slaves were brought directly from Africa, and for all I knew this might still be the case. My breathing slowed on another recollection, one that went back to the day I'd made rounds with Matthew. Bitterly I'd commented that Negroes were probably still being smuggled into the country. His tightening expression and lack of response had made me wonder if he knew that for a fact.

I hardly slept that night, and when I left the bed in the morning I was tired and in no mood to ride into the city and look for a place of my own. I tried to appear cheerful when I went down to breakfast, but Lizzie noticed the smudges beneath my hazel eyes. "Is you not feelin' well, Miss Alexandra?" There was worry in her tone.

"I had trouble sleeping," I admitted, then ventured after a momentary pause. "I heard strange noises in the night again."

Lizzie's eyes widened for a flutter of a second. "Did you see anything?"

"No." I kept my gaze on her face. Was that relief coming into her eyes?

"You should've called for Eustace," she reminded me, then shook her head in quick dismissal. "I expect there was jest another supply boat. That man of mine done said something about shingles for the repairs. I is sorry the noise troubled your sleep. Maybe you should moves to the front of the house."

Five times now I'd heard that suggestion, and I hadn't even a smidgen of doubt that it had anything to do with my comfort. "Thank you, no." I sat down at the table, my spirits even lower than before, though that hardly seemed possible. Lizzie had lied about a shipment last night. I'd been awake through most of those hours, and I would have heard a boat being unloaded. She'd probably lied about the nails, also, because that so-called delivery was on the night I'd first heard the grating. I knew now that sound was the sliding tombstone. Moreover, Tyler had seemed clearly unaware of the nails when I'd mentioned them.

That entire day was a jumble of thoughts, and I could scarcely concentrate on the pattern for Hester. Rory was the only bright spot in the long hours that dragged by, and when I sat down to supper with Felicity and the men, I felt as if I didn't know them.

Actually, as it now stood, I had never known them. The Steeles with their secret glances and false graves.

Throughout the meal I surreptitiously eyed Matthew, wondering how I could still have even one iota of love for him. But that feeling had not changed. Once or twice when I looked up, I saw him watching me, and with a longing that increased my yearning. The attraction between us defied all reason, and I couldn't even imagine myself ever feeling this way about another man.

As we moved from the table, Matthew urged me aside. When we were alone in the dining room, he asked with a softness that turned my insides to jelly, "Are you still angry with me about last night, Alexandra?"

For an instant my mind went blank, and then all I could remember about the previous evening was the picture of the Negroes running from the cemetery. Certain Matthew wasn't referring to them, I simply said, "Over what?"

"The way I snapped at you outside the study." The hint of a smile touched his mouth. "Obviously you're not mad, or you wouldn't have forgotten."

And obviously Lizzie hadn't told him that I'd heard noises again, for surely he, too, would try to find out if I'd seen anything. "No, I'm not angry, just preoccupied with business matters."

His smile broadened. "I'm glad it's gotten off to a good start."

Was he really? Although it hardly mattered now.

"Would you join me for a walk through the gardens, Alexandra? I think we have quite a bit to talk about."

Despite doubt, I still couldn't trust myself to be alone with him. And I had no reason to believe that Matthew would suddenly take me into his confidence, especially if he and his family were up to something shady. "Another time, maybe," I said, noting disappointment alter his features. "I'm tired and would like to turn in."

He nodded in understanding, then to my distress he pulled me near and kissed me lightly. Matthew's mouth on mine was warm and inviting, and it took all the willpower I possessed to withdraw and move away. Had he thought that maybe I wouldn't, that one kiss would lead to another and he would eventually have his way?

As I ascended the stairs to my room, my heart and my body urged me to whirl and return to him, but thank God, my brain remained in control. And when I changed for bed, I reflected on his reminder of the study and the words he'd hurled at his brother. What had Matthew meant by "I'm the master"? He couldn't have been referring to Belle Haven, which the brothers ruled jointly.

Slave owners were called masters. But the family no longer owned any, and even if they did, it wasn't against the law. Matthew's neck wouldn't be at stake. Actually, in all I'd heard and read since coming to Belle Haven, only a small fraction of the Southern white population had any connection to slave ownership. Master of what, then? Unless those involved in smuggling Negroes into the country were called—

I broke off that horrid thought and threw back the bed covers. As I extinguished the flame in the bedside lamp, I heard someone on the veranda, and I glanced around. Through the partially open French doors and the moonlight falling into the room, I saw Felicity pass by. She paused just beyond my room, then continued to the far end. Two or three minutes later she returned. This wasn't the first time she'd meandered by my quarters at bedtime or the first time I'd wondered if her seemingly casual strolls were more of the watching over me. Was she on patrol? If so, did that mean more activity in the cemetery?

Determined to stay awake and see if anything developed below, I refused to let my eyelids, growing heavier by the hour, close. Twice, though, I lost the battle and dozed off, but only for scant minutes. And I was pacing like a caged animal when I thought I heard the grating, only this time the sound wasn't nearly as pronounced.

Once more I quietly moved to the veranda railing, and once more, in the light of the moon, I saw Negroes coming up out of the fake grave and disappearing in the grove of trees. I also saw a boat. It, too, was being maneuvered upstream by men with poles that were soundless in the water.

🌿 20

THE next morning, after the men had left for their offices and Felicity had also gone into the city, I went out to the cemetery. It was windy and storm clouds were gathering, but I'd bundled against the threat in a light wrap. On the chance that one of the servants, or perhaps even Hester, might be watching me from the windows, I forced myself to move casually among the headstones.

I paused at Charlotte's grave, then meandered to the one just beyond. My heart fluttered against my ribs, and in my mind I heard the grating. But that sound only came after dark, and this stone wasn't apt to be slid open now. It was smaller than most of the others, the width and depth of its base covering a hole that I remembered was only big enough for one person at a time to pass through. Engraved upon this marker was simply the given name George, which struck a familiar chord. But I'd known two or three Georges back home.

Glancing up, I furtively scanned the grounds and the verandas. There didn't appear to be anyone about, though I couldn't see beyond the curtained windows. Praying that I wasn't being observed, I touched the tombstone, thinking it might be lightweight, imitation marble. The stone was genuine, and when I gave it a mighty push, it didn't budge. I looked it over carefully, but saw no levers or any other operating device. Apparently, it was opened from somewhere inside. What was below—a tunnel? To the house? Hester had remarked that it was unique. A secret passageway to the family plot would certainly make it that, and also fit the character of the ancestor who had built this place during the French Revolution. As I recalled, that was Hester's great-grandfather, the privateer, who had also ridden with the Swamp Fox.

The muscles in my face tightened. Would people who were

descended from pirates, and whose family fortune had been amassed through murder and pillage, have any compunction about selling Negroes for profit? For all I knew that might be where the money came from to maintain Belle Haven and perhaps had even kept the family from losing the home that was Grandmother Hester's obsession. It might also be the source for the comfortable lifestyle Felicity and Tyler favored and might have funded the opening of Matthew's free clinic. Charlotte had vehemently insisted he hadn't the capital for that venture, and since it didn't appear he'd helped himself to her money—

I shook my head in swift denial. But there was no dismissing the fact that something illegal was going on at Belle Haven, and whatever it was, Matthew was in the middle of it. How could a man who gave so much of himself to the needy and to those in bondage be involved in anything as loathsome as selling human beings? Unless that giving was nothing more than a means by which to ease his conscience. But would the servants support the Steeles in the slave trade? Lizzie and her family were born and reared at Belle Haven. This was the only home they, and perhaps the others, had ever known, and they could fear losing it.

Shoulders drooping, I started back to the house. As I climbed the veranda steps, I remembered that George was Great-grandfather Steele. Hester had mentioned his name several times. George the pirate and murderer. My stomach churned and nausea rose. If I'd felt this way a week ago, I would have worried that the upset was linked to the lovemaking rather than the family plot and slaves.

If there was a secret passage to the house, where would I even begin to look for it? And if I found out what was going on and my worst fears were realized, what then? That answer was all too clear: I would have to notify the authorities, no matter how painful that would be. Silence in the face of moral injustice would be more than I could bear. But what about Rory? His father's neck could well be at stake, and perhaps the rest of the family's, also.

I wrestled with that question as I entered the house, but even at that, I knew the answer. If the Steeles were involved in something sinister, I would be doing my nephew an injustice by turning my back and allowing him to follow in their footsteps. No matter what the cost, I had to protect that sweet little boy.

So while the house was still quiet, I searched the main floor, scrutinizing shelves and anything else that might conceal an entrance to hidden hallways. Nothing so far, but there was still the study, with its cypress-paneled walls lined with books. Carefully I went over each shelf. As I was coming to my feet, after running a hand along the bottom row, I spotted a small lever in the corner of the shelve above. My heart raced, and I could hardly breathe. Lifting the lever with one hand, I pulled mightily on the shelf with the other hand. A three-sectioned square swung out; behind was a crawl space. Throat constricted, I leaned in, but it was too dark to see.

Quickly I lit the desk lamp and held it up inside the opening. A narrow passageway went straight back, then veered right. Where did it go from there? As much I wanted to know, when it came down to it, the thought of exploring between the walls was a bit frightening. Especially when I didn't know who or what might be in there.

Swallowing, I closed the panel, returned the lamp to the desk, and went to my room. The wind had picked up substantially and rain beat down. Out on the veranda servants hurriedly moved the rattan furniture into the library next door, and I suspected the shutters across the front of the house were being closed securely over the panes of glass. I paced, trying to decide what to do about the passageway. Actually, and as much as I hated to admit it even to myself, I was endeavoring to work up the courage to explore. I'd never been the brave and adventurous kind like Charlotte, and I wasn't sure if now was the time to start.

At my desk I lifted the sketch I'd done of my nephew a few weeks back and gazed upon his handsome face. How very much he resembled his father. In many ways I hoped the little boy would grow up to be like him, though scrupulous beyond question. That last thought confirmed what I knew I must do, even though I still didn't feel particularly brave. Inhaling a fortifying breath, I caught up the small desk lamp, for I daren't use the one in the study. Someone might notice it was gone and become suspicious. Then I went back down the stairs.

Certain I wouldn't be missed until lunchtime, which was still two hours off, I lit the lamp and crawled into the dark passage behind the bookshelves. I sealed the panel shut, taking comfort in the lever on the inside for reopening it. With faltering courage I came slowly to my feet and held the lamp aloft; its flame cast eerie shadows that made my flesh crawl. I was alone, and it was quiet. I couldn't even hear the wind and rain. Blood rushed in my ears, but it was the thick walls that kept me from hearing the outside noises.

I took one hesitant step, then another. The air was cool and thin and musty, and I was grateful that I was dressed in warm muslin. Thank goodness, it didn't swish or rustle, sending out an alert. As I moved along the narrow passage, I spotted more square panels with levers. Clearly, I'd missed secret openings in the other main floor rooms I'd searched.

At the end of the dank corridor, I peered around the corner. A few feet ahead were two staircases, one went up, the other down. If there was a tunnel to the cemetery, it was undoubtedly below. Still holding the lamp high, I descended the wooden steps, carefully and without making a sound. Thank heaven, there were no creaking boards, though with luck no one else was about. At the bottom the passage veered right again. I paused on the damp stone floor and listened. No sounds.

As I rounded this corner, a breath stuck in my throat. Ahead was a small room, with several beds, a table and chairs, and two racks of clothing. People were housed here. For how long? Hours? Days? Beyond were a pair of corridors. Inching forward at my snail's pace, I lifted the lamp to the mouth of the one headed toward the front of the house, then swung to the other. I followed it to the rear for some distance. The passage ended at an earthen wall, with a half-dozen embedded iron rungs that served as a ladder to the marble slab overhead. Clearly it was opened by the thick rope and pulley rigged to a nearby iron bar. During the Revolution this tunnel must have been a means of escape from threatening troops, for it was a straight line to the river and boats to safety. Now the tunnel was a path to human bondage and suffering.

Heart weighted, I followed the other passage. Whatever was at its end couldn't be any worse than coming up under the gravestone in the cemetery, could it? This tunnel seemed to go on forever, well beyond the house. All about me were walls of earth, shored with thick timbers every few feet to prevent caving. The air was a little warmer but uncomfortably thin, and my lungs strained for every breath.

Just as I was about to turn back, fearing I might collapse from lack of sufficient oxygen, the flickering light of my lamp revealed more embedded iron rungs. I stopped before them and glanced up. A trapdoor. Opening into what? In my mind I retraced the path from the house. Matthew's office. That made sense. At the

ime of the Revolution anyone being pursued on the road had
only to duck into what had once been the gatehouse, and disappear into this tunnel.

That thought took me instantly back to the carriage accident.
It had occurred to me then that the two riders who sped past
were being pursued. And as I'd lain sprawled alongside the road,
I'd heard Matthew shout, "Keep going! You know where the entrance is!" Had he meant to this passage? And if he was being
chased, by whom and for what reason?

Lungs begging for air, I set down the lamp. As I climbed the
five rungs to the trapdoor, I prayed it wasn't locked. I pushed
at it and nearly cried in relief when it inched up. If this was Matthew's office, I knew he wasn't about, and I wouldn't be caught
sneaking in. Although at the moment all that mattered was huge
doses of fresh air. I inhaled as I crawled out of the tunnel and
into another place almost as dark. Vaguely I could make out
shelves about the walls that closed in, and there was a door on
the left. Overhead, rain pounded deafeningly on the roof, and
the wind howling beneath the eaves sent chills sweeping over my
flesh.

I crossed to the door and eased it open. Matthew's pharmacy,
and I was in the supply closet. I tiptoed out and looked around,
reassuring myself that I was alone. The bed in the examining
room brought back unwanted visions, and I was grateful for the
slamming gust of wind that startled me back to the present.

A glance out the window confirmed what I had suspected: I'd
be soaked and blown all about if I tried to return to the house
by way of the drive. Worry twisted my heart for Matthew and
the two other Steeles, who would have to battle the storm home
from the city. But the memory of what I'd seen in the cemetery
the past couple of nights reminded me that they weren't worthy
of concern.

I returned to the closet and was about to slip back through
the trapdoor, when I spotted the trunk in the corner. Matthew's
initials were embossed in gold on the fine leather. I stared at it
for a long moment. Then without really knowing why, I knelt
and ran my fingers over the initials. More unwanted memories
came forward, happy times, the closeness. On a deepening ache
I opened the trunk. I don't know what I'd expected to find inside,
a few treasures from abroad perhaps. Instead, all that met my
eyes were a dozen or so medical volumes and a crumpled out-
of-date suit coat. A corner of white paper protruded from be-

neath a sleeve. Curious, I pushed it aside. My blood turned to ice. Charlotte's letter, the one that had been taken from my handbag. Burning tears clogged my throat, and with trembling hands I lifted the coat. "Oh," I choked. A diary! It had to be the one I'd been looking for. I withdrew the volume from the trunk and turned to the first page. Rising tears spilled over and ran down my face. Matthew had known all along where my stepsister's latest diary was; he'd lied about it, too. My brain urged me to flip through the pages and devour every word, but my heart held me back.

The blast of wind rattling windows reminded me that the storm could bring Matthew home early. If that should be the case, there was always the chance he might stop in here before heading up to the house. I didn't want him to catch me, but most of all, I couldn't bear to look at him now.

With the letter and diary in hand I closed the trunk. Then I let myself back down through the trapdoor, lowered it into place, and hurried along through the tunnel. I was so upset that I was scarcely aware of the thin air, or maybe I just didn't care. This time I didn't even glance at the room with the beds as I passed through. But when I mounted the steps and the flight going up loomed, I stopped dead. Were there secret openings into the rooms on the other floors? A hidden door to my quarters?

Shuddering, I lifted the lamp higher and ascended. Another flight rose to the third floor, but for now it held no interest for me. As I moved along, my nerves became a tightened, coiled spring, and a gasp escaped my lips when I reached the area of my room. On the walls to each side of the passage were the telltale square panels and levers.

Trembling now with anger more than any other emotion, I opened the panel on the left. Something heavy blocked the way. If this was my room, the obstacle would be an armoire. It would take more than one strong person to shove it aside to gain entry. Unless . . . the back swung in like the shelves in the study. I pushed. Nothing. I tried in the other direction. To my horror, the back slid easily open and my gowns were hanging before me. I straightened, my mouth gaped. Had anyone spied upon me or sneaked into my quarters?

Furious, I extinguished the flame in my lamp, set it down beside the shoes I'd pushed aside in the armoire, then parted my gowns and crawled through. In my room I shut the armoire doors and wished I'd had a length of sturdy rope to secure them.

In this house I'd been lied to and my privacy probably invaded. What next?

Grimly I gazed at the diary I still clutched, and the pain ringing my chest tightened. The French doors shook on a blast of wind, which flung rain against the panes of glass. The sky was ominously dark, and I could see the tops of trees bending and dipping. Again I thought of Matthew and the two others, but I forced myself to blot them out.

It took several minutes to gain a semblance of control over my emotions, then I sat down on the chaise and opened the diary. Heart in my throat, I turned to the final entry, penned on the night before Charlotte's death. The words here were much the same as those she'd written in that last letter to me. Matthew had taken money from her account, she'd insisted, and probably had been secretly helping himself all along. He couldn't have done so without his brother's knowledge, though, I reminded myself. If that had also occurred to Charlotte, she hadn't jotted it down.

My pulse leaped as I read the next several lines. My stepsister had seen the ledgers on the day before she died. But how was that possible if the books weren't out, as Tyler's office clerk claimed? Had he also lied? To what purpose?

"Something is terribly wrong with the accounts," Charlotte had written, and she was going to talk with Tyler in the morning about the missing funds, then confront Matthew. Only, as far as I knew, she hadn't done, either. Unless she died before she'd had the chance to make note of it. A deep chill crawled through me, and I reread the passages pertaining to Matthew and the money. Charlotte had written with such vehemence. Why, even the letters in this section were heavy with that emotion. Whatever she'd seen in the ledgers had been obvious; she'd never been one to pore over figures. But I had with the accounts, on both visits to Tyler's office.

I shook my head, trying in vain to dismiss what I knew might be a real possibility: another set of books! If that was the case, if Charlotte had talked with Tyler or Matthew— "Oh, God." Tears burned behind my eyes. To save their hides, might one of the brothers—?

Sickened, I pushed aside the diary and jumped to my feet. Murder? No! They weren't capable of it. I paced, my mind stubbornly hauling forth what I didn't want to remember, the lies, the Negroes in the cemetery. Worst of all, the grim reminder that the Steeles were descended from thieves and murderers.

Before the French doors I stared numbly toward the cemetery. But all I could see was the storm-darkened sky and the solid wall of rain. Charlotte hadn't written a single word about the false grave and the Negroes, so I assumed she hadn't known about either. But maybe that vile business hadn't even started until after her death, and after the accounts had fallen under my scrutiny. Although if there were two sets of books, what would that matter? Except the family could feel as if I were breathing down their necks and feared I might catch on to something.

All the little hints about opening my salon in New York flew back, and I jumped when Lizzie knocked on the door. "There you is, Miss Alexandra." She came into the room. "I been huntin' the house for you. You wasn't in here a bit ago, and I be gettin' worried you gone outside."

I shook my head but didn't volunteer anything. "Did you want something in particular?"

"Jest to call you for lunch. You usually isn't late for meals."

"I'm sorry, I lost track of the time. I'm not hungry, Lizzie."

"You isn't gettin' sick, is you? You look a little pale." She glanced at the doors I stood before, and the angry sky beyond. "Is you frettin' 'bout the storm? In this big house we always manages jest fine."

"Yes, the storm," I lied. One false excuse was a good as the other, only I couldn't think of another.

"I knows jest the thing that will relax you, a nice hot bath."

"Thank you, I appreciate your concern, but—"

She lifted an insistent hand "You lets me take good care of you, Miss Alexandra. I been seein' to people most all of my life, and I does a good job."

Her concern was comforting, and I just couldn't bring myself to even chance hurting her feelings. Besides, what difference did it make if I soaked in a tub, or continued to pace?

Within an hour I was in the tub behind the ornate screen, and Lizzie even brought in a glass of warm milk. "I'll puts it here on the night table," she said. "Jest like I used to do for Miss Charlotte most afternoons. Now, you drinks this up when you is finished with the bath, then maybe you can takes a nice long nap."

I didn't care for warm milk or a nap, but I thanked her anyway. "Has the family returned from the city yet?" I peered around the screen but couldn't see the area by the bed where Lizzie stood.

"Jest Miss Felicity and Mr. Tyler. I expect Dr. Matthew be on his way, 'fore the storm gets worse."

No Matthew yet. My nerves tightened another degree. How could I still care? With my thoughts racing in what seemed an endless circle, I scarcely heard the housekeeper leave the room. But little could be heard above the horrid weather. The hot bath did feel good. Nevertheless, I was still tense when I left the tub, and my stomach felt as if it were afire with anxiety. I didn't know what to think about Charlotte's death and the Steeles anymore, and how in the world could I find out if there were two sets of ledgers? Even if I came right out and asked, Tyler wouldn't admit to wrongdoing. And if he was innocent, the insult to his integrity could cause an irreconcilable rift.

With a helpless sigh I toweled dry and put on fresh clothes. Then once more I sat down with the diary. But it was pointless to go over it again; I'd practically memorized the last few entries. The increasing ache in my stomach reminded me of the milk. Hoping it would soothe, I crossed and slowly drank the now tepid beverage, then returned to the chaise.

Tipping back my head, I closed my eyes. In my mind I saw Charlotte, and for countless minutes I relived many wonderful memories. I could almost hear her playing the piano, all the lively melodies we'd both loved. The emptiness of her passing became overwhelming. As if to console myself, I climbed the stairs to the cupola and ran my fingers over the instruments she'd cherished. As odd as it seemed, I felt her presence here, felt a sense of peace.

Beyond the encircling windows, the storm raged. Trees were blowing every which way, and the rain being flung against the panes of glass sounded like tiny pebbles. I prayed Matthew was safely home by now, but that thought seemed distant and my eyes were growing heavy.

Yawning, I sank down on the settee and lay back my head. The fury of the late spring storm faded as I drifted into a dreamless sleep. I don't know how many minutes passed before I was shaken awake by the wind hammering the windows. My lashes fluttered and I glimpsed someone in dark clothes. I looked up. My heart stopped. Felicity loomed before me, her face contorted. In her raised hands she gripped a mallet.

21

TERROR awakened every nerve and muscle in my body as Felicity brought the mallet down. Instinctively I rolled away, narrowly missing the crushing impact. "I'll get you," she hissed, "just as I did Charlotte."

Charlotte? Rage coiled and I hurled myself forward, knocking Felicity off her feet. The mallet flew out of her hands. I dived and pushed it away as she reached out to reclaim what had become a weapon. She caught me by the hair and jerked me back. A scream ripped from my lips, and before I could wrestle free, a heavy, wind-propelled branch crashed through a window, hurling glass in every direction and smashing the spinet. Wind and rain poured in. Amid the deafening commotion, piercing pain shot through my arm. But there wasn't time to think about the cut I'd sustained. Felicity was back on her feet. Unscathed, she scrambled for the mallet. In self-defense I caught up a sharply pointed shard of glass. Fear blazed in her eyes and she shrank back, glass crackling beneath her shoes. Brandishing the shard, I eased to my feet. Felicity lunged. I ducked and struck her across the waist. Blood spurted through the fabric of her gown and her lips twisted in pain and horror. Whirling, she flung aside her weapon and bolted for the door.

Biting back slicing pain from the shard cutting into my hand, I dropped the jagged glass and darted after her. She would pay for what she'd done to my stepsister. Down three flights of stairs I was on Felicity's heels. Clearly the wound I'd inflicted was superficial, for her step never faltered.

In the entrance salon Felicity shot me a frantic look over her shoulder. Her eyes widened at the distance I was narrowing between us. In a second she yanked open the front door, and it crashed against the wall as she darted onto the veranda. A blast of wind whipped my skirts and sent pictures and vases flying off tables. My heart drummed and every breath was a painful gulp.

By the time I reached the door, Felicity was starting across the lawn, headed toward the side of the house. Already she was soaked from the pounding rain. Without warning a wind gust picked her up and slammed her to the ground, littered with leaves and branches and palmetto fronds. As I raced crossed the veranda, Felicity pulled herself up and continued forward. And I kept going. For every two steps I took, fierce gusts pushed me back one.

The beating rain stung like hurled pebbles. My hair fell about my face in sodden strings and my clothes became plastered weights. As I pushed against the elements, struggling to stay on my feet, I glimpsed Matthew leaving his office at the base of the drive. Pausing, I cupped my hands over my mouth and screamed for help, but the plea was flung back in my face. I couldn't even tell if Matthew saw me.

As Felicity rounded the corner of the house, on her way to the stables, a gust straight from the devil scooped us both up and flung us to the hard earth. The air was knocked from my lungs, and my head reeled. Overhead, branches snapped like twigs in a child's hands and flew in every direction. Dazedly, and through bright swirling colors before my eyes, I saw a heavy limb above Felicity break and crash down. I screamed, but the sound was drowned by the wind. Then the world spun, and all I saw was peaceful blackness.

By the time I came around, I had been carried into the house. "You'll be fine, thank God," Matthew said softly as he caressed my cheek with a gentle hand.

Through the fog still engulfing my brain, I once again saw the heavy limb plummeting. "Felicity?" I choked.

Matthew shook his head sadly. "Her injuries are severe. She hasn't much time. She'd like to see you if you feel up to it, Alexandra."

Tears stung at my eyes, though she certainly didn't deserve sympathy. Somehow Felicity had murdered my stepsister and had also tried to do me in. Why? I swallowed. "I'd like to see her, too." Gently Matthew cleansed and dressed my cuts, then left me to Zalea's care. After she helped me into dry clothes, I joined the men at Felicity's bedside. Tyler held her hand, his face wreathed in deep sorrow. Felicity's face was pale, and her breathing almost nonexistent. The rage I felt for her dipped a little.

"Alexandra is here," Matthew said slowly.

Her lashes fluttered and she looked up at me. Felicity's eyes were apologetic, and her whispered voice when she spoke held the same expression. "I'm sorry for trying to hurt you. For what I did to Charlotte."

Matthew inhaled a sharp breath of what sounded like shock, and Tyler's hand on Felicity's tightened in what I assumed was the same emotion.

But she would have . . . found out about . . ." Her voice faded.

"Found out? About what?" Matthew pressed, leaning near.

Tyler shifted uncomfortably and gave Felicity's hand what looked like a warning squeeze. Her apologetic eyes met his for a second. Then she moistened her lips and said in a voice that could hardly be heard, "The money."

"Money?" Matthew murmured, and I felt a moment of joy at his obvious confusion. He hadn't dipped into Charlotte's funds as she had insisted.

Tyler's grim expression conveyed that he knew what she meant. But he didn't intrude on the confession Felicity couldn't seem to stem, and I sensed she was making peace with herself.

With tears running down my face I strained for every word. And for as long as I live, I will remember them. On the day Charlotte died she had told her dearest friend Felicity about the discrepancy in the ledgers, and that she was going to talk to both men. Matthew had no knowledge of the missing funds, but Felicity knew he would demand to know what had prompted his wife's accusation. The truth would come out, and Felicity had feared charges would be pressed. "I couldn't let that happen," she whispered as Tyler continued to hold her hand. To protect herself, she had laced Charlotte's afternoon glass of milk with a heavy dose of sleeping powders. After she'd fallen into deep slumber, from which she could not be roused, Felicity had struggled Charlotte through the secret passage and threw her into the rain-swollen river. Felicity had also hidden the diary and the letter she'd taken from my handbag. "I couldn't leave anything about that mentioned the missing money," she choked. She'd put them both in Matthew's supply closet, certain they would be safely hidden in the old trunk. "I should have destroyed them." Once again her voice was barely audible.

Tears flooded Felicity's sapphire-blue eyes in those final moments of life. "We all thought Matthew would inherit if anything happened to his wife."

I looked up at Matthew in surprise. "Charlotte never told you about the stipulation in our father's will?"

He shook his head, and Felicity went on. "If he . . . had inherited, I . . . wouldn't have tried . . . to . . . harm you, Alexandra. But I . . . couldn't chance you . . . would find out . . . the truth." She closed her eyes for a long moment, and when Matthew urged her to rest quietly, she whispered, "No." Then she continued to unburden herself. "If only you would . . . have gone somewhere else . . . to live," she said to me. "That would have . . . been less threatening. But I begged you to make the gown, I . . . stupidly helped you get . . . your business started . . . here."

Felicity paused again, then confessed she'd sneaked into my room through the armoire while I was in the tub and put sleeping powders in my glass of milk. Through choking tears, she said she had planned to shove me over the veranda, hoping it would look like I'd been the victim of the vicious storm.

Grandmother Hester was brought to the bedside for a few moments. She wasn't told about the confession, and the men and I agreed to forever shelter her from the truth of Felicity.

In the month of June, at the zenith of a hurricane, Felicity died as Tyler held her in his embrace. For a long time the three of us stared numbly at her lifeless body. Then Tyler, slowly and and with heavy emotion in his voice, confessed how he had borrowed money from Charlotte's accounts to finance investments for himself and Felicity. Yes, he'd kept a double set of ledgers. Apparently, Charlotte had seen the fraudulent books he'd been working on when he was called out of his office on the day of her last visit. "I left in such a rush that I forgot to lock them away in the safe," he said. "What Felicity and I did was wrong, Alexandra. But we never really cheated Charlotte. Every penny was repaid, with interest. You're welcome to bring in your Boston attorneys to look over the accounts. They're all in order; I haven't touched a cent for my own use in months."

Matthew was furious with his brother, and if I hadn't stepped between the men, there would have been blows. "How many other clients did you steal from?" Matthew demanded of Tyler.

"I never borrowed from anyone else," he answered quietly. "I'll open the books to every account in my office, if Alexandra wants."

"You will open every one of them," Matthew insisted.

I was so dazed and sickened by all the truths that I couldn't bear to hear another word. Yet there were many more explanations I sought. But tomorrow, I told myself, and allowed Matthew to walk me to my room. He held my hand so tenderly, and when his gaze met mine, I saw apology and sorrow reflected in his dark eyes. How could Charlotte have stopped loving him? How could she have failed to tell him about Father's will? In truth, I should have suspected that possibility. She'd never been able to discuss anything associated with death.

Two days passed before I was able to talk again of all that had happened. By then the storm had come and gone, and I was standing on the rear veranda, enjoying the warm night air, when Matthew came out to join me. As he stood near, I asked about the cemetery activity, and he responded without hesitation. "Hester and I wanted to take you into the family confidence some time ago, but Tyler and Felicity were afraid you might not support our effort. We have much to lose, if that should be the case."

"Whatever you're doing is illegal?"

"Yes, though the law isn't always rigidly enforced. My family and I operate a safe house. Runaway slaves come to us, and we help them escape upstream and, with luck, to freedom in Canada."

My lips parted in a combination of surprise and relief. "I had no idea that people who once owned slaves would go to such lengths to help free them."

"I told you I believe slavery is morally wrong. My family shares that belief." He shook his head. "Considering what Felicity did, it seems incredible that she was capable of all the good charitable work."

"Yes," I murmured. "Unfortunately, money and luxuries were far too important to her."

"There is one more thing about her. I wasn't going to mention it, Alexandra, but I think it's best if everything is out in the open. No more secrets between us."

I nodded in wholehearted agreement.

"It has to do with the snake in the sewing room closet."

The mere mention of that reptile sent a shudder coursing through me.

"As I said before, we'd never had one in the house until then. And after Felicity's confession, I began to wonder if she might have had anything to do with it."

"Are you saying she did?"

"I'm afraid so. The boys around here make a game of trapping them," Matthew explained. "So I asked around and learned that she'd had one of our worker's sons capture a snake and put it in a covered basket. The boy had no idea why she wanted it, and it wasn't his place to ask."

"Who put it in the closet, then?"

"She must have. It was securely in the basket and couldn't have bitten her."

"She and I were the only ones who had reason to be in and out of that closet," I murmured. "So she must have hoped the snake would bite me." My throat closed, and for a spine-chilling second I heard that horrible rattle and the hissing. Then my mind flashed to the rope lying across the trail on the day of my riding accident in the woods. Felicity had been home that day and had known I would be on the path through the trees. Might she have pulled on the rope and tripped my horse?

I thought to mention my suspicion to Matthew, but how could he know the answer any more than I?

There was a quiet moment, then Matthew asked, "What are you planning to do about Tyler and the accounts?"

"Have the books examined, as he suggested, and return the accounts to my Boston attorneys."

"Will you press charges?" The words came slowly.

How could I, when I loved his brother? Especially if the money had been returned. "No, but if any other accounts were mismanaged, I have no control over those clients."

Matthew nodded in understanding and gave my hand a gentle squeeze. We strolled to the end of the veranda. A glance at the cemetery brought back a memory. "What did you mean when I overheard you tell Tyler you're the master?" I asked.

In the light of the moon Matthew looked into my eyes. "Those in charge of safe houses are called stationmasters. At Belle Haven, that's me."

"Have you helped many slaves since I've been here?"

"Yes, quite a few."

"But I only heard the gravestone being moved twice."

"You were probably asleep the other times. At least, we hoped you were." A boyish smile touched his lips, and I couldn't resist leaning near.

"When I first came to Belle Haven, I heard a woman crying pitifully. I thought it was Felicity, but now I wonder if it could have been one of the slaves?"

"Probably. Felicity wasn't one to cry.

"What did you think was going on in the cemetery, Alexandra?"

I couldn't admit that I had, even for a second, considered him capable of dealing in slaves. Maybe if there hadn't been the doubts, the thought never would have occurred to me. "I wasn't really sure," I fibbed a little. "What about the day of my carriage accident, Matthew? You were one of the riders, weren't you?"

"Yes. I was with a group of abolitionists that day. We'd freed some runaways from the courthouse, and one of them was with me."

"You were with the group who attacked the Federal Marshal's office?"

"You heard about that, then?"

"A handful of woman were marveling over it when Tyler and I were having lunch in the city one day. They called what you and the others did daring."

"To a handful of women, I suppose it was."

"To me, also," I admitted. But then I'd always liked daring men. As long as they weren't pirates or worse.

Smiling again, Matthew drew me close. "Do you think you can love a daring man, Alexandra?"

"Yes, but only if he can love a woman who designs ladies fashions and also wants two or three children."

Matthew's eyes sparkled. "I know someone like that, a doctor who loves you very much."

On an overpowering surge I raised up on my toes and met Matthew's mouth in a fiery kiss that held a provocative promise.

After a long time he lifted his head and teased, "Are you positive you can manage both a family and a profession?"

"As I once told you, put me to the test."

The set of his mouth told me Matthew was remembering that afternoon alongside the river. "You can bet I will."

That wasn't exactly a storybook proposal. But the moon and stars were the romantic setting of my dreams.